# everyone else's girl

MEGAN CRANE is a full-time writer and she lives in Los Angeles with her husband and various pets. She is also the author of *English as a Second Language*, *Frenemies* and *Names My Sisters Call Me*.

## Praise for Megan Crane

"Brilliant . . . hugely enjoyable . . . It's romantic, funny, believable and gripping" Marian Keyes

"Megan Crane rules!" Meg Cabot

"If you enjoy a giggle, this novel . . . is the perfect read for you" *Inside Soap*

"A breathless, gossipy read that you'll giggle your way through. When it comes to love, we're not so different whichever side of the pond is your natural home" Carole Matthews

"Delightfully wicked" *U Magazine*

"Amusing, heartfelt and emotionally sophisticated" *Kirkus Reviews*

"Crane's style captivates and brings the story to life" *Buzz*

# everyone else's girl

Megan Crane

Quercus

First published in Great Britain in 2010 by

Quercus
21 Bloomsbury Square
London
WC1A 2NS

A CIP catalogue record for this book is available
from the British Library

ISBN 978 1 84916 212 8

This book is a work of fiction. Names, characters,
businesses, organizations, places and events are
either the product of the author's imagination
or are used fictitiously. Any resemblance to
actual persons, living or dead, events or
locales is entirely coincidental.

10 9 8 7 6 5 4 3 2 1

Printed and bound in Great Britain by Clays Ltd, St Ives plc

*To Adrianne, Marshall, and Noelle.*
*And to Catie, who said I should write a book about family.*

# Chapter 1

I would rather parade naked through the streets than find myself in the backseat of a tacky stretch Hummer, cruising from bar to bar in bright banana-yellow splendor. Unfortunately, no one had offered me this choice.

It was just a bachelorette party. I would survive it.

Probably.

Not that I was out of options entirely. I could always throw myself under the wheels of the eyesore we were riding in. Suicide by Hummer, however, seemed like it would only add insult to injury at this point. Besides which, Washington Street in Hoboken was not really the ideal place to stage my death. Entirely too many drunken frat boys for any kind of emotional resonance.

It wasn't *that* bad, I told myself philosophically, trying to rally. I looked down the narrow interior of the Hummer toward Jeannie Gillespie, my former best friend from high school and, more recently, my brother Christian's fiancée. Jeannie was waving around a bottle of champagne and looked to be having a blast. She met my gaze from down the long, long interior and grinned.

"Come on, Meredith!" she cried, lurching forward with the champagne bottle in her hand.

She misjudged the distance between the plush leather seat and the console, and ended up crumpled facedown on the floor in a tangle of expensive sandals. Being Jeannie, she merely shook with laughter and ordered the legs out of her way. The other bridesmaids let out earsplitting cackles and turned up the radio, the better to rock out to some eighties anthem. They also moved out of Jeannie's way.

I wasn't too proud to admit my own foot was tapping along. After all, everybody had to cut footloose. It was practically hardwired into my generation.

Jeannie laughed up at me as she fought her way through the tangle of legs, and then handed me the bottle when she reached my feet.

"Drink, for God's sake," she said, struggling to her knees. "You've got that killjoy face on again."

"I am not a killjoy," I retorted immediately, extending my hands automatically for both the lukewarm champagne bottle and Jeannie's arm. Together, we hauled her from her knees to the seat beside me.

She flopped into place and heaved a sigh like she'd just conquered Everest. Given the amount of Jell-O shots she'd consumed at Bahama Mama's, our previous stop along the bachelorette Trail of Tears, getting from the floor to a seat really was an incredible achievement.

"I can't believe you came all the way up here from Atlanta to be the Queen of Killjoys," Jeannie told me, leaning close.

"Hey—" I'd come all the way up from Atlanta because I had been informed in no uncertain terms by various members of my family that my presence at Jeannie's party was nonnegotiable. And to be honest, I kind of agreed, and had left the comfort and safety of my usual weekend plans with my boyfriend, Travis, to travel north and take my place in the ceremonial Hummer.

Which made my sister Hope's absence all the more offensive, but I wasn't going to think about that. Not with Jeannie tipsily pontificating three inches from my right ear.

"Meredith," Jeannie intoned, entirely ignoring my attempt to speak, "this is a sacred ritual. It is up to me to make an ass out of myself without actually crossing any lines that might endanger my relationship with your brother. I have accepted this challenge." She swept a dramatic hand over herself, inviting me to look.

Jeannie had the requisite tatty veil pinned to the back of her head and was wearing the expected sexually explicit T-shirt. She was even sporting a headband festooned with wobbly pink penises, which had made two of her sorority sisters spit out mouthfuls of their apple martinis at the very *sight* of such *naughtiness*.

"That's right," she said now. "I'm wearing a penis headband. I'm allowing myself to be *photographed* while wearing a penis headband."

I felt my mouth twitching, but tried to control it. She saw it, though—I could tell from that glimmer in her eye.

"And why, you ask?" Jeannie leveled a look at me. "Do you think I like parading around the streets of Hoboken, making a spectacle of myself?"

I tilted my head at that one and opened my mouth to respond.

Jeannie snickered. "Don't answer that." She took the bottle back from me and took a swig, then returned it. She glared at me until I surrendered and tilted the bottle up to my lips. Warm and bubbly liquid filled my mouth. I choked on it, but drank.

I wasn't too proud to drink, either. Bachelorette "events" made me suspicious, true, but really I just didn't like Jell-O shots, which had been hard to convey in a dark, deafening bar in the middle of a screaming pack of bridesmaids. It was a texture thing.

But I could make up for that now, I figured, no matter how unpleasant cheap champagne was when warm. And it got notably less unpleasant with every sip I took.

"I'm doing this because it is the Girl Code," Jeannie was saying in that same serious tone. She could have been delivering a sermon to the troops. "It is my *responsibility* to prance around like an idiot, making single women sneer and then weep over my engagement ring, wondering how anyone would want to marry a drunk loser like me. This is my *duty*, Meredith."

"You're a giver, Jeannie," I agreed solemnly. I took another gulp. Or three.

"I'm happy to sacrifice my dignity for the amusement of others," Jeannie said. "It's the least I can do." She pointed at me again. "In turn, however, you have to do your part. I can't allow any slacking."

"After all, the bachelorette party is really nothing more than a preemptive strike," I drawled, sinking back against the pink seats.

"Too true."

We'd discussed this before, years ago when we were closer than close, and even more recently, when the topic of Annoying Weddings was one of the few we could navigate without stepping on any of the private land mines that littered our relationship.

But I wasn't thinking about any of that tonight, I reminded myself. Sternly. I took a hefty, restorative pull from the champagne bottle.

"It's the bridesmaids' only revenge for ugly dresses and uncomfortable shoes," I continued instead. "Not to mention the horrible posed pictures that will hang on the happy couple's wall for the rest of their lives."

"Ashley Mueller made us wear petticoats," Jeannie told me in a whisper. "And hats. All of it very, very green."

Ashley Mueller herself—she of the pinched mouth and ruthlessly blown-out blonde hair—had a new last name that I couldn't be bothered to learn and was perched at the other end of the limo, clutching a checklist of humiliating and sexually charged activities for Jeannie to perform in the bars. Ashley Mueller took her maid of honor duties entirely too seriously. She was *exactly* the sort of person who would obscure the relative attractiveness of her bridal attendants in butt-ugly petticoats with matching hats. Moreover, she would do it for that very reason. Not because she had some green petticoat fetish, but because she, by comparison, would look like a supermodel angel in white.

I'd never been happier that she hated me—a sentiment I had returned since sometime in the seventh grade—and had thus excluded me entirely from her wedding drama sometime last summer.

"I don't believe you," I told Jeannie with a shudder. Although I definitely, gleefully did. I took another swig. It was amazing how the rush of warm bubbles against the tongue got less and less repellent.

"Remind me to show you the tragic photographic evidence," Jeannie murmured. "I cry over it once a month when the PMS gets really bad. But the *point* is, I was forced to retaliate, and that is why Ashley was required to wear a strap-on throughout her bachelorette event. A big, hairy, revolting strap-on. Picture *that*."

The image penetrated even the champagne.

"You're lucky Christian is so hot!" one of Jeannie's sorority sisters brayed at her suddenly, jerking both Jeannie and me out of an appalled contemplation of Ashley Mueller and a strap-on dildo. We both choked back laughter.

"He's pretty damn hot," Jeannie agreed lasciviously, and toasted my absent brother with my champagne bottle. I eyed her as she drank a big gulp, and then swiped the bottle.

"Hell yeah!" shouted another. "You won't even *want* to stray, with him around!"

"You guys have big mouths," yet another one admonished them in a stage whisper they could probably hear across the Hudson River in downtown Manhattan. She pointed down the long interior of the car at me. Her arm wobbled dramatically, but they all looked at me anyway. "One of his sisters is *right there*!"

"Let's definitely not talk any more about how hot he is," I agreed hurriedly.

That sort of thing had been bad enough in high school, when Christian and I—at ten months apart and often confused for twins—had been in the same grade and I'd had girls falling all over me in attempts to get near him. All these years later, he was still too cute for his own good, but he and I weren't as close as we'd been. No one would bother trying to get to him through me, not anymore.

But there wasn't any time to nurse the pain on that one, because the Hummer was pulling up in front of yet another

Hoboken club. I upended the remains of the bottle down my throat and climbed out of the limo. It took a group effort to dislodge Jeannie, but eventually we had her upright and past the surly bouncers. Sometimes it was actually useful to be part of a group of scantily clad sorority girls. I made a mental note.

Inside the club, dance music was pumping and immensely breasted women in gravity-defying bikini tops circled through the crowd dispensing bright-colored liquid from little boxes that hung around their necks. Everything seemed particularly blurry and frenzied—or, possibly, the champagne had gone to my head. Our group staked out a position near one of the three bars and Ashley commenced ticking off the items on Jeannie's checklist.

Which she kept brandishing around ostentatiously, in case anyone forgot for five seconds that she was In-Charge.

I reminded myself that I had to deal with her only tonight, and then at the wedding, and then, if there was a God, never again.

"Don't look at me like that," she snarled at me when I accidentally ventured too close to her.

"Was I looking at you?" But it was Jeannie's party, so that came out nicer than I meant it to. A little more warm champagne and that wouldn't be a problem.

"You have no idea what Jeannie put me through at my bachelorette party," Ashley barked at me. I looked at her mean little eyes and thought about dildos, which made whatever other nonsense she was spouting more than okay in my book. I only realized I was smiling when she smiled back. "Jeannie has to follow the rules," she told me.

Jeannie herself had been swept up in the giggling arms of some of her sorority sisters, and was even now leaning in and whispering in various ears. Hopefully about Ashley and her strap-on.

"It's time for body shots!" Ashley commanded, loud enough to perk the interest of several eavesdropping gentlemen. The shortest and—not coincidentally—loudest of the group stepped up and offered his services in an accent straight from *The Sopranos.*

Jeannie caught my eye briefly and waggled her brows at me.

She was right, I thought. This was about duty.

And I was nothing if not capable of doing my duty.

So I ordered myself a margarita, and dove in.


Sometime later, I was reclining in a plush booth, just barely keeping my head above the table. Not because I was drunk—although let's not kid around, I was pretty drunk—but because Jeannie was singing.

Normally, Jeannie didn't sing, thank the gods. She was tone-deaf and music-dumb, and made the Cameron Diaz character in *My Best Friend's Wedding* sound like Whitney Houston. Usually, Jeannie used her singing voice as the weapon it was: she would sing along in car rides to the worst songs, thereby ensuring that the driver would play only her favorite tunes.

But this was a bachelorette party. More than that, it was Battle of the Brides.

The freaky emcee at the karaoke place had been delighted when we all trooped in, none of us particularly steady on our feet.

"You're the second bride tonight," he smarmed at Jeannie. Luckily for him, she was too wasted to reply in her usual fashion.

The first bride was draped in tulle and had clearly had a recent mishap at the hairdresser's. Either that, or she preferred to have bright orange Ronald McDonald hair. She watched our party approach with the light of battle in her eyes and a pitcher of margaritas in one fist.

"You and me, sweetheart!" she bawled at Jeannie.

"You and who?" Jeannie asked, blinking at her.

"Winner takes the happily ever after!" Tulle Bride shouted. With that, she took to the stage and began belting out "Love Lift Us Up Where We Belong"—the extended version. Her bridesmaids hooted and hollered like she was winning the Super Bowl.

"No way is some clown-haired bitch taking my happily ever after!" Jeannie slurred, breaking for the stage.

It was maybe inevitable that she chose "I Will Always Love You," shattering glasses and eardrums with every syllable she sang.

Or, more precisely, yowled.


There was absolutely no sign of my brother Christian's trademark grin when he swung the door open sometime after 3 a.m. He squinted at me, and then scowled when he took in his fiancée's condition.

"This is your idea of keeping an eye on Jeannie?"

We both swiveled to look at her.

Jeannie was more or less unconscious, emphasis on *more*. She had one arm slung across my shoulders and most of her body propped up against mine. She kept mumbling vowel sounds. Her hair was matted, and though I had had the presence of mind to remove the T-shirt with the risqué inscriptions, it was putting it mildly to say she looked the worse for wear. At least she was upright.

Well.

Mostly upright, anyway.

"She's not facedown in a gutter," I pointed out in the sweetest voice I could muster at that hour, and staggered a little bit when Jeannie flopped hard to the left for absolutely no reason.

What I didn't point out was that we were all equally lucky that I was not in a similar condition. After all, I'd had several margaritas. And the better part of a bottle of champagne. It was just that when the other girls had opted for wacky drinks involving colored liquors and naughty titles to drown the pain of the karaoke, I'd opted for water and diet Coke.

Hence my ability to speak in complete sentences.

Christian held out his arms—despite the dubious look on his face—and we transferred Jeannie's body from me to him with only minimal fuss. He moved inside the apartment and deposited Jeannie in a heap on the couch. She moaned slightly and muttered a few words toward the sofa cushions before lapsing into silence.

Or a coma, call it what you will.

"She'll be up and puking within the hour," Christian said, frowning at his wife-to-be—probably because he'd finally gotten a whiff of her brewery breath. Although, I reflected, it could also be the prospect of the night he had ahead of him. That would be enough to make anyone frown.

"Anything I should know about?" He gazed at me expectantly, and then his eyes crinkled up in the corners. "This isn't Vegas. What happens here needs to be shared."

I gazed back. "There's nothing to share."

Because of the Girl Code and because, let's face it, he didn't really want to know. He should count himself lucky he hadn't had those Alpha Beta Whatever girls screeching in his ear all night. I might be permanently deafened.

In any event, there had been no sex, no kissing, and no stripping. That pretty much covered the bases. Why fill in the blanks? What fiancé wanted to know about the dancing, or the body shots, or the lewd commentary?

"I'm trusting you on this, Meredith," Christian said, laughter in his voice. "I don't want to turn into an urban legend, with some bozo passing out photographs on my wedding day."

"Everyone was on their best behavior," I assured him.

Given the assortment of people present, this was undoubtedly true.

"I'm trusting you," he said again. Significantly, as if he really did trust me, which I doubted. "And don't slam the door behind you. I'm hoping she'll just sleep it off."

"Yeah, right," I muttered, but I still didn't slam the door when I left.


When I tiptoed into my parents' house later on that night, reenacting whole years of my adolescence in ways I was too tired to analyze, I stopped in amazement when I heard the sound of the television from the family room. Peeking inside, I saw my younger sister Hope crashed out across the couch. She had just graduated from college and had nothing to do with her life, as far as I knew. Yet she had been "too busy" to attend our soon-to-be sister-in-law's bachelorette party.

I goggled at her supine form. She didn't look particularly

busy. In fact, if the junk food littered around her was any indication, she'd been in that same position all night.

"Oh hey," she said when she saw me. "Check it out, there's a teen movie festival on."

"I thought you had other things to do tonight," I said, and I could hear a little too much Snotty Big Sister in my voice.

Hope sighed. "How bad was it?"

"It was fine," I told her. "It would have been better if you were there."

"I really doubt it." Hope looked at me. "You want to watch the rest of this movie with me?"

"I have to get to bed," I responded. Hope was like an alien to me. I didn't understand the things she did or said, and it always seemed to require way too much energy on my part to make the effort to bridge the six years between us.

I left the room without looking back.


But upstairs in my narrow twin bed, the one I'd slept in throughout my youth, I was suddenly wide-awake. I felt tired, but more than that, the strange kind of loneliness that seemed to go hand in hand with being awake when the world was sleeping all around me. Maybe I missed my boyfriend, Travis. Maybe it was just late. Or maybe it was a perfectly normal reaction to spending a whole evening in my past.

Once upon a time, Jeannie and I were best friends, and Christian really was like my twin. The three of us did everything together. Whatever boyfriends Jeannie or I had, or whatever girlfriends Christian had, what mattered was the three of us. We'd been that way since Christian and I had met Jeannie when all of us were toddlers. And we'd continued that way until the summer after my freshman year of college, when Jeannie's and my friendship fell apart. I'd never expected to talk to her again until she'd started dating Christian the summer after we all graduated from college.

Fast-forward almost eight years and they were getting married, I was a stranger to them, and we all pretended things were exactly the same as they'd been in high school. I smiled and kept my thoughts to myself, Christian grinned and looked adorable, and Jeannie made us all laugh. We did the same dance every holiday I came home, and we would do it this weekend too.

Sometimes I forgot that everything was different, and just relaxed in the familiarity of it all. And then sometimes I wondered what would happen if we were forced to deal with each other for longer than the odd weekend here and there. Would everything explode? Or would we decide it wasn't worth dredging up the past?

Happily, I wasn't ever likely to find out.

# Chapter 2

In the basement, my father had created an aquarium to rival the one we'd visited in Baltimore as kids.

I was only slightly exaggerating.

Fish tanks of varying size and containing different numbers of fish covered the many tables he'd erected across the concrete floor. They all gurgled and hummed, and inside them the fish swam back and forth, back and forth, without end. I stared at the nearest tank, which contained tiny little ones, barely the size of my fingertip.

"Babies," Dad told me, following my gaze. "I had to take them away from their mother. She was trying to eat them all."

"That's horrible!" I said, looking around for the cannibal fish, but they all looked the same to me.

"That's nature," Dad replied. "Next time you come home, you should spend some more time down here. I'm doing some interesting things with fins." He smiled at me, the kind of smile he'd been using since he retired from Wall Street. He kind of aimed it in your direction but there wasn't much to it. "I know you used to get a kick out of science."

Actually, that was Hope. She was the kind of irritating person who would roll her eyes into the back of her head, pronounce all homework "dumb" and "boring," and then effortlessly ace her tests. She'd slouched and shrugged her way through school, never appearing to pay attention or crack a book, and had somehow ended up with a 4.0. Christian had once theorized that it was an elaborate ploy, and that in reality, Hope hid out under her covers at night, feverishly cramming.

In any case, I didn't bother to correct my father. No need to correct people when what they thought was true was more favorable than what was *actually* true.

I walked closer to the nearest tank and peered into it. There were ferns waving sluggishly in the water, a bright pink rock, and a few plump fish.

Unlike Hope, I'd always hated science. And I'd never understood the fascination with fish. Who wanted to spend all that time and energy with tiny, slimy creatures who couldn't love you and forgot you existed by the time they turned around at the edge of their tank? *Finding Nemo* was cute and all, but a real pet, I'd always thought, had to be a mammal of one sort or another.

Nonetheless, the fact that my father loved fish was practically the only thing I could say about him now with any certainty. It had been easier before he'd retired: Goldman Sachs, Ivy League schools, an addiction to the *Wall Street Journal*. Now there were just the fish tanks, scattered around the basement like clues.

"It looks like you have more fish tanks down here than you did at Christmas," I said, trying to take an interest.

"Oh, a few."

"Wow."

So much for that.

I snuck a look at him as he puttered around a table. He

looked the way I half imagined Christian would look eventually, and he liked to engage in political debates over Sunday dinner, but only if they could be wrapped up in time for *60 Minutes*. Was I supposed to know him better? Were grown children supposed to *want* to know their parents better? It was different with my mother—she was a constant voice in the back of my head, and, when I wasn't screening my calls, she was directly in my ear. In comparison to all that, my father was just a quiet background noise. Kind of like wallpaper.

He looked up then, as if he'd heard me, and smiled slightly. "I think your mother wants to talk to you," he said. "Before I take her to the airport."

At least it was comforting to learn that some things were genetic, I thought, staring around my parents' familiar bedroom. My mother's suitcase was open on the bed and just about every garment I'd ever seen her wear was piled around it. Packing light was not in the McKay family genes.

Mom looked up from a consideration of what appeared to be two identical black Talbots sweaters, and her brow wrinkled slightly.

"Aren't you up late today," she murmured, in that *amazed* tone of hers. The one that suggested she was *astounded* by my laziness.

It occurred to me every now and again that she didn't actually mean things the way they sounded, that my internalized Mom Voice was already cranked up to high and I responded as if she was deliberately trying to be evil when really, she was just commenting.

I took a few deep breaths, and tried to let this occur to me more forcefully.

"The bachelorette thing took all night," I said, hating that I felt defensive. Not that hating it either (a) stopped me feeling that way or (b) stopped me *sounding* that way.

"I hope Jeannie had a good time," Mom said, totally unperturbed by my tone. "She pretends to be so relaxed about these things, but I'm not sure she is."

"She seemed pretty relaxed," I said. Or, you know, wasted drunk, but I kept that to myself.

"It was so nice of you to come up for the party." Mom beamed at me. "I know that meant the world to Jeannie."

Apparently we were pretending that she hadn't expended some serious energy during our weekly chats making sure I would come.

"Your trip is going to be so amazing," I said, changing the subject and fingering the edge of her suitcase. "You and Aunt Beth are going to have a fantastic time."

Back when they were girls, my mother and her sister had dreamed of taking the Grand Tour like the heroines in the novels they read. They'd talked endlessly about touring the great capitals of Europe, but life had intervened and they'd never quite gotten around to it. This summer, however, things had changed. Aunt Beth had finally divorced Uncle Richard and had declared that come hell or high water, she was taking that trip at long last. Shortly thereafter, Mom had announced that she saw no reason why she shouldn't accompany her little sister on the trip they'd always meant to take, particularly *at such a time*. They were taking off for some six weeks of a Grand Tour this evening.

"I'm just pleased that your father can spare me," Mom said, choosing one of the identical sweaters and placing it in her suitcase. She walked over and put the other one back in her bureau.

I couldn't tell what the difference was between them, but knew better than to ask. I'd made that mistake once before, with nightgowns. The woman had *a system*. End of story.

"Dad said you wanted to talk to me," I said, settling on the edge of the bed. "I was looking at his fish."

"He loves those fish," Mom said. She turned back toward me then. "I've left the makings for dinner in the fridge," she said, suddenly brisk. "Your father will drop me off at the airport and then come straight home, and you should all have a nice dinner before your brother takes you to catch your flight later tonight."

"You shouldn't have gone to any trouble," I said. Much less intricately plotted everyone else's every move while she was going to be at cruising altitude above the Atlantic Ocean. The woman was detail-oriented on a pathological level. "I could have made dinner."

"It wasn't any trouble at all," Mom countered. "I'll like thinking of my family gathered around the table together as I head off on my adventure."

"You should have been concentrating on your trip, not on us." I smiled at her. "You do too much, Mom."

"It was easy enough to pull together," Mom demurred, but I thought she looked pleased.

"She's been puking her guts out since last night," Christian muttered around a yawn.

He was slumped over the kitchen table, unshaven, with bloodshot eyes. Jeannie had made a brief appearance in the kitchen, ascertained that no parents were about to perform for, and headed directly upstairs to lie down in Christian's old room. Perhaps she derived comfort from the remains of NHL stickers (Go Rangers!) that still clung to the windowpanes, or from Christian's extensive collection of Douglas Adams novels.

"I told her I didn't think it was fair that I had to deal with the consequences of *her* ridiculous bachelorette behavior, and she just got sicker." Christian rubbed his jaw and cracked a smile. "And also told me to go to hell, of course."

"Your relationship is so tender and sweet," I teased him, and his smile widened.

"Yeah it is," he said. "I held her hair back. For *hours*."

"Are you going to give us a chunk-by-chunk breakdown here or what?" Hope demanded from her seat. "Because I already have too much information, thanks."

"I don't even want to talk to you." Christian eyed her. "How could you bail on Jeannie's party? What kind of sister-in-law are you?"

"The kind that was busy *and* doesn't want to hear anything else about vomiting," Hope retorted.

"There must be traffic," I mused, ignoring both of them and staring at the clock. Mom's plane was at three-thirty. It was nearing five.

"There's always traffic," Christian said, but he was still frowning at Hope.

"Maybe Dad stopped along the way to buy himself a snazzy new fish," I suggested. "Maybe one with extra-special fins."

I wasn't sure if fish were the sort of thing one just impulse-bought, like clothes, or if they required planning and thought, like furniture. Or possibly even an emotional commitment, like puppies. Fish were obviously part of a whole world I knew nothing about.

"What time is your plane?" Christian asked me, obviously giving up on Hope. She just smiled to herself and returned her attention to her glossy magazine. Neither one of them addressed the fish question. Deliberately, I was pretty sure.

"Nine-thirty," I said.

And at about nine-twenty-five, I figured, the cheery goodwill that we all put on for show would dissipate like a fairy godmother's spell, and there we'd all be, rolling around in the lumpy pumpkin patch of our actual relationships.

I intended to be deep in the bowels of Newark Airport well before that could happen.


An hour later, Jeannie was up and in the kitchen and even Hope was moved enough out of her disinterest to register that it was unlike our father to be late for anything, much less *this* late, and to a *meal*.

When the phone began to ring, we all stared at each other. And especially at Christian, who held the receiver in his hand.

*Ring.*

"That's probably him now," Jeannie said. Her voice was scratchy, but her eyes were fixed on Christian. "Right? That'll be him."

"Answer the phone," Hope told Christian.

*Ring. Ring.*

"I'll get it," I said, but I didn't move.

And so we all watched while Christian picked up the receiver and bit out a greeting.

And then we watched as the color drained out of his face.

*    *    *

The last time I had been to the local hospital was back in the eighth grade, when I'd had my tonsils removed. I had been anxious about the surgery, but excited about Christian's tales of endless ice cream to soothe my aching throat. I had been outraged to discover that ice cream was out because of the way dairy produced phlegm, and I was expected to make do with ice chips. Ice chips! Looking around the hospital lobby, I realized I was still holding on to that outrage.

*Is this really what you're thinking about?* I asked myself in astonishment.

But it was better than the alternative.

We knew only the basic facts: there had been an accident, and Dad had been taken from the scene of the accident to the hospital. Beyond that, we knew nothing. And so we gathered in a little group, with scared eyes and tight mouths, and waited for more information because there was nothing to do *but* wait.

Time stretched out and trapped us in that same aquamarine waiting room. It was just one night, but it felt like years. In the morning, Dad was groggy but okay, with just a badly broken leg to show for it.

"Don't be ridiculous," he barked when I suggested letting Mom know. "I hope none of you tried to talk her into coming home?"

"She's been on a plane," Christian said.

"We were going to call the hotel," I said.

"Obviously," Hope said, "she'll want to come back and make sure you're okay."

"Don't you dare call that hotel!"

I jumped at his tone.

"Don't get upset," Christian said at once, looking uneasy.

Dad blinked up from his hospital bed. "She's been looking forward to this trip since she was a little girl," he said, far more calmly. "There's no way she'll miss out on it on *my* account!"

"Which is all well and good," I said later that day.

We had broken for naps, calls to our respective lives, and had regrouped at the kitchen table. Hope and Christian looked as bleary as I felt. Jeannie had been too wiped out to even attend this little summit meeting.

"But he can't take care of himself with that leg. He's going to need help. This house is almost entirely made of stairs." I looked from Christian to Hope.

"Mom has to come home," Christian said at once. "Right?"

"Once-in-a-lifetime trip, yadda yadda yadda," Hope said. "She's not coming home."

"Her husband had a *car accident.*" Christian frowned at her. "Of course she's coming home!"

"You go right ahead and wait for her to appear in the arrivals hall at Newark Airport," Hope suggested. "In fact, I'll drive you. But it's going to be a long wait."

"Dad was pretty adamant that he didn't even want her told," I agreed. "I think he'd flip out if anyone suggested she come home."

"I don't understand this," Christian said, still wound up. "If Jeannie was in a car accident, no one would have to *suggest* I come home! What the *hell*?" But he wound himself down even as he spoke, and sounded more resigned than anything else.

"Whether or not Dad should tell Mom, or Mom should come

home, or what either of those things says or doesn't say about their marriage . . ." I shrugged. "I can't deal with any of those things right now. Worst-case scenario is she doesn't come home and we have to handle it, right?"

"Someone already lives at home and can take care of him," Christian pointed out. He looked at Hope. "Someone who doesn't have a job."

Hope laughed. "Yeah, right." She wasn't at all moved by our two pairs of eyes upon her. "I can hardly take care of myself. Anyway, I don't have time. I'm traveling."

"So far, 'traveling' looks an awful lot like bumming around the house, staying out all night, and sleeping all day."

Christian sounded more jealous than angry, I thought. Of course, he'd done the same when he graduated from college. In fact, I was the only one who had gone directly from graduation into the workforce, with no "finding my feet" time at Mom and Dad's. Not that I planned to bring this up. I jerked my attention back to my sister.

"What do you care, *Dad*?" Hope was sneering at Christian. "Did I ask you to comment on how I live my life?"

"You don't actually have a life," Christian snapped. "You're a post-graduation freeloader who can't be bothered to get off her ass and get a goddamned job!"

"Come on, Christian," I murmured reprovingly.

"I graduated all of five seconds ago!" Hope retorted. "Anyway, I'm saving up my money and going backpacking in Costa Rica. So back off."

Christian rolled his eyes and sighed. "You're the best option, Hope," he told her firmly. He stared at her, as if that would transmit his authority. "It's not like you'd be on your own. We'd all be around, helping you out."

"Sure you would." Hope laughed mirthlessly. "Meredith lives in Atlanta and you like to pretend Hoboken is in another galaxy instead of a half-hour down the Turnpike. Which adds up to Hope alone, waiting hand and foot on Dad. No way."

"Hope," I said carefully. "Of course you feel that way, but it would be—"

"Listen closely," Hope interrupted coldly. "Maybe you want to ruin your summer playing nurse, but I don't. I don't want the responsibility, thank you very much."

And with that she knocked back her chair and stalked off into the night.

"That selfish little bitch," Christian said, but in a kind of awe. He was almost smiling.

I sighed. "Oh come on. What did you think she was going to do?"

We both shook our heads, and even laughed a little bit.

Christian sat back and crossed his arms across his chest. "There's no way I can take any time off. The partner track waits for no one. And Jeannie has her hands full with the wedding."

Jeannie was a tenth-grade teacher, which should have left her hands pretty empty from about 3 p.m. on, while Christian labored away in his Newark law firm. Not to mention the approaching summer vacation. I didn't find it at all difficult to believe that Jeannie had thrown herself into their wedding preparations. The fact that Christian thought that was a reasonable excuse for avoiding family duties was something else altogether.

"I'm sorry, Meredith," Christian continued, although I didn't think either one of us believed that he was really sorry.

I already knew where this was going. What surprised me was how easily I accepted it as inevitable. I would do this because I was the responsible one. Wasn't that the way it always worked out? *But I just want to go home!* a plaintive voice wailed in my head. I silenced it. It was more important to be the good daughter than to be happy.

"I'll speak to my boss," I said, hearing what sounded—horrifyingly—like the trill of martyrdom in my voice. I tried to ignore it. "But I don't really know what to tell her. Do we know how long his rehabilitation will take?"

"The doctor said it's about six weeks until he gets the heavy cast off his leg," Christian said, poking at the table as if he could hurt it. Or maybe he was reacting to the martyr tone himself. "And then I think there's a walking cast, and after that I guess he can take care of himself."

"I've been at Morrow almost five years, so I have some leeway, but taking off the rest of the summer?" I shrugged as if to say, *Who knows?*

Christian blinked at me. "So you quit. Right? You don't really care about that job." He looked confused. "Since when was it your life's dream to work in the alumnae association of a school you didn't even attend?"

"I'm not sure how thrilled I am at the idea of moving home," I continued with only a sideways look his way, not up for a discussion of my life's dreams with Christian just then. "Even just for the summer."

"It wouldn't really be *moving home*," Christian said hurriedly. He glanced around at the familiar kitchen walls. "That would be suicide. It would just be helping out the family, which is totally different."

For a brief moment I thought, *What if my boss says no? What if I don't want to help out? What if I'm not so dependable after all? What if I demanded that you take care of someone else for a change? What if I got up right now and stormed off out of the house like Hope?*

But that wasn't me.

And in any case, it wasn't going to happen. Doomsday scenarios courtesy of Hope aside, what wife didn't rush to her husband's side the moment she heard he was in an accident? It was great that we had a plan B, but surely the fact we had it practically *guaranteed* we wouldn't have to use it.

"Obviously," I said to Christian then, "none of this is going to matter anyway, because I'm sure Mom will be on the next plane home."

"Of course she will." He sounded relieved I thought so too.

"It's just a question of telling her." I rubbed at my eyes. "And of making Dad see reason."


"Here's the thing," Christian said in his "I am so reasonable" voice. He was playing Dad *to* Dad—a risky proposition at best. "I know that you want Mom to have a great time and that you don't want her to come home, but we have to think about it from her perspective."

"Exactly!" I agreed heartily, as planned and briefly rehearsed in the completely beige hospital lobby, with Hope playing a very surly version of Dad, perched on a bench next to a rumpled businessman who clearly believed we were both destined for the psych ward. Possibly because Hope's version of Dad used a great deal more profanity.

"How would you feel if the positions were reversed, Dad?" I asked. "You might very well choose to stay in Europe, but you'd definitely want to be the one to make that choice."

"Meredith makes a really good point there," Christian chimed in. "Mom has to have all the facts, so she can make an informed decision."

"The real issue here is that you believe she's going to come home," Hope interjected, looking at Christian as if he amused her greatly.

This part was not scripted. I turned to gauge Dad's reaction. His leg was splayed out before him in the narrow bed, looking both small and bulky beneath the hospital gown. So far, he hadn't said a word.

"Hope—" Christian was trying to send a warning while remaining reasonable. It came out kind of strangled.

"*Christian*," she mimicked him. "If anyone cares what I think—"

"No one does," Christian assured her. With far less bite than he would have used if our father wasn't in the room.

"—I don't think she'll come home." She shrugged at Christian's glare. "I'm sorry, but I don't."

"That's not really the point," I hurried to say. "The point is, she has to know." Hoping to forestall any more sibling drama, I looked toward Dad. "Right? Dad?"

"I appreciate how concerned you all are," Dad said, sounding surprised at all the energy we'd put into the topic. "Of course we can tell your mother, but I can't imagine she'll come home, Christian. Why should she? I'm perfectly fine."

Which is exactly what he told her when we called her later that morning.

And exactly what I told her when she demanded to speak to me and I assured her that I was delighted with my new role as primary caretaker.

"It's practically like being on vacation myself," I assured her. Happily!

"I'll have to call the airline," Mom said, my happy tone apparently unconvincing. "I can't let you risk your job. And what will Travis do without you all summer?"

"Mom, please! There's no risk and Travis will be fine! Believe me, if there's one thing people in the South understand, it's having to put family first!"

Speaking in exclamation points was actually exhausting, I discovered. I rubbed at the back of my neck.

"I just don't know what to do," Mom said. "I'd hate to let your aunt Beth down, but if it's truly not as bad as it sounds, I just don't know. Do you really think it's something you can handle?"

She'd programmed me well. I practically fell over myself assuring her that not only *could* I handle it, I *couldn't wait* to handle it! I *wanted* to handle it!

"This is *your* time!" I chirped at her like some refugee from a theme park, ignoring Hope's derisive snort from behind me.

By the time we got off the phone, I had convinced the both of us that Dad had a hangnail and I was hanging out around the house as my summer vacation, nothing to worry about, enjoy the Louvre.

"Congratulations," Hope said as I replaced the receiver. "You've just become a Stepford Wife."

"Don't be ridiculous," Christian said, in that through-his-teeth way he used to talk to Hope in front of Dad. I thought he should maybe either stop doing that, or see the dentist about jaw strain. "Meredith lives for things like this, don't you, Meredith?"

"Of course," I said, beaming at Dad. As brightly as possible, to avoid looking at Hope's smirk. "There's nowhere I'd rather be."

# Chapter 3

It was depressingly easy to sort out a summer up north. My boss was incredibly understanding when I reached her and only too happy to grant me compassionate leave—but then, summer was always our dead time. She might have been far less supportive had it been closer to the end of the fiscal year.

"I don't understand why you have to move home," Travis said yet again. I moved the phone from one ear to the other and stared at the kitchen sink. "The rest of your family lives *right there*."

"Whining is so unattractive." I was striving for a light tone, which was hard, as it had just occurred to me that the dishes in the sink were my responsibility. "Anyway, it's not *moving home*. It's *visiting*, with a little nursing thrown in."

"I'm serious," he said. "What am I going to do all summer without my girlfriend? Have you thought about that?"

"I have the least important job," I said, not for the first time. I waited for Travis to defend my job, but he didn't. And why would he? I hadn't mounted any defense myself. "Plus," I said, "can you really see my brother nursing my father? Would *you* nurse *your* father?"

"What about Hope?" Travis asked. But he knew better. "That's just wrong," he said when I only sighed. "You let that girl get away with murder."

"It's a McKay tradition."

"We have about a hundred barbecues to go to," Travis groused. "I hate doing that stuff on my own."

"You'll be fine. You have all your friends to keep you company," I reminded him. "Not that I trust *them*."

"They all love you," he assured me. "They'd never let me do you wrong."

I shook my head. "Your friends are dogs!"

"Our friends," he corrected me. "And they're perfectly well-behaved dogs, when the ladies are around."

"Exactly my point!"

He sighed again. "I'll send you some clothes and stuff," he said finally. And then, teasing me: "And I'll try to keep the apartment exactly the way you left it."

We both knew the place would be a mess of his laundry, his meals, his lack of interest in housework of any kind, and maybe already was. I decided not to think about my beautiful apartment left in his careless hands, because that might make me cry. And I was determined not to cry. I was just taking care of my father for a few weeks. I wasn't being sucked into the vortex of my past. I wasn't *trapped* in my childhood home.

"I'll call you," I promised.

"You better," Travis retorted. "I don't know how you can stand to miss out on the traditional Sweat-lanta summer," he drawled. He was a local boy, born and raised with parents in Buckhead and that lovely drawl. He said it "Sweatlanna."

"It's not much better in New Jersey," I pointed out. "The humidity is already disgusting."

"Baby," he said patiently, "New Jersey is the armpit of the nation. What do you expect?"

I ignored the slur on my home state with the ease of long years' practice. Highway jokes, exit sign cracks, "armpit of the nation," *The Sopranos*, and the side-splitting irony of calling the place the "Garden State." No one ever came up with a new one.

"I'll be home soon," I promised him. Maybe with more ferocity than it warranted.

Home meant the comfortable ease of our life together: the friends we saw several nights a week, the parties and celebrations. The routine of our life as a couple. The simple pleasure of the two of us on the couch at the end of the day, so comfortable we didn't need to talk to each other. It was all about being on the same page. We wanted the same things. We liked the same people. We'd built the perfect life for ourselves with all those things we shared.

This place I'd grown up in wasn't real to me anymore, not the way Atlanta was. I was just a visitor here, pretending to belong to the people around me. But I didn't belong. It wasn't home any longer.

The first few days as nursemaid were a blur of visiting the hospital and preparing the house for a mostly immobile invalid. Christian and I made up the family room so Dad could get up and get downstairs—with help, of course—and have a place to watch television, snooze, and not have to be in his bed. Which worked better in theory than in practice.

The first day he was home, my father was too groggy to do much.

The second day, however, he was impossible.

Christian had taken off work to help with the transition, and by the time night rolled around and we'd put Dad to bed, the two of us were ready to leave him there.

For good.

"If he asks me one more time about those stupid fish, I'm killing him," Christian moaned, slumped against the kitchen counter.

"I don't think he was kidding." I shook my head. "I think he really does have a flowchart somewhere. Possibly several."

"If he hands you a flowchart, or even something that just *looks* like a flowchart, you have my permission to leave him upstairs. Permanently."

"Do you think he just made up the flowchart for fun one day?" I mused. "Or do you think he was anticipating the possibility that he might be incapacitated and someone else would have to feed the fish? Do you think the flowchart—"

"If you say the word 'flowchart' one more time," Christian informed me, his eyes narrow, "I'm killing both of you."

When I woke up on Saturday morning, it was like I was back in high school. I shuffled down the carpeted stairs to find Jeannie in the kitchen, slamming in and out of the refrigerator with unnecessary force and malice. As if the refrigerator had been getting smart with her and she had to teach it who was boss.

She had never been a morning person, I remembered with a smile. My mother had chirped—repeatedly—that "anyone can be a morning person if they put their mind to it, girls," but Jeannie had been evidence that some people just couldn't crack a smile before noon. Or before consuming seven large cups of coffee, whichever came first.

Jeannie was putting together a breakfast tray. Her hair was pulled back into a tight ponytail, and she was wearing the glasses she normally pretended not to own. She was also wearing the same patented scowl of outrage at being awake that I recalled from the entirety of our childhood, when she'd been the unofficial fourth McKay. Now my brother's ring sparkled on her finger, which I guess made it official.

I stood in the doorway and watched her crash around, hit suddenly with the force of all we'd lost. Losing a friend was like losing a language. The jokes were just never as funny if you tried to explain them to someone else. Whole private vocabularies disappeared. I smiled, thinking of those lost days, when we'd all scrambled around, grumpy and giggling on our way to school.

"What's so funny?" Jeannie asked, seeing me in the doorway. She sounded as if she was still mostly asleep, and blinked at me as if she too was confused into thinking I was the high school version of myself.

"This," I said, maneuvering around her with remembered ease to grab a mug and some coffee. I smiled. "What year is this?"

Jeannie yawned. Then she smiled slightly. "Junior year in high school, at least," she said, crossing her arms across her body. "Lord knows there was never any breakfast in my house. My mother still thinks it's funny that I had to come over here on my way to school every morning if I wanted to eat something before lunch." She shook her head. "Just one more thing to talk about in therapy."

We grinned at each other. Jeannie gave me an affectionate elbow to the stomach, more like a nudge. It felt like old times in a way I had never believed could happen again. I felt a rush of something, some emotion, and opened my mouth to comment on it. Maybe build a bridge.

Which is when Hope came stamping in from the outside. I turned away from Jeannie and the moment disappeared.

"Ah, the delightful Hope McKay chooses to grace us with her presence," Jeannie said smoothly. "And look, it's only nine in the morning. Have you been out all night?"

"When I want your opinion on what I do, Jeannie," Hope said, unperturbed, "you'll know because I'll *ask*."

"Hey, Hope," I greeted her mildly. "Were you somewhere fun?"

Hope stood in the doorway, as if about to take flight. She was wearing what was probably a clubbing outfit, which was all about her perfect legs and perfect abdomen. My younger sister was a hottie. And she knew it.

"Nowhere you'd know about," she said, in perfect seriousness. She rubbed at her eyes. "Are you making breakfast?"

"For your father," Jeannie said. She eyed Hope. "You know, the one you can't be bothered to take care of, because your life of debauchery and clubbing is more important."

"I know you *feel* like you're my older sister," Hope said, "but you're not. Try to remember that. And it is *way* too early in the morning." She collapsed into the nearest chair.

"Has anyone heard from Mom?" she asked.

"She called last night." I flicked her a look, but she looked only politely interested. "Christian talked to her. She's having a great time, although, of course, she's worried about Dad." I tried to sound as if I supported and understood this, but I wasn't sure I was successful.

Hope stared at the surface of the table and said nothing.

"Maybe it's for the best." I tried to sound reassuring. "Dad seems to think it's really important that this trip happen for her."

Hope's gaze was incredulous when it swung to me. "You can stop the Miss Perfect act, Meredith," she said. "Because there's no one here to see it and applaud."

Miss Perfect. My default family role. I hated it when they called me that—or, even worse, Saint Meredith—with that *tone*. As if it was outrageous that I tried to help out, to make things better. As if they were somehow better for sulking about everything (Hope) or demanding praise for lifting a pinky finger (Christian).

"The topic here is Mom, not me," I replied, stung. "And I'm not putting on any *act*, Hope."

Like *she* was in any position to judge anyone else.

"Whatever," Hope snapped. She lurched to her feet. "I have to crash."

"She's completely out of control," Jeannie said with a sniff when the sounds of Hope stamping up the stairs faded away. "She's probably still drunk."

"I wish I was," I muttered, and turned my attention to the breakfast tray.

"You don't do anything to help, Meredith," Jeannie continued. "Catering to her isn't going to make her change."

I watched her as she put the finishing touches on the tray. Jeannie thought she was such a big expert on Hope, but I noticed she hadn't opened her mouth on that topic until Hope had left the room. I also noticed that her fiancé was nowhere to be seen.

"Oh," she said when I asked. "He's at the gym. But he definitely wants to do as much as he can for you when he gets back. Before we head back down to Hoboken."

"It's nice of you to help out." It was a deliberate tone, that one. It suggested Jeannie was a helpful stranger at best.

She stiffened.

"Of course," she said. I'd obviously thrown her off-balance.

Score one for me, I thought, and took the tray upstairs.

The enforced rest was clearly not sitting well with Dad. His broken leg stuck out straight and unavoidable before him. His bare chest was patterned with bruises and yellow remnants of tubes and IVs. Medicine was much more violent in real life than it seemed when George Clooney was waving syringes around and smiling bashfully over gurneys. My father's body was marked and scarred. Maybe for good.

All of my early mental images of my father involved him in motion. Laughing, shouting, tossing footballs in the backyard with Christian, or dancing around the kitchen with Hope. He told long stories at parties that circled in and around themselves and always ended somewhere unplanned, and he had a merry laugh that was impossible to hear without smiling.

After his retirement, he'd seemed to shrink a little bit more every time I saw him. I could even hear it in his voice on the phone. The accident had made him even smaller, and worse— mortal.

I thought back to our small, insignificant talk in the basement right before the accident and it made heat pool behind my eyes. What if he had died? What if that was the last time I'd spoken to him? How would I ever deal with that?

"I love you, Dad," I told him as I settled his tray on the bedside table, before I knew the words were coming.

Once said, they seemed to ricochet around the room.

Dad looked startled, and uncomfortable. He blinked at me, then at the food, as if he suspected the cantaloupe might have precipitated this emotional outburst.

"Well," he said. He sounded baffled. "Well, Meredith. I love you too. Sweetheart."

It wasn't exactly violins swelling and the credits of a Hallmark Channel movie rolling, but it was something.

I knew better than to exhibit even the hint of tears—he might have a coronary, and a broken leg was quite enough drama, thanks—and so busied myself instead with fixing the tray, fluffing his pillows as he sat up, and other such mindless tasks until I got myself under control.

"I'm not sure I need a nursemaid," Dad said, clearly trying to curtail any further emotional declarations. He took a pillow and wedged it behind him, which required more movement than his leg could handle. Wincing, he tried to cover by swiping a piece of toast from the tray. He bit into it and chewed like he could get rid of his pain with his teeth.

"I'm not a nursemaid," I soothed at him.

This was not a man who could bear to show any weakness. I had distinct memories of him succumbing to colds or flus over the years. Each time he'd carried on as if his body had deliberately betrayed him and we, by implication and by being healthy, were in on it.

"I'm just going to help out around here, so you can concentrate on getting better."

"I appreciate the gesture, Meredith." He sounded weary, but he met my eye.

"You'll hardly notice your leg is broken!" I promised him. Rashly.

"But I will notice you hovering over me like a vulture," he

said, with a glimmer of exasperation. He tried to hide it, and sighed. "Can I just eat my breakfast in peace, please?" he asked. "I'm sure I'll be in a much better mood once I have my coffee and read the paper."

This didn't exactly surprise me. My dad could be sweet, but emotion? Forget it. Any concrete sign of love made him freeze up. Our version of hugging involved him stiffening, angling his torso away, and patting me awkwardly on the back. It was hardly intimate.

Being forced to accept this much help was probably just about the worst thing my father could imagine.

Out in the hallway, Jeannie was waiting for me. She straightened away from the wall and moved with me down the hall to my old—and current—bedroom. Jeannie sunk onto the bed, and I sat next to her out of habit, before I could think better of it.

I could admit it: I wasn't feeling very positive. About Dad or anything else. Why had I agreed to stay home in the first place? No one in their right mind would want this particular job.

"Is he any better today?" Jeannie asked. "Christian said yesterday was pretty bad."

"It must be tough for him," I mused aloud, trying to make myself feel better, if nothing else. "Think about what a control freak he is normally. This is his worst nightmare."

We sat quietly for a moment. I stared at the wall where my six-foot Wham! poster had hung throughout my youth. My mother had replaced it with a tasteful watercolor, and redone the once blue room in a palette of pinks. Nothing in the house—or in the family, for that matter—was safe from the force of my mother's attention.

I snuck a look at Jeannie from the corner of my eye. She was frowning at the same wall, as if she couldn't figure out what had changed.

"The Wham! poster," I supplied.

Her brow smoothed. "Of course. I was thinking Duran Duran, but I knew that wasn't quite right." She sighed. "I was always so jealous that you had that poster. My mother refused to let me hang stuff on her walls."

"When I came home for the summer after my junior year in college she'd overhauled the entire room." I shrugged. "The Wham! poster was long gone by then, but it was still a little disorienting."

"That's your mom," Jeannie said, with a sigh.

But I could hear the affection in her voice, and wondered why other people seemed to have no trouble at all seeing the great side of my mother. I seemed to only ever see the other side. The one involving that voice in my head.

"I think the real reason Dad didn't want to tell her about the accident is that it will prove what she's been saying for years," I said then. "You know, that he's a terrible driver."

"Who are you telling?" she asked with a chuckle. "Do you remember that time he almost killed us by driving the wrong way down that street? I *knew* we were going to die!"

She laughed that rich belly laugh of hers. It was so contagious I grinned. She'd always been able to do that. Growing up, we all would have done anything to make Jeannie laugh and then to bask in it.

Which is when I realized that I was slipping back into my old role again, confiding in Jeannie as if she was still my best friend. How did she do that? How did she make it so easy to feel comfortable around her, even when I knew better than to believe it?

I could tell that she was encouraging me to laugh along, maybe bond a little bit and patch things up between us, but something perverse stirred in me despite my wanting exactly that back in the kitchen. We weren't in high school anymore. She couldn't bridge the distance between us just by laughing, just by making me feel relieved to be back there laughing with her.

"Thanks for making my father breakfast," I said coolly, as if she was some distant acquaintance who'd mouthed a pleasantry about the weather. "I know he might not show it, but I'm sure he appreciates it."

Jeannie was quiet for a moment, then shook her head. Her mouth tightened.

"I can sense your appreciation," she said. "Whatever, Meredith."

She jumped to her feet and was through the door before I could react. She slammed it shut behind her, leaving me to blink into the silence.

Everything about her made me angry and sad at the same time. Maybe there would always be that part of me that yearned to relax back into the old embrace of our friendship. It was so tempting, after all. I'd known her forever. There were no surprises, easy laughter, a hundred shared stories.

But there was also something toxic in it, something that swirled around and exploded every now and then. I'd decided I was finished with those explosions after that last one, the summer before our sophomore year at separate colleges. But then Jeannie started dating Christian after college, so I'd sucked it up during the holidays, smiled hugely, made empty promises, and concentrated on my new life in Atlanta, the one I could control. The one that made sense.

I told myself I never looked back.

# Chapter 4

In the hot and airless week that followed, I threw myself into my new routine. I cranked up the AC, concentrated on one room in the house each day, and cleaned it from top to bottom. Scoured it, actually. When Mom got back, she'd find her house sparkling even brighter than when she'd left it. The very idea gave me intense satisfaction.

"You'd be surprised how much dust can accumulate in hidden corners," I told Travis on the phone. Smugly.

"You'd be surprised how little I want to know about dust accumulation," he replied. "How long should I put this chicken thing in the microwave for?"

The cleaning was for my own purposes, and I wasn't so sure I wanted to look too closely at my rationale. I reported my progress to Dad in half-hour intervals. Dad didn't care about cleaning wars or my need to prove myself through Lysol to my absent mother, of course.

What Dad cared about was his fish.

The flowchart Christian and I had been so afraid of was real. Terrifyingly, unavoidably real.

It wasn't a chart, exactly. It was a sheaf of papers attached to the sort of clipboard I associated with overenthusiastic coaches and mirthless retail managers. The papers included a map of the fish tanks in the basement (drawn to scale); a breakdown of the number of fish per tank; and several pages of incomprehensible scribbling I took to be either scientific data vaguely pertaining to the composition of the water in the tanks or (and far more alarming) some crude form of experimentation with fish DNA.

Clearly, retirement was driving my father stark raving mad.

Dad frowned at me anxiously as he watched me flip through the pages.

*All* the pages.

"It's very important that you follow the instructions *to the letter*," he insisted.

Which is when I saw that the final set of pages detailed how much fish food was to go into each tank at each feeding, complete with drawings of the *actual amount* of food Dad believed constituted "a pinch."

"When did this happen?" I wanted to know. Because this was a little bit scary, frankly. "Christian had one single goldfish. Once. There were never any other fish around the house, were there? When did you become the fish guy?"

"I've always liked fish." He sounded distracted.

"Really?"

I tried to remember any particular interest Dad had paid that lone goldfish, but all I could recall was the elaborate funeral ceremony Christian had insisted upon, and how angry he'd been that I'd failed to keep a straight face when he started reading *The Tenth Good Thing About Barney* over the toilet.

We'd been in fifth grade. It had been halfway through the seventh grade before Christian had fully forgiven me.

"I had fish as a boy," Dad said, definitely impatient now. "And much as I'd like to talk about them, it's the fish I have *now* that need your attention . . ."

"I'm on it!" I promised—cheerfully—and descended the rickety old stairs into the basement.

In the dark, and without my father there, the fish tanks took on a decidedly sinister cast. What was he *doing* with all those equations, so many that they filled up whole clipboarded pages? Was he brewing up some biological weapons here in our suburban New Jersey basement? Look at the Unabomber—a good education was no guarantee that a man wouldn't go completely nuts, given the right set of circumstances. Should I be calling Homeland Security instead of searching for the fish food?

Weapons were probably out, I decided, because that would involve carrying out attacks, which would in turn require *leaving* the basement. Dad didn't seem too keen on that idea. If he'd had his way, he'd probably prefer that we set up his recovery room down here in the middle of his creepy, tank-filled hobby.

As I looked around, however, I began to feel as if I was in some seventies sci-fi movie. It really was eerie. Maybe he wasn't making bioweapons—maybe he was breeding something horrible. Like monsters. Was my father some kind of mad scientist? *God only knew* what he was whipping up down here—Frankenstein with fins? Exactly what was that squiggly-looking thing, lurking right behind that rock in the nearest tank? Was it a tentacle? Was it *moving*—

"What are you doing?"

I lurched backward and screamed bloody murder, scaring Hope as much as she'd scared me. She scrambled back up the stairs and glared at me from halfway up the steps. I glared back from where I'd plastered myself against the nearest wall.

"You scared me half to death!" I told her. When I could breathe.

"You need to get a grip on yourself, Meredith," Hope retorted. "I almost swallowed my tongue!"

From upstairs, Dad shouted, "What happened down there? Did you break something?"

"Everything's fine!" I yelled up the stairs.

I rubbed at my heart, trying to manually convince it to stop beating so fast, and eyed Hope as I retrieved the clipboard from the foot of the stairs. Apparently, I'd planned to beat off my assailant with Dad's flowchart.

"I'm feeding the fish," I told her. With great dignity. "According to this chart, it should take me just about forty-five minutes."

"Yeah," she said. "That's because he likes to talk to them. Mom thinks he names them. Anyway, you can do it in five."


I cooked nutritious meals to keep my father from ballooning up to blimp size without any exercise. I knocked myself out trying to make them appealing.

"What the hell is this?" Dad demanded with equal parts outrage and disgust over the dinner table one night. "Did I die and turn into a rabbit?"

"I think we call them *salads*." Hope exaggerated that last word into about ten syllables.

"Don't you use that tone with me, young lady." Dad's eyes glinted when he looked at her. "As far as I know, I'm your only source of income."

"Dad," I interrupted, sharing a quick glance with Hope. "It's a salad, yes, but there's all that good stuff in there. A little bacon—"

"Turkey bacon," Hope amended. She caught my expression. "Which you can't even tell."

Later, I washed the dishes with some of the aggression I was trying to hide from my father. He was watching reruns of *NYPD Blue* on cable in the family room, with the volume turned up so loud I thought Sipowicz was inside my head.

"You want to go out?" Hope asked. She paused in the kitchen doorway. "Why don't you just leave those? Jesus, Meredith, you're not the hired help."

"Who else is going to do them?" I asked, maybe with a little hostility. Definitely with an extra helping of self-pity.

Hope whistled. "That sounded so much like Mom it actually sent a chill down my spine. Did you know you could channel her like that?"

"Very funny."

"I'm not kidding. Sneak up on Dad and do that. See if he jumps." She sashayed past me and helped herself to a cookie. "In the meantime, please spare me the martyr routine. It's frightening."

I wiped my hands dry on one of my mother's decorative dishtowels. "I think I got your point about five minutes ago."

"You need to get out of this house," Hope advised me, her expression serious. "You probably forgot, since you've been living hundreds of miles away, but it's poisonous here." She waved her hand at the walls. "Emotional asbestos."


For fun, or something else—something much closer to obsessive-compulsive disorder than I was comfortable admitting—I cooked meals nobody ate. I made stews and soups and so many desserts I had to start freezing them. I fed the freaking fish twice a day, as ordered, and marked down changes in environment—also as ordered—on the intricately plotted graph Dad had provided for that very purpose. I cleaned and scrubbed, and then, finally, exactly ten days after I'd come north to help out, it occurred to me that I had turned into a housewife. Possibly even a Stepford Wife, as Hope had predicted.

It was different at home, for Travis, because I paid half the rent and held down my own job, as boring as it was. I *wanted* to cook and clean for Travis. I enjoyed it. In fact, I'd practically made it into an art form.

We had a comfortable routine in Atlanta—a routine I'd worked hard to perfect. I was good with the details of things, and my life with Travis was a triumph of details. From the moment he woke up to the moment he went to sleep, I made sure our life together flowed smoothly and easily. I spent hours at work trolling the Internet for recipes I thought he'd like, and tried never to repeat any single recipe too often—in case he thought I'd lost interest in cooking for him. I anticipated the work clothes he'd be likely to want each week, so I could be sure to either wash them or get them to the dry cleaner in time. I liked the glow of pride I got when he noticed the things I did for him, or when he told me how great our life together was.

And it was great, all right. I made sure of it. The weather was good, and unlike the East Coast, the people were cheerful. It was sweet and easy, and we lived in the shade of magnolia trees.

It was the perfect life.

Here in New Jersey, the same things felt entirely different. Here, working out the details seemed to be another chore like the ones Mom had assigned when we were kids. Here, I was an angry and bitter housewife with perfectionist leanings and the early signs of OCD.

Not just any housewife, then. My mother.

Kill me now.

I packed the cleaning supplies back onto their shelf in the laundry room and then approached my father in his den. He lay with his leg elevated in his recliner, books and remote controls within easy reach. I exchanged his soda for a new one, and crooked his straw into just the right angle.

"Dad," I chirped brightly, "do you need anything else?"

"I'm just enjoying a little peace and quiet," he said with a slightly battered version of his usual grin.

"I'm going to go out, then." I frowned. "The phone is right here. If you feel even the slightest pain—"

"I was in a car accident, Meredith," my father said impatiently.

Maybe my chirpy voice was getting to him—Lord knew, it was putting my own teeth on edge.

"I did not have a lobotomy," he continued in the same tone. "I believe I can remember how to dial a phone."

"All right then," I said in my normal voice, ignoring *his* tone of voice. No one wanted to be the daughter who got in fights with her incapacitated father. "I'll be back soon."

It felt good to leave the house without being on an errand involving my father's needs or groceries. It felt good to leave the house, period. It felt even better to drive a little bit too fast on the highway, almost like I was escaping, and drive around in my mother's ridiculously oversized SUV—which, naturally, she required for all the suburban off roading she did.

I had the geography of northern New Jersey imprinted on my brain, from the thousands of hours I'd wasted as a teenager just driving the same streets again and again. On weekends or after school, Jeannie and I would drive aimlessly until we were lost, and then try to find our way back home again. The towns blurred together, a mess of tunnels and bridges and New York City glimmering in the distance, peeking up over this hill and across that ridge.

Eventually, I headed back into town, staring at the familiar streets and sights of the place I'd grown up. At one end of the main thoroughfare were the train tracks that carried so many residents to work each morning in Manhattan. At the other was the impressive-looking high school where I'd marked my time and allowed Jeannie and Christian to sweep me along in their wake. The public pool where we'd all learned to swim was just a stone's throw from the public library and the town hall with all its policemen, whose days could hardly be considered difficult, what with the dangerous jaywalkers and illegal parkers. It was a deliberately, self-consciously nice place to live. Safe when very little was safe anymore—or it had been. I could remember some truly poor adolescent decisions—Christian's decisions, of course, which I got caught up in—that had ended well enough, simply because it was so safe. It was hard to believe that New York City was only some fifteen miles away.

It was even harder to believe I was home again. It was different at Christmas. My visits were packed full and I rarely had more than a few days. No time to reexplore the place where I'd grown up. No time to even *want* to.

I parked near the shaded green lawn of the central square and wandered. Gentrification had claimed the place, bringing shiny chain stores and a booming restaurant business. It was a different town entirely than the one I remembered: face-lifted and sleek, and filled to bursting with Saturday day trippers from the city and New Jersey ladies who lunched across three counties.

It was blazingly hot in the afternoon sun, and I ducked into the bookstore to escape it. It was the last remaining independent bookstore in town. There were three separate corporate giants out on the highway, an easy drive, and so the bookstore was forced to cater to the many elitists who lived in town and could be convinced that waiting to order a book was better for their intellectual health than going out to the larger highway stores and picking it up immediately.

I smiled automatically at the woman behind the counter and wandered around the display tables. I picked up a signed copy of the latest Stephen King novel, and then set it down again without reading the back. I liked the weight of books, their shape in my hands. I ran my fingers along a stack of brightly colored paperbacks. Pinks and lime greens, all begging to be bought.

And then I looked up and saw a familiar figure standing at the table, facing me but frowning down at the book in his hands.

I hadn't seen him in years, but I recognized him immediately. Scott Sheridan.

He'd grown up across the street from us. Christian had spent long years tormenting Scott simply because Scott was there and Christian could. Scott had been forever branded a loser in our class in school because he'd had the misfortune to cry once in the third grade and to thereafter express a lack of interest in team sports.

But the fact that I recognized him didn't mean he looked the same.

From his dark hair to the fine, lean lines of his body, he bore almost no resemblance at all to the version of him I carried in my head—that gawky teenage boy, all elbows and skinny legs. This Scott Sheridan wore casual shorts and a T-shirt with the careless grace of a man entirely comfortable with himself and his body. A man who was not looked down upon because he'd burst into tears in the third grade. A man who was more hot than cute, but was, shockingly, both.

I tried to make the versions match.

He looked up, and I was trapped in his gaze. It made my stomach clench. This Scott Sheridan was all gray eyes, dark hair, and a mouth that inspired several choice fantasies. In rapid, vivid succession.

I was so surprised I took a step back.

"Meredith McKay," he said, sounding out my name. As if he was remembering how to say it.

"Scotty Sheridan," I replied. And no more fantasies about his mouth, please. My heart could only take so much.

His smile crinkled up the corners of his eyes, and my heart skipped a beat. "I pretty much dropped the 'y' when I turned ten," he said.

I felt myself flush red. "Of course you did," I said. "I'm sorry."

He considered me for a long moment, and then flicked his eyes back to the book in his hand. He shut it with a snap and returned his gaze to mine. There was a smile lurking somewhere in there, somewhere not quite hidden.

"I heard about your father," he said politely. "I hope he's doing well?"

"He's better every day." Which was technically true.

Scott nodded. "That's great," he said. "You're up visiting?"

"Oh."

I hadn't yet had to explain my presence to anyone. It had occurred to me that my mother's failure to return to her husband's side might possibly be seen as a curious decision. Even a negligent decision. And I certainly didn't want to be responsible for casting my mother in an unfavorable light, even if only in front of a former classmate, who, if I remembered right, had had a ferocious crush on me for the better part of puberty. It made my cheeks heat to think of it.

When I focused on him again, Scott was smiling.

"Was that a trick question?"

"No!" I laughed. "Of course not! I'm just here to help out."

There was something about him, about the way he looked at me, as if he delighted in what he saw. He made me nervous. He also made me wish I had paid some attention to my appearance before racing from the house. I was blushing again, which could only draw attention to the state of my hair and the less-than-pristine tank top I'd pulled on earlier. I tugged at it.

*Why, exactly, do I care what I look like in front of Scotty Sheridan?* asked a small voice within me. I ignored it.

"I was about to get some coffee," Scott said after a moment, his smile deepening. Almost as if he could read my mind. "Want to come?"

I was so surprised that I froze. The invitation hung there. Scott laughed.

"Come on," he said. "You danced with me at the senior prom. What's a cup of coffee next to such a supreme sacrifice?"

"I did?" Even as I asked, I had a hazy memory of some slow song and Scott's oddly formal swaying. "I completely forgot about that," I said quickly, before his smile could do something more dangerous. Maybe to my respiratory system. "But I'd love to have a cup of coffee with you. We can catch up."

His mouth twitched, but he only gestured for me to precede him toward the door and arched an arrogant brow. He was definitely hot, I thought. But nothing as nice and safe as *cute*.

We walked back outside into the summer glare. I was entirely too happy to slip my sunglasses back on. I wanted the barrier.

"So," I said as we walked into the coffee shop. "Why are you in town? Summer vacation?"

"I live here," Scott said.

"Oh."

"Not 'oh,'" he said, sliding me a look heavy with amusement. "I'm not the loser your family thinks I am, Meredith. I work in the county prosecutor's office, and I live here because my mother is old and frail and I'm all she has. I live out by the baseball field." He threw me a cheeky grin. "Ironic, I know."

"I didn't say anything!" I protested.

"You didn't have to." He looked down at me and his eyes sparkled with mischief. "Your sister gave me the entire Scotty Sheridan Sucks story at Christmas."

"The what?" I asked weakly, but I was horrified. A swift glance from him told me he wasn't fooled. I had actually forgotten that too—but it quickly flooded back.

Scotty Sheridan Sucks had been a family game, played on car trips or to while away boring family events. Ring-led by Christian but always egged on by Hope's evil imagination, we tried to top each other with fabricated Scotty Sheridan Sucks stories. *Scotty Sheridan sucks*, someone would begin, *because he eats his own gym shorts*. And so on. It had begun because of the notorious third-grade crying incident, but had taken on a life of its own as a sibling bonding ritual. It hadn't been about the real Scott Sheridan at all, or at least it had only been about him at first, but how to explain that?

"What exactly did she tell you?"

"Enough," Scott said. He grinned. "Scotty Sheridan sucks because he vacuums his—"

"Oh my God, please stop!" I was appalled.

"She was pretty drunk." His eyebrows arched upward. "But I think I got the idea. I had no idea I inspired such creativity."

Once at the coffee shop, we ordered iced coffee drinks and sat outside on one of the benches. The sun was hot and traffic eased by on the street in front of us. I was too aware of the man sitting next to me, and for once I was at a loss for words.

"Scott," I ventured when the silence had drawn on too long. "I'm really sorry. Hope should never have told you any of that."

What was *wrong* with my sister? Did she even live in the same world as the rest of us?

He laughed again. "It's nice of you to apologize," he said. "But I'm not sure you can."

"What do you mean?"

He looked at me. "It's like high school. Can anyone really apologize for things they did in high school? I think you'll find no apology will do."

I thought about some of the grudges I still held from back then. None of them were *gone*, necessarily, I'd just incorporated them into my adult self. And Scott was right, no apology could change that.

"So you won't accept an apology." I sipped at my drink and felt like smiling for some reason. "I have nothing else to offer you."

"I'll keep that in mind." He smiled back at me. "But I'll note for the record that the apology was *offered*. It's not as if you can pay restitution for dragging my good name through the mud for decades, now is it?"

I groaned. "So you're saying I'm stuck in your debt?"

"Maybe." He sipped from his drink and stretched his legs out in front of him. "That could be interesting, exploring debt and restitution with Meredith McKay."

Our eyes locked and held, and I felt something turn over inside of me.

As if he could feel it himself, Scott grinned.

# Chapter 5

In future, I would do my best to avoid having intense conversations, brimming with undercurrents I chose not to explore, with old acquaintances from high school, I told myself sternly while driving back from coffee with Scott.

Especially high school acquaintances who once had a crush on you, and were now entirely too interested in telling you all the reasons they held long-term grudges against your family. *All* the reasons. In detail.

In fact, high school in general was better avoided entirely, as a personal policy. Who had anything nice to say about their high school experience? And if they did, why would you want to talk to them? If that wasn't irrefutable proof of mental illness, what was?

I picked up my cell phone to call Travis and rant about Scott, high school, and anything else that came to mind about being trapped in my hometown. When his office phone shot me straight to voice mail, though, I hung up. The truth was, Travis would be fairly alarmed to discover I had a rant in me. I wasn't much of a ranter, and Travis didn't really like surprises. Me in a full-on rant might make him nervous.

And if I was really honest with myself, I didn't *want* to tell Travis about Scott. Like his once-upon-a-time crush on me, back in the day, was something private. Something that was only mine, that might make being here better somehow. Or maybe because I knew Travis would demand to hear the entire Scotty Sheridan story, and would start mocking him too.

In any case, I didn't leave a message.

When I turned down our street, I had a near-giddy urge to slam my foot against the gas pedal in Mom's huge car and roar off in a cloud of exhaust—anything to escape the figure loitering near the front lawn.

Of course, I knew better.

Gladys Van Eck knew the make, model, and permitted list of drivers of every vehicle within a five-mile radius of her home, which was, tragically, right next door.

Gladys Van Eck had been old when I was a kid, which meant she now had to be at least two hundred, and she'd been in a bad mood for at least the last hundred and seventy-five of those years. She owned a succession of mean-tempered, snotty-looking Yorkshire terriers whom she adorned in bows twice the size of their heads and paraded through the neighborhood. She claimed she was exercising them, but no one was fooled by this claim.

The woman was a spy.

Gladys Van Eck—known, inevitably, as Mrs. Van Ick to the neighborhood kids and not a few of their parents—knew everything about everyone. She tattled on teenage parties and called the town to report derelict cars in driveways—or even more hideous suburban offenses, like chipping paint on garages and recycling in the wrong garbage bins. She clocked the speeds of cars past her house and called in reports on habitual speeding offenders, particularly if said offenders were under the age of eighteen.

She was the most hated woman in the neighborhood, and, therefore, every single neighbor kissed her ass and bent over backwards trying to appease her. Each attempt to curry favor made her more suspicious.

"Meredith McKay!" Her voice rang out like a school bell. It had the same effect, too—I winced, immediately reduced to somewhere around the age of thirteen, and obeyed. My half-formed plan to break for the back door died in infancy.

"Hi, Mrs. Van Eck," I said as politely as possible. There had been a Mr. Van Eck and even kids, I remembered hearing years ago, but that was long before my time and I wasn't sure I believed it.

"You're looking well enough, Meredith." She strode toward me. No osteoporosis for the neighborhood menace, naturally. She'd be outrunning us all for decades yet in her obnoxious pastel pantsuits and that awful little sun hat.

"Is that little Athena?" I cooed at the dog. Like her predecessors, the dog sported a droopy bow clinging to a vertical tuft of brown hair on her tiny head. The bow was robin's egg blue. The dog sniffed, quivered, and then commenced barking as if I'd tried to kick her.

Mrs. Van Eck glared at me as if I had.

"Her name is Isabella," she barked.

"Little Isabella," I simpered on cue. The dog bared its teeth at me from beneath the quivering blue bow. Little runt.

"I can't help noticing that the grass in your mother's front lawn is overgrown," Mrs. Van Eck snapped at me, her eyes narrowed. She clearly suspected that the overgrown grass was part of a larger plot she had yet to uncover. Her expression warned me that she was on the case. Isabella yipped in agreement.

"Is it?" I peered past her at the lawn. It looked fine to me, but then, what did I know about grass? What I did know was this: if there was a certain length suburban neighbors were supposed to keep their grass, Mrs. Van Eck would be out there with a ruler ensuring compliance.

"I know your father is laid up with that leg of his, but that's no excuse to let the yardwork slide," she continued. From a distance, it probably looked like she was concerned. I was closer. "I think your mother would be beside herself if she imagined that she'd left her house in such a state that the neighbors had to step in."

*Neighbors*, she said. Like she was an entire coalition of the concerned, instead of a lone gorgon on a rampage.

"I'll get my brother to mow the lawn," I interjected, because I felt like kicking at her or the dog and that would be A Very Bad Idea. "But I'm sorry, I'm in a big rush to get some lunch for Dad . . ." Diversionary tactics were my only option. Next she'd be talking about the state of the pachysandra beds and we could be there for days.

I could practically see the steam come out of her ears. She didn't like being foiled.

But then, the woman packed her own arsenal.

"I thought I heard you were engaged by now," she said, looking pointedly at my notably ringless left hand.

We both stared at my bare fingers. My hand twitched entirely of its own volition, and it almost hurt not to clench it into a fist. Isabella howled with what sounded like doggy malicious laughter and danced around on her hind legs, the vicious little cur.

"I remember now," Mrs. Van Eck said, relishing the moment. "It was that Gillespie girl you were always running around with. But then, she was always so pretty."

When I got inside, I found Hope and Jeannie seated across from each other at the kitchen table, squared off as if they were preparing to debate.

Or possibly tear each other's hair out.

I wasn't sure which of the two I would find more diverting. Okay—the hair pulling, definitely. Tough as Jeannie might be, I'd long suspected that my baby sister could kick ass in the literal sense. And the truth was, after dealing with that horrible woman, I was interested in a little violence.

"What's going on?" I looked from one to the other. "Is Dad okay?"

"Your father is fine," Jeannie said, never taking her eyes off Hope. "Little Miss It's All About Me—"

"I think she means me," Hope contributed in an exaggerated stage whisper. I fought the urge to laugh.

"—and I were just having a little talk about family responsibilities," Jeannie continued as if Hope hadn't spoken.

"Meaning our family, not her own," Hope drawled, and smiled up at me. "Would it be rude of me to point out for the eight trillionth time that Jeannie isn't actually a member of my family just yet?" She turned her smile on Jeannie, and it went wide and fake. "I'm making the most of my last few weeks of freedom, you know."

"It's obviously unfair to you that Hope lives here and refuses to help out with your father," Jeannie carried on in her teacher mode, the one that paid no attention whatsoever to Hope's comments and yet—make no mistake—heard them, filed them away, and planned to use them later.

It occurred to me that Jeannie, having been the Mean Girl Supreme when we were in high school, was probably an excellent teacher for that very reason. She could see those teenage girls coming a mile away. It was an interesting concept.

"Did I miss something?" I asked, getting back to the task at hand. I took the chair at the end of the table, placing myself between them. Like a mediator. "When did the two of you declare yourselves mortal enemies?"

"When I was born," Hope said at once. I recalled that Hope, unlike the rest of the family, had never been overly impressed with Jeannie. It must have been the years of unjust torture at her hands. That kind of thing was only forgivable from a blood relative.

"Jeannie's always been jealous of the fact that while she *wanted* to be the other sister in this family, I *actually am* that sister," Hope continued merrily. She batted her lashes at Jeannie, leaned forward a little, and mouthed, *Sorry!*

Jeannie's eyes narrowed, and Hope smirked. It was about to get ugly.

"I just saw Scotty Sheridan in town," I said abruptly, hoping to forestall the bloodshed.

As bombshells went, it rated pretty high on the shock and awe scale. They both quit trying to stare down the other, and stared at me instead.

"We had coffee." I shrugged. And wished I hadn't said anything.

"With Scotty Sheridan?" Jeannie looked lost. "Why?"

"Scotty Sheridan is a hottie now," Hope said. "Hard to believe, but true. My friend Katie says that guys who were geeky in high school almost always end up hot. They have so much more motivation to use their twenties to their advantage."

"Are we talking about the same Scotty Sheridan?" Jeannie asked. "*The* Scotty Sheridan? The one who lived across the street?"

"It's just Scott these days," I told them both. Then I glared at my sister. "And what possessed you to tell him about Scotty Sheridan Sucks? Are you insane?"

Hope looked blank, and then laughed. "Oh yeah. Oops."

"No one needs to hear that they were the butt of jokes for years," I told her with a bit more heat than necessary. "How do you think hearing about that made him feel?"

"Aren't you going a little overboard?" Hope shook her head. "The man is what? Thirty years old? What does he care what we said about him twenty years ago?"

"No one likes to hear something like that," I repeated. Stubbornly. "It was mean to tell him about it, pure and simple."

"And if he *does* care," Hope continued, "he should do some more work with his therapist. Because who comes out looking like the asshole in this story?" She leaned back in her chair. "Not Scott Sheridan, let me tell you."

"I can't process this," Jeannie moaned. She looked at me. "Are you standing up for Scotty Sheridan? Did you actually *have coffee* with Scotty Sheridan? *And* he's hot?" She shook her head as if to clear it. "I knew something was weird when I woke up this morning. Silly me, I thought it was too much cheese before going to bed last night."

"Maybe it's just you," Hope suggested. Jeannie rolled her eyes, but didn't respond.

"He's cool," I told Jeannie. I didn't want to get into the 'hot' thing, or even near it. It was too disturbing. Obviously, that left only a good offense. "He's a lawyer now. Which should worry you, in case the statute of limitations hasn't run out on being a teenage drama queen at his expense."

"Like you're one to talk!" Jeannie fired back at once. "You would have thought dancing with him at the prom was a freaking virgin sacrifice, the way you carried on about it."

"You danced with him at the prom?" Hope asked me, looking delighted. I frowned at her, but returned my attention to Jeannie.

"You were the one who told me that being seen dancing with him would be the same as dating him," I reminded her. "You told me it would be like 'social suicide,' and I did it anyway, didn't I?"

"Oh please," Jeannie scoffed. "You take selective memory to a whole new level. Like anyone cared who you danced with."

"Was the high school a John Hughes movie when you guys went there?" Hope asked. "Because when I was there, it was just a high school."

"You certainly had a lot to say about who I danced with," I threw at Jeannie.

"Here's a news flash, Meredith," Jeannie snapped at me. "I wasn't as obsessed with you as you were. If Scotty Sheridan had asked *me* to dance—"

"As if he'd dare. You'd have ripped him into pieces for daring to talk to you in public."

"—I would have *just said no!*"

There was a small silence as Jeannie and I glared at each other, broken by Hope's amused chuckle.

"I can't believe you guys are fighting about the senior prom," she said. "I'm not sure I can even remember my senior prom." She frowned. "Actually, I don't think I *went* to my senior prom."

Jeannie looked away and I took a moment to reflect that Hope was frighteningly right: it was embarrassing that I was even *discussing* the senior prom. It was one thing for Jeannie— she taught in a high school; she had to deal every day with teenage drama and it no doubt reminded her of her own.

I had no such excuse.

This was obviously the sort of horrifying thing that happened if you were foolish enough to move back home with your parents. You reverted back to yourself at seventeen, with everything that entailed. On the one hand, I wouldn't mind fitting into the jeans I'd worn at seventeen. On the other, it's not like there was a call for high-waisted, tapered-leg jeans in today's world of low-cut, boot-legged denim, and anyway, who in their right mind would ever want to be seventeen again? I'd barely survived being seventeen the first time around. What was next? Fights with my father about curfew? Prank-calling boys? *Where did it all end?*

"I just think this is a tense time," Jeannie said, snapping me out of rising hysteria. "Your father's accident, your mother's trip, the fact that you uprooted yourself to move all the way up here because Hope is too wrapped up in herself to take any responsibility for her family . . ." She let her voice trail away.

"Make sure you get that last part in there," Hope said with a sigh. "It might distract attention from the fact that you *want* to be in this family and yet there's been no sign of you around here since Meredith came home."

"I have a wedding to plan," Jeannie said, giving in and responding directly to Hope.

I, meanwhile, had a strange out-of-body moment. I could feel the part of me that felt seventeen again respond to Jeannie, making me want to join in and snap at Hope. But the other, older part of me took a step back and wondered. Neither one of them was helpful, really, but at least Hope was around the house. The last time I'd seen Jeannie she'd stormed out of my room and slammed the door. There'd been no sign of her or my brother since then. I might want to kill my little sister, but at least she was *here*.

I opened my mouth to say something about that, to take a stand for once instead of doing my usual routine, which was to run away and live in another state or—over holidays—to pretend everything was hunky-dory. But before I could say anything, the phone began to ring.

I told myself that I was annoyed at the interruption as I hurried to answer it, but I knew better. I was relieved.


Things to talk about with your mother on the telephone when she's cavorting about Europe with her sister while you are trapped in the house, taking care of her husband and driving yourself crazy having arguments about events that were meaningless ten years ago:

"Oh!" I said merrily. "The weather is all right, actually! The humidity hasn't been *too* bad, and today's just beautiful! Hot, but beautiful! August will probably be a different story!"

Exclamation points again! I could actually taste them.

"I knew I could count on you, sweetheart," Mom said from across the ocean. "But I do worry that you left Travis on his own like that. Men don't like to come second best, Meredith. You'll learn that you have to put them front and center, or they'll find someone who will."

Apparently, that was what you talked about when you were cavorting about Europe with your sister while your daughter

abandoned her life to live the one you left behind in New Jersey.
I rubbed at my temples. I never could seem to understand my
mother. Why should that change now?

"Travis will deal," I said, with perfect confidence I didn't actually feel. "He's completely supportive of my being here."

What Travis *actually* was, I chose not to say, was frustratingly
incapable of talking on the telephone. He could discuss football
teams for hours on the phone with his college friends, but talking to his girlfriend? Forget it. It was one thing to lounge about
in comfortable quiet on our couch together. It was something
else entirely to have to work so hard at conversation on the
phone. He was such a . . . *guy*.

But I wasn't about to tell my mother that.

"If you say so, dear," Mom said.

As if she suspected otherwise, but was too well-bred to say
anything.

I wanted to scream. Instead, I asked about Italy.


"I only have a few minutes," Christian said in his phone voice,
the one that reminded me that some people probably didn't
think it was weird that he was a lawyer. "Jeannie's really down
about the wedding, Meredith. She thought you and Hope
would be honored to be such an integral part of our special
day, and instead it's like neither of you can even be bothered
about it."

"The wedding? What's going on with the wedding?" I stared
at the phone. Was he kidding? Of course he wasn't kidding. He
never used his Speech Voice when he was kidding, because
probably he didn't know how silly it sounded. "I offered to help
about a thousand times when you got engaged, but—"

"Jeannie asked both of you to be in the wedding party," Christian cut me off. "You've been her best friend since we were three years old! I can't believe you aren't more into this!"

How to even begin answering that?

"Well, Christian," I began. "I'm surprised that all of a sudden you've forgotten that ever since, oh, sophomore year of college, Jeannie and I have kind of stopped—"

"You have no idea how stressful the entire process is!" Christian interrupted fiercely. "Jeannie wants the bridesmaids' stuff all taken care of as soon as possible—and let me tell you something, Meredith, I think you should ask yourself what kind of person makes her own sister-in-law *cry* while she's getting ready for what *ought to be* the happiest day of her life!"

There was a small pause while I inhaled and told myself that I wasn't touching that one with a ten-foot pole. After all, the first thing that came to mind was to reiterate what Hope had said days before—that Jeannie wasn't my sister-in-law *yet*, and let's not rush into anything.

But this, I was pretty certain, was not what my brother wanted to hear.

I opted for: "I'm sorry that Jeannie's upset."

Christian heaved a sigh. "I didn't mean that," he said. "Jeannie's just freaking out, usually on me. It's not your fault." Nor was it his, he didn't say, but I inferred from the sigh.

"I was calling to tell you that dinner tomorrow is at seven," I said, powering through. "You're still planning to come, right? You seem to have disappeared on me," I couldn't help adding.

"I'm busy, Meredith." Christian's tone was ever so slightly patronizing. "I can't be there every night."

"You're not here *any* night."

Petty? Perhaps. But also true.

"Do you have any idea how tough this is for Jeannie?" Christian continued as if I hadn't spoken. "All she asked is that you *try on* a stupid dress you already own. How hard can that be?"

"I don't know what you're talking about!"

"Jeannie is actually really bad at standing up for herself when it comes to personal shit," Christian informed me.

In direct contradiction of everything he or I had ever known about Jeannie Gillespie since we were all in preschool. Who was he kidding?

"I want the dress thing dealt with, Meredith."

And he hung up.

"Oh yeah," Hope said later when it occurred to me to ask her. "Jeannie did call." She looked up from the television and smiled. "I tuned out when she mentioned the word 'salmon' again. Like I don't know that's pink, and no way am I wearing pink, which I told her a million times when we tried on all those dresses at Christmas." She finally noticed that I wasn't reacting, and was in fact just staring at her. "What?"


The mornings were the only time the temperature was bearable, and so I started running then, before the sun had a chance to do its damage. I thought longingly of the gym Travis and I belonged to in Atlanta, beautifully air-conditioned with treadmills all in a row. There was nothing close to cool on the New Jersey streets. The cicadas hummed, gearing up for the long, hot day ahead, and I picked my way through an obstacle course of landscaping trucks and trailers and the heavy, sweet smell of the linden trees.

I did the short loop that I'd run when I was in high school and running was the only time I ever had to myself. I was walking a bit in a vain attempt to cool down when I headed back toward the house. As I approached it, I saw a car pull into the Sheridans' driveway across from ours. Scott emerged and went around to the trunk to pull out some grocery bags.

The thing was, I really didn't like the way Jeannie had spun that whole prom story. *I* wasn't the drama queen, *I* was the nice one. In fact, I'd made *being nice* my career.

Also, he really *was* hot. Shockingly so, considering what he'd looked like at fifteen. On a purely biological level, it was fascinating.

"Hi!" I said brightly when I came closer. He looked up, letting his eyes settle on me. I knew then that he'd seen me coming from a long way off.

I kicked my smile into high gear. To match my heartbeat.

"I make this amazing lasagna," I said. "I made the sauce last night, because it takes a while, and letting it sit makes it even better. I'm going to serve dinner around seven. You should come by, if you feel like it."

Scott's jaw worked for a moment, as if he might laugh.

"Are you for real?" he asked finally.

"It's a lasagna," I said. "No big deal. My brother and his fiancée are coming over. All very casual."

"You're inviting me to sit down and have a cheery family meal with Christian McKay?" Scott asked, laughter threaded through his voice. "Christian McKay who was the bane of my existence from the age of five when we moved here until the glorious day of our high school graduation? Are you mentally ill?"

Definitely a valid question.

"He's mellowed a lot," I offered.

Scott shook his head and laughed. It was real laughter, and it made his eyes brighten. I blinked.

"Unreal," was all he said. He looked at me, still laughing, and then he hoisted up his bags and headed toward his mother's front door.

I watched him go. When the door thudded to a close behind him, I turned and made my way across the street.

And thought, *What the hell are you doing?*

"Sorry we're late!" Jeannie sang, pushing in through the door.

She looked like an advertisement for something swanky yet laid back, in a cute little sundress and her hair in a casually chic up-do. I immediately felt grungy, in a pair of old jeans and a tank top liberally sprinkled with lasagna sauce. I grimaced at the hot oven and shoved my hair back from my face.

"You're not late," Hope said from where she slouched at the table. "Ten minutes still counts as on time." She looked past Jeannie pointedly. "Unless you're anal."

Christian came in behind Jeannie, already frowning, and missed Hope's dig. "Where's Dad?" he wanted to know.

"He couldn't be bothered to engage in a family dinner," Hope said dryly. She pursed her lips. "You go and argue with him if you want, but I don't think he gives a shit."

"Nice language, Hope," Christian said, and shook his head. Hope smiled sweetly and gave him the finger. He rolled his eyes and then frowned at me. "He's really not coming down?"

"You can go up and say hello," I suggested. I leaned back against the counter. "Nice to see you, big brother. And since you're here, Mrs. Van Eck thinks the grass needs mowing. I think that's officially a guy thing."

"Yikes. Van Ick strikes again," Jeannie murmured, amused.

"My theory is she died in the last world war and this is just one of a series of clones," Hope offered. "Those awful little yip dogs too."

"Yeah," Christian muttered. He frowned at Hope and me in turn. "I'm going to go up and see Dad." He left the room, and we could all hear him take the stairs two at a time.

Dad had had a rough day, which I thought had a lot to do with my mother's latest call. It was probably hard to be upbeat about healing when your wife was having *such* a good time in Italy, but what did I know? As Mom continued to point out, I'd be lucky to still have a boyfriend when I got back to Atlanta. A boyfriend whose version of sending me clothes had involved the selection of the ugliest pieces in my wardrobe—but that was neither here nor there.

Jeannie settled herself at the kitchen table and smiled.

"This has been such a crazy week," she announced. "You wouldn't believe how ridiculous some of these wedding people are. It's a complete racket."

Neither Hope nor I really responded to that, and Jeannie's smile disappeared.

"You look ragged," she told me, her voice dripping concern. "I thought good little southern girls never let anyone see them sweat."

This was the kind of thing that Jeannie had done so well when we were younger. Somehow, she always knew what button to push. It was so close to what I'd already been thinking that I felt the urge to smack her. Instead I turned and fiddled with the stove until the urge went away. It took a while.

"Not everyone has time to primp all day," Hope was saying. In my defense? I slid a look her way.

"You just can't stop pushing, can you?" Jeannie asked Hope with a sigh.

"You know, I can't," Hope drawled. "I wonder what it is about you, Jeannie, that makes it impossible?" There was a smirk in her voice, if not on her face. I bit back my own smile.

"He's not doing so well," Christian announced, coming back into the kitchen. He had a definite edge in his voice. "What the hell, Meredith?"

"Excuse me?" I was taken back.

"I mean, what are you doing out here? He hasn't even shaved!" He threw that fact out as if it was proof of neglect. *Did you check him for bedsores?* I asked him acidly. And silently.

"You shave him then," Hope suggested. "Because I'm not going near that man with a razor. But you knock yourself out."

"Please, Hope, give it a rest!" Christian snapped. "You couldn't be bothered to help out—remember? You're not involved in this!"

Hope's eyes narrowed, but she only shrugged.

"I think he's a little depressed," I announced.

"Depressed," Christian repeated. As if he'd never heard the word and had to sound it out.

"Wouldn't you be?" I asked.

Hope laughed. "Think about it," she said. "It's got to suck to know that romping around Italy trumps your broken leg."

"I'd be depressed about the leg alone," I said.

"Okay, but this is *Dad*," Christian scoffed.

"Dad probably has emotions too, Christian," Hope said. "Just because no one's ever seen them doesn't mean they're not there."

Christian ignored her.

"This is all getting crazy," he snapped at me. "You think Dad's depressed but Jeannie said you were out on some *date* with Scotty fucking Sheridan the other day—"

"Date?" I didn't know whether to laugh or yell. I chose something a little closer to the latter. "I wasn't on a *date,* I was out in town and I ran into him, and what does it matter what I was doing?"

"You were *out*?" Christian's voice was rising in both pitch and volume. "What does that mean? You're running around shopping while Dad's declining? What the hell are you *doing*, Meredith?"

The timer buzzed loudly, as punctuation.

Shaking a little bit, I turned and pulled the lasagna out of the oven. "Dinner's ready," I announced.

"Fuck *dinner*!" Christian yelled.

"Everybody needs to calm down," Jeannie said.

"My family is falling apart, in case you haven't noticed!" Christian barked at her. She flinched.

He turned to me. "This isn't supposed to be some vacation for you!"

"Why don't you stop yelling at me?" I asked him. Through my teeth.

"And thanks for stopping by," Hope added, with malice. "It's nice of you to take time out of your busy yuppie life to check up on your sick father."

"Hey, Hope? The day I ask for your input?" Christian scoffed. "Is never going to come. Why don't you shut up for once?"

"Or what?" Hope retorted immediately, springing to her feet. "You'll beat me down?" She stepped toward him, arms wide, like she was about to get physical. It clearly surprised Christian, who actually took a half step back.

"Both of you, please calm down!" I cried, visions of a brawl dancing in my head. Hope whirled to face me at once.

"Why don't you defend yourself?" she demanded. "Why don't you tell him to leave you alone?"

"I told you to back off!" Christian shouted at her.

"I'm not Meredith!" Hope shouted right back at him. "I'm not even a little intimidated by you! You want me to back off? You fucking try and make me!"

"Christian!" Jeannie was up, pulling on his arm, but he was still moving toward Hope.

"You spoiled little bitch—"

They were primed to spring—

"Sorry if I'm interrupting," Scott said from the doorway, his voice like a bucket of cold water. "I brought wine."

# Chapter 6

Scott and I stood in the kitchen, in the wake of all that shouting and near-violence. My gourmet lasagna sat untouched on the table, cheeses oozing sullenly. We both stared at it, as if it might offer some kind of explanation for the family implosion.

"I lost my appetite," I said.

I heard Hope slam out of the front door, and winced at the noise. Christian and Jeannie had stormed away almost immediately, and by now were long gone, Christian no doubt shouting all the way down the Parkway. Lucky Jeannie.

"Well, I'm hungry," Scott said, unperturbed. He sat down at the table and began helping himself. I stared at him. He ignored that too.

"You're just going to eat?" I demanded. "Like nothing happened?"

"Nothing did happen," he replied easily. He looked up and his eyes laughed at me. "To me."

"I can't figure you out," I snapped, because what I wanted to do was laugh along with him. "Are you really this much of a jerk, or are you just putting on an act?"

It felt kind of good to snap. It felt as if snapping was something I should do more of, it felt so good. And Scott didn't seem in the least bothered. He just grinned.

"That's an excellent question," he said. "Why did you invite me to dinner, Meredith?"

If I was far more honest than I ought to be: because he was so surprisingly hot. He was hot, and he'd had a crush on me when we were young. And I practically owed him dinner after the Scotty Sheridan Sucks thing.

I had a boyfriend, after all. It was just a meal.

So:

"Guilt," I retorted at once.

"Guilt," he echoed. "The funny thing about guilt is that nothing helps get rid of it. It just sits there." He forked in a bite of lasagna. "Cold lasagna can't make up for thirteen years of torture from the McKay family."

It didn't look like all that torture was interfering with his appetite, much less his grin. And he'd certainly ranted enough on the subject over coffee. I felt unsettled, and found that glaring at him made me feel a little bit better. So I kept glaring as I took a seat, and poured myself a huge glass of wine, which was guaranteed to do the rest.

"You might consider getting over your childhood sometime soon, since you're almost thirty," I suggested. "You beat this subject into the ground already. And anyway, you're exaggerating."

"Not entirely," he said, snagging the bottle of wine. He filled his glass and toasted me. I made a face, and he only grinned.

I watched him clear a plate, fill a new plate, and clear that too. I tossed back a couple of glasses of wine and opened the bottle he'd brought with him.

"Are you going to eat everything in the house?" I asked.

"I might," he said, but pushed his plate away. I rose and reached for it. "Don't"—he slapped my hand away—"clean up after me, Meredith."

"What would you like me to do? Leave it here for the kitchen fairies to take care of during the night?"

"I'm not who you're mad at," he pointed out. "Although I guess it's nice to see you actually *get* mad."

"What does *that* mean?" I demanded.

"It means you barely react," Scott said at once. Which meant he'd given it thought, before being asked. I blinked, surprised. "You just smile and try to make everyone else happy and let your whole family tap dance all over you. You did it when you were a kid and, from what I saw tonight, you still do."

"I do not," was my mature response.

"Okay." He sounded amused.

I sat there, scowling, as he picked up his plate and took it over to the sink.

"You don't know anything about me," I continued. "You hate my whole family, so you aren't exactly the best judge of them. So what do you know?"

"Why do you let your brother talk to you like that?" Scott asked mildly. "How come you came all the way up here to 'help out' when both of your siblings already live here?" He slapped the water off, and turned around to watch me. "And don't you get sick of being so well-behaved and reliable?"

"No." I glared at him. "This is who I am. I don't owe *you* any explanations."

"No," he agreed. "You certainly don't."

We stared at each other. The kitchen fell away, and there were only those eyes of his, for a moment that went on too long.

I took a deep breath, and poured another glass of wine.

"You're not going to find any answers at the bottom of a glass," Scott told me. "I would think you'd know that already."

"I'm not looking for answers," I shot back. "I'm looking to get drunk."

He let out a laugh.

"I can get behind that," he said.

"So," I said, a long time later, when I was buzzing along nicely and we were sitting out on the back porch surrounded by the hot night. "How do you live in this town?"

"Is this a trick question?"

"High school is everywhere," I said with unnecessary melodrama. "Don't you get sick of it?"

"High school is everywhere for you, maybe," Scott said. "But let me assure you that the county prosecutor doesn't really care what happened to me in high school. And neither does anyone else."

"If you say so." I looked at him. "You've brought up high school a few times, for someone who's so over it."

"Because it's the last time I saw you, I guess," he said, tilting his beer toward me in a sort of toast. "And besides, it's not like we had the same experience in high school. I went through the usual soul-crushing misery. You're one of the aliens who enjoyed themselves in high school." He laughed. "You people scare me."

"I *felt* like an alien half the time." I still did sometimes. "Doesn't that count?"

"Nope." He tilted his beer bottle toward me. "You were *happy*. It violates natural law."

I rolled my eyes. "What's your problem with me, anyway? I never beat you up."

"Neither did Jeannie Gillespie," Scott pointed out. "And believe me, I bear her some ill will. You remember," he said when I just stared at him blankly. "You know the kind of mouth she has on her."

Did I ever. Jeannie wasn't a subject I wanted to get into, even with an almost-stranger I knew would take my side over hers in an automatic reaction to his adolescence.

"I guess," I conceded. "But wasn't everyone horrible as a teenager?"

"You weren't," Scott said, but he didn't sound particularly complimentary. He was propped up lazily against the back door, a beer bottle dangling from his fingers.

"Why does that sound bad?"

"You made it your job to be the nice one, and you were nice. That's not necessarily a bad thing."

"And again, it sounds bad when you say it."

"I used to wonder how you could be so nice when everything was so terrible," Scott said, looking at me in a way that made me shiver.

"Maybe I'm not that nice," I said, although I had always wanted to be. I rubbed at the goose pimples on my arm. "Maybe I wasn't then, either."

"I just wonder what you were so afraid of," Scott said. He sat up, which brought our faces closer together. "Your brother? Jeannie? What are you afraid of now?"

"I'm not afraid of anything!" I didn't quite look at him. "I'm not afraid of *you*!"

"I can see that."

"I don't know what you're talking about." I took a swig of my drink. I was feeling bold and brash. "You grew up cryptic."

He muttered something that sounded a whole lot like, *At least I grew up.*

I chose to ignore it.

"You still haven't told me why you hate *me*," I reminded him.

"Who says I hate you?"

"You want to hate me, anyway."

"Are you a little tipsy there, Meredith?"

"I guess I am."

I looked away from him and up toward the stars, where it was less dizzying. I decided it was time to stand up, and wandered out into the backyard. I could feel the grass beneath my bare feet, and it made me feel young again.

"I had a crush on you, growing up," Scott said quietly from the porch.

I could feel him watching me. I didn't turn back around, because what I knew was one thing, but his saying it out loud made it something else. Something perilous.

"Pretty little Meredith McKay. Never a bad word to say to or about anyone." His tone was mocking, but whether it was directed at him or at me, I couldn't tell.

I heard him get up and walk across the lawn toward me.

I wanted to start running, through my backyard and into the next, and on and on until there was no breath in my lungs and nowhere left to run. So I turned around instead, because it felt like the same thing.

He stood before me, too close, and I had to tilt my head up to look at him.

"And now?" I asked quietly.

"And now . . . here you are," Scott said, in the same hushed tone.

I didn't stop him from bending his head. I didn't dodge his mouth when it touched mine, or protest when he angled his head for a deeper, better fit. I didn't question my own arms circling his waist, or the pounding in my chest, or the dizziness that had nothing to do with alcohol.

He pulled away slightly, and his eyes slammed into me, looking for something.

I didn't run. I hardly breathed.

And whatever he was looking for, he found. He smiled, and my toes curled.

And when he tumbled me down into the grass, he made me feel lost and beautiful and sexier than I could remember ever feeling before.

I never said a single word.


"I used to dream about you," Scott said.

We were lying side by side in the grass. I might have been paralyzed. I felt battered and bruised. And wonderful. I felt like someone else entirely. I could hear him breathe next to me, and fancied I could feel it in my own chest.

"I imagined what you would be like when you were all alone," Scott continued in that same quiet voice. "When you weren't following after your brother and Jeannie, thinking your smile made up for the things they did. Sometimes, though, it almost did."

I thought I had slept, although I wasn't sure, as I couldn't entirely remember waking up. I should sit up soon, I knew. There were clothes to hunt around for, and the long walk back to the house from where we lay. But I knew that as soon as I sat up, I would have to think. I was afraid of what would happen then.

"I never forgot about you," Scott said, his voice still low. "When I got to college and started being who I wanted to be, instead of that loser everyone thought I was. The thing is"—he sat up so he could look down at me—"it made me hate you."

I stopped looking at the stars and warily turned my attention to his face, intent against the night.

"Do I want to hear this?" I asked.

But I still didn't move.

"Doesn't really matter," he said. "You're hearing it."

I sat up too. As I'd suspected, it was unpleasant. I blinked, and fumbled for my T-shirt. I could see him reach for his own clothes from the corner of my eye.

I was trembling—visibly, I realized when I pulled the ball of my jeans and underwear toward me.

"Is this the way you always act after—" But I couldn't say it, because I didn't know what to call it. His smirk kicked in.

"After what?" he taunted me. "This was an exorcism."

I pulled on my clothes quickly and not necessarily correctly, and jumped to my feet. Emotions were buffeting me in rapid succession, too quickly to identify or name. But there was a unifying theme: shame. I bolted for the back door, as quickly as I could move without actually running.

He caught me before I could make it up the steps to the porch, grabbed me by the arm, and whirled me around into one last kiss.

I hated myself with a searing pain, because I could feel that kiss flood through my senses and down my legs to the soles of my bare feet.

I shoved him away, and he fell back willingly enough, but I was all too aware that it had taken me crucial moments to push him away at all.

I wanted to curse at him, yell at him, hurt him, but nothing came to mind. He only watched me, that damnable smirk like a slap, and waited. And I had never wanted to scream as much as I did then, but when I opened my mouth, nothing came out.

"Yeah," he said, his voice rich with amusement and satisfaction. "That's what I thought you'd say. See you around, Meredith."

He turned around and sauntered back toward the yard, presumably to locate the rest of his clothes. I didn't stick around to find out. I ran into the house, and then came to a complete standstill in the kitchen. My brain was flooded with lurid images, and I starred in every one of them. What I had done. How I had moved. What could I possibly have been thinking?

I ran for the stairs, and didn't stop until I was standing naked under the hottest shower spray I could take, as if I could shower away my behavior, or at the very least blame it on anyone other than myself. Fifteen minutes later, I had to admit defeat. I wrapped myself in a towel and shuffled toward my bedroom.

"That good, huh?" Hope was reclining across my narrow little bed, looking far too pleased with herself.

"I didn't hear you come in," I said, blinking at her.

"No," Hope agreed. "You sure didn't."

She couldn't possibly mean . . . ?

But of course she did. I knew she did.

I tried to hold out.

"I was in the shower," I said. "I think I got that lasagna sauce all over me."

"Uh-huh," Hope drawled. A huge grin crept across her face. "I'm in complete shock, Meredith. If I hadn't seen it with my own eyes I never would have believed it!"

"Believed what?" I asked through my teeth.

"My big sister, Saint Meredith the Perfect," Hope said with slow delight, "is a *slut!*"

I winced, and had to close my eyes for a moment.

"Was that really Scotty Sheridan? Does he actually suck? In either sense of the word?" Hope giggled. I folded my arms over my chest, mostly to protect myself.

"You should never have told him about that," I said. I tried to loosen my neck by rolling my head around, and Hope laughed again. "I'm glad you think this is funny!" I moaned.

"I think that you're actually human," Hope retorted. "Who knew? I wasn't even sure you *had* sex."

Since Hope wasn't going anywhere, and I really didn't want to answer her, I moved around the room as if she wasn't there. I very deliberately did not look out my window and across the street, and why would he be at his mother's this late anyway?

"I feel it's my duty to tell you that Van Ick the Horrible spends more than a few of her evenings with her face plastered to her windows," Hope told me, still lounging. "This I know from tragic personal experience. Only in Peter Dworkin's wildest fantasy did anything happen between us, yet Van Ick told Mom there was a guy in my room, and boom! I was grounded. You should be prepared for the possibility."

"Fantastic," I moaned. I entertained the hideous mental image of Gladys Van Eck at her window, watching scenes I wished I could delete, and then reporting them in scandalous detail to my appalled mother.

I actually felt faint.

I pulled on the coordinated summer pajamas Travis's mother had given me for Christmas and crawled into the bed as if Hope wasn't sprawled across the foot of it.

"I didn't know you and Travis broke up," Hope said.

She ignored my feet when I tried to forcibly dislodge her, moving over on top of them and pinning them both down with a roll of her hips.

"Doesn't surprise me, though," she continued calmly. "He was such a frat boy." She picked at one of her nails. "I just thought that's what you liked. It's kind of nice to find out you don't. Scott's all . . . edgy and sexy, don't you think?"

*Travis*, I thought, and the shame deepened and flooded through me, threatening to drown me.

I had been deliberately—very deliberately, so that it required all my concentration—*not* thinking about Travis. Not once all night, not really, and not much in the days before.

It was just a phase, I'd told myself. Our relationship was about taking care of details, and that was harder to do on the phone than in person, obviously. Things were a little bit strained, not that "strained" *meant* anything. He just sounded kind of distant and I found myself sort of nagging . . . It was just the long-distance thing.

But then tonight. The backyard. Scott's hands—

"Hope!" I barked out desperately. The words poured out of my mouth. "Travis and I haven't broken up as far as I know so actually I really *am* a slut and I just can't deal with having this conversation, okay?"

Hope looked startled. I held my breath.

"Well," she said. She took in my flushed face and what I imagined was the beacon of self-loathing emanating from within. "That makes things more complicated." She shrugged. "But this is the kind of stuff I can deal with."

"What does that mean?" I was almost afraid to ask.

"You know," Hope said, and shrugged again carelessly. Her smile then was genuine, and something else I had never seen before—a combination of wicked and bashful. "I get into a lot of these situations."

I frowned. "Define 'a lot.'"

Hope grinned. "That's not the point. The point is, you feel bad and you shouldn't. Nobody knows but me."

"*I* know!" I moaned.

"Tell me what happened," Hope commanded.

It occurred to me to feel strange about sharing anything with Hope, who had long been, at best, a complete mystery to me. But as the story crept out of me—first haltingly, and then when Hope exhibited no judgment whatsoever, like a torrent—I forgot that it should have been strange. And she was right—this was definitely the kind of stuff she knew how to deal with.

"Exorcism?" she hooted. "I can't believe he actually said that!"

"I haven't let myself think about it yet." I shuddered. "But it may be the most horrible thing anyone's ever said about me. Much less *to* me."

"It's not nice," Hope agreed. She was lying on her back, having long since released my feet from underneath her, and had propped her head up on her hands. "But he completely played himself with the parting kiss."

"He did?" I could only remember the heat of it, and how much I had wanted to be disgusted and repulsed. And how much I wasn't either of those things.

"Totally he did," Hope said. "Maybe he planned the whole

scene with the exorcism line, but he should have just left, hate-fuck accomplished, so you could feel bad about it for the rest of your life. But running over and having to have that one last kiss? I don't know, it seems to me that he liked the mechanics of the exorcism more than he wanted to. I bet he still has a crush on you."

"It doesn't really matter," I said quickly, although it did. "It's not like I plan to ever see him again." I buried my face in my hands. "What am I going to tell Travis? How can I ever face him again?"

Hope was quiet for a moment. Her eyes searched my face.

"I wouldn't tell him, actually," she said at last.

"You mean I should betray him a second time by not telling him I betrayed him the first time?" I demanded.

"If you want to be a complete drama queen about it, yes," Hope said. "What he doesn't know really won't hurt him. And this isn't a normal situation. He doesn't live here. He really *doesn't* have to know, and it's not like you have to stress about running into Scott somewhere when you're with Travis, or someone else telling him 'for his own good.'" She made a derisive noise in her throat. I sensed Hope was familiar with those situations, although she didn't elaborate.

"I don't know . . ." I murmured.

"I don't see any benefit at all in confessing," she said matter-of-factly. "Maybe it makes you feel better, but it's only going to make him feel bad. An ongoing affair is one thing. That's different, I guess. But one night after a lot of drinking? Stuff happens. To everyone."

"I don't know," I said again. "Lying by omission is just as bad as lying directly, isn't it? That's how you get into terrible relationships. The next thing you know you're conducting secret fish experiments in the basement and your wife is too busy traveling the old country to visit you after you have a car accident."

I wasn't sure where that had come from. Possibly the alcohol still sloshing around my system. Anyway, it seemed like an obvious slippery slope to me.

"Meredith, come on." Hope snickered. "We're not our parents."

"*You're* not," I agreed immediately. "You're not like anyone in this family. But I'm sure you know that."

"I just know what I can get away with," Hope said. Her hazel eyes were ripe with mischief. "If they think you really will go nuts, they stop provoking you. So I get to do what I want. Look at the alternative."

"Meaning what?"

"Meaning Christian, who was a bully when he was younger and is a fuckhead now, and why? Because he got treated like the little maharajah his entire life and thinks it's his role as 'the son' to boss the rest of us around."

"I always forget that he really was kind of a bully," I mused, thinking of Scott's undying dislike. It wasn't exactly undeserved.

"Or," Hope continued as if I hadn't spoken. "You. Miss Perfect. Saint Meredith. Selfless, dependable, and reliable to a fault."

"What's wrong with that?" I demanded.

"Not a thing," Hope said. "Except it's not real. Who made you responsible for this family? Who told you it was up to you to take care of us?"

I think my jaw actually dropped open, but I was silent.

"And I get to be the wild, unmanageable brat," Hope said

softly, when it was clear I couldn't find any words. "It might be just as fucked up, but at least it's real, and I get to do what I want." After a beat, she continued quietly, "Of course the bad part is that this is the first time you've ever treated me as something other than a pain in the ass."

Much later, I lay wide-awake in my bed and wondered if I would ever sleep again. My mind leapt from one thing to another as if pausing on any particular thing might force me to self-destruct. Had I put my mouth *there*? When had Hope become so wise, and how had I never noticed a whole personality behind the brattiness? Had he really done that *thing* with his hands?

I turned over and punched the pillow, and then, in a rush, hurled it across the room.

My entire life had plodded along on course, until tonight, when it had suddenly become someone else's life. I didn't do things like this. I wasn't that girl. I couldn't be.

Hope might be able to navigate a world where people could do the things that I had done in the backyard with Scott Sheridan and then go on with a normal, reasonable, presentable, and happy life in Atlanta, never a word to anyone, but I couldn't. I couldn't possibly live with a deep, dark secret. I was no good at secrets and deceit. I didn't have to give it a try to figure *that* out.

Filled with something almost as horrible as righteousness, I leapt out of bed. It was just before three, but I didn't let that stop me. I padded down the stairs, through the sleeping house, and grabbed the phone in the kitchen.

I dialed the number and played with my bottom lip when it rang. Once. Twice. A third time.

"Hello . . ." His voice was groggy and asleep.

"Travis." I could barely say his name. The sobs were sudden, silent, and huge, and racked my whole body.

"Darlin'," he drawled, though muffled. "What're you doing? It's three in the morning. You okay?"

"I'm fine," I whispered. I shoved a fist into my stomach.

And thought: *How do you blurt that out? What do you say? "Sorry to wake you, honey, but I just wanted to let you know that I spent the better part of the night rolling around naked in my parents' backyard with some guy I went to high school with who my brother used to beat up. How's work?"*

"Are you sure?" Travis asked, sounding slightly more alert. "Is your dad okay?"

And I couldn't do it.

"He's okay," I whispered. "We're all okay. I'm sorry. I just . . . wanted to hear your voice."

It was the hardest sentence I'd ever uttered. I thought for a moment that my vocal cords might defy me, that the truth would blurt itself out and make me the honest person I'd always believed myself to be.

But only the lie came out. And it was easy.

After I hung up the phone, I stood like a statue in the dark and wondered if I would ever feel like me again.

# Chapter 7

It wasn't enough for her to *watch* me mow the freaking lawn," Christian said, outraged. "Oh, no. That woman kept stopping me to tell me all the ways I was doing it wrong. Is she kidding? I'm still pissed off about the time she ratted me out to Mom and Dad about that party senior year." He shook his head. "One more word and I would have shoved that drop-kick dog of hers down her throat."

"Honey, please," Jeannie said. "The manly posturing is cute, but Van Ick could eat the likes of you for breakfast."

They smiled at each other.

We were standing around a Saturday night barbecue, out on the back porch. I was scanning the backyard for signs of my bad behavior the week before. Something subtle, I thought—like a huge scarlet *A* scorched into the earth. The freshly mown grass was green and unscorched, however. Which didn't exactly make me feel better.

Meanwhile, Jeannie had taken over the grill, having claimed that a new recipe she'd found—presumably while surfing the Web, too busy to handle her future in-laws—would force us to worship her as a god.

Needless to say, I was skeptical.

Behind me, the soon-to-be-married couple was getting silly.

"Are you saying that a seven-hundred-year-old woman could take me?" Christian demanded with mock bluster. "This is the kind of faith you have in me?"

Jeannie grinned up at him and stuck out her tongue. She squealed when Christian grabbed her in a complicated sort of headlock, and then kissed her.

"You're awfully quiet," Christian said, releasing Jeannie and looking at me.

"It's been a long week," I said shortly.

I didn't paste on my usual smile, and Christian looked a little bit thrown. His form of rallying was to head back inside, muttering something about spatulas.

"What's going on with you?" Jeannie flicked me a look and flipped a few chicken breasts on the grill. Her flip was tentative. I figured she was just winging it with the whole Goddess of the Grill routine. "Christian has been insane all week about the whole Scotty Sheridan thing. What was that all about?"

I flinched—and looked at the grass again for burn marks— but then remembered. They couldn't possibly know what had happened a week ago. They meant the dinner they'd walked out on, the one we had all pretended hadn't happened when Christian called to announce they were coming to hang out for the weekend.

"A better question is why the two of you stormed off into the night like two gigantic babies," I said. Because a good offense is always the best defense. "What was *that* all about?"

"Are you kidding?" Jeannie pointed her spatula at me. "You invited *Scotty Sheridan* over for dinner and then were *surprised* when Christian didn't think it was appropriate to have a *stranger* sitting in on a *family* discussion?"

I *really* hated that tone. Complete with audible italics and the assumption that whoever she was speaking to was a total idiot. I'd hated it in elementary school and I hated it now.

"That's funny," I retorted with a definite edge in my voice. "I don't remember any *discussion*, I just remember Christian having a tantrum and then ranting and raving some more when it turned out there were witnesses."

I took a sip of my beer, as if I was unconcerned, to disguise the fact that I was trembling slightly. I hated that I was such a coward. That I couldn't even defend myself to her without practically breaking into a rash. I didn't think of myself as such a fragile thing, so when had that happened? Why did she have such *power* over me?

"Is the food going to be ready before I die?" Hope drawled, stepping through the door and saving me from a panicked contemplation of the fact that I couldn't seem to escape my adolescence.

She had on her sultry nighttime eyes, and a pair of jeans about a thread away from obscenity, they were so low. Hope was about the only person, aside from Britney Spears, who actually looked good in low-riders. It was unfair that a real person could be in possession of a body that good. I reminded myself that Hope was twenty-two. She had yet to become acquainted with gravity.

"Careful." Jeannie smirked at Hope. "Inhale and you'll be cited for public indecency."

"By who?" Hope asked sharply, her eyes raking Jeannie from head to toe. Jeannie pursed her lips and returned her attention to the grill.

"Anyway," Hope continued in a smoother tone. "Everything's ready in here. Whenever you are."

She flounced back inside.

"I can't believe she's actually helping with any part of dinner," Jeannie said when she was gone. "What did you do? Hypnotize her? You bribed her, didn't you?"

"Hope and I reached an understanding."

I took another swig from my beer. A longer, deeper swig.

"About what?" Jeannie asked caustically. "How much she needs to get over herself?"

"I'll carry that platter in," I said. I slid a deliberate look her way, and took a deep breath. "And she's not the only one around here who could stand to get over herself, Jeannie."


Dinner was a strained affair.

Dad eyed Hope across a bowl of salad. "Is it Halloween?" he asked her. Being Hope, she was completely unfazed.

"It's actually Estee Lauder," she replied, fluttering her extra-long lashes at him. "I almost went for glitter, but decided that was too much of a statement for suburban New Jersey."

"I don't think anyone was complimenting you," Christian tossed at her.

"I don't think anyone was even *talking* to you," Hope retorted.

"More vegetables, Dad?" I asked sweetly.

"The zucchini is hardly going to draw my attention away from my twenty-something children squabbling like toddlers," Dad said, shooting me a look.

And so on.

For once, Christian had the pleasure of helping the patient

back up the stairs with the cast and the cursing and the "I can do it myself" nonsense. The rest of us did the dishes and then sat in the family room.

"That was ridiculous," Christian said with a sigh when he returned. "I was about to leave him on the landing."

"You should have," Hope said carelessly. "Maybe that would make him reconsider his charming attitude about the stairs."

She wandered over to the mirror on the family room wall and turned from side to side.

"You're still gorgeous," Jeannie said dryly. "As I'm sure you know."

"I was checking my ass," Hope murmured. She arched her brows. "And not because I think it's fat."

"Of course not," Jeannie said with a laugh. Christian just sighed again.

"So what are we supposed to do about Mom?" he asked abruptly. "Are we supposed to run after her and beg her to come home? Or just hope she decides to show up before he completely falls apart?"

"I choose door number two," Hope said. She shrugged when we all looked at her. "Oh, come on. Like it's not better around here without her daily crucifixion routine. You guys aren't fooling anyone."

"She and Aunt Beth have been planning this trip for years," I said, throwing out the party line. It sounded pretty convincing, if I did say so myself. Most things did after you repeated them a million times—funny how that worked. "I'm here to take care of Dad. It's not as if we're in some dire situation." I looked at Christian. "You can call and tell her how depressed he is if you want, but I don't think that's going to get her home any sooner."

I knew I wasn't going to call her myself. Not after our most recent conversation, in which she had made more completely unsolicited and dire predictions about my relationship with Travis. Which was exactly the last thing I needed to hear after the Scott episode.

"Don't look at me," Christian replied. "I'm not getting involved in their marital stuff. I was just curious about whether or not we think we *should* be involved."

"You guys talk about it as if your mom is deliberately not coming home and it's like she's flipping your dad the giant bird from Rome," Jeannie pointed out. "Do you actually know that? Or do you guys just think that?"

We all sort of looked around at each other.

"I don't know what we know," I said, finally.

"I'm pretty clear on what I know," Christian contradicted me. "It would be one thing if she was actually doing something important, but hello—she's on vacation."

"It's a once-in-a-lifetime foreign vacation," I argued. "It's not like she went down to the Shore and refuses to drive back up."

"No, she just doesn't care enough about her husband to cut short her trip," Christian said, disgusted. "I love this family."

"I do love this family!" Jeannie said, and flushed when we all looked her way. "Well, I do," she said defensively. "I know you guys have issues with your parents, but I wish you could see what you have from my perspective." Her shoulders hunched up around her neck. "I don't know, they kind of fit. They work."

"They don't *work*," Christian said, staring at her. "My father has to breed fish as friends and my mother has more interest in eating pasta at the source than in the fact Dad had a car accident. How does that *work*, exactly?"

"I know," Jeannie said helplessly. "But as upset as you guys are right now, you don't know what a really bad family is. No one's wasted drunk here. No one's getting whaled on, no one's throwing dinner plates around or calling the cops. This is just a weird situation, not a lifetime of therapy."

I thought, then, of all the hours Jeannie and I had spent when we were kids, holed up in my room talking through our dreams about the world. Jeannie had wanted to be safe and secure more than anything. She wanted her own house, her own family. I had pretended to want the same things, but when she would drift off to sleep I would dream instead of being free, flying away to some exotic place and being someone completely different. Jeannie had never really discussed what went on in her house, but I'd known then it was bad. We'd always known.

Christian rubbed at her shoulders to ease the tension.

Hope perched herself on the edge of the couch.

"Well, I'm definitely not calling her," she said matter-of-factly, as if there'd been no silence. I doubted she could deal with reminders of Jeannie's truly nasty family any more than I could. "I don't think anyone should butt into their marital problems. Christian's right."

"I'm sorry, I didn't quite hear . . . ?" But Christian was grinning. Next to him, Jeannie smiled.

"Don't get used to it," Hope warned. "I very much doubt you'll be right again. I'm going out," she announced abruptly. She turned to me. "Want to come?"

There was a small, shocked silence. Everyone was suddenly looking at me.

"Yes," I said, surprising everyone in the room. Including myself.

"Cool," Hope said, but swept a critical glance over me. "But you definitely have to change." That clearly troubled her. "In fact, let me go pick something out." She charged away.

"Are you kidding?" Christian gaped at me. "Why the hell would you go anywhere with her?"

"I'm tired of being in this house," I said, very simply. "You and Jeannie are here if Dad needs something, so I feel like going out. And why not with Hope? I get the feeling she has more fun than I ever did at her age."

"Yeah, but . . ." Christian was nonplussed. "I thought we were going to hang out."

"I hang out here every single day, all day," I pointed out as lightly as I could. "If you came over more, we could hang out more."

"I'm really sorry I have a *job*, Meredith!" Christian retorted, immediately on the defensive. Maybe he felt guilty. But for once, I decided I didn't care.

"I don't feel like having this conversation," I announced evenly, and stood up. "I have to go make myself look hot enough so as not to embarrass Hope."

Which meant submitting to Hope's beauty regime and clothing selections. After a few of my protests were shot down, I surrendered to the process. Worst-case scenario: I looked like an ass. Hardly a new look for me this summer.

Hope even did my makeup. I had been going with the same quick and efficient slick of mascara and lipstick for years now, but this suggestion was met with only a cold stare from my sister.

"I've been wanting to do your makeup ever since I discovered what mascara was for," she told me, wielding the tiny brush with accomplished ease. "Your eyes are amazing, and you should showcase them more."

"My eyes are brown."

My head was tilted at an unnatural angle, which made my voice sound funny. Hope stood between my legs and held her face close to mine as she worked. It was a strangely intimate thing, I reflected, to be that close to someone else. Just one more example of the casual intimacy women took for granted. What did men have? Football tackles?

"Your eyes are brown, yeah, but with this whole gold thing going on," Hope said, sounding distracted. "Plus, you have to stop dressing like a middle-aged matron."

"I do not!" I was outraged.

"You do," Hope replied easily. "You're not a member of the royal family, Meredith. You're hot. You need to show it off."

"Sure." I couldn't quite hide my disbelief. "Tonight we'll show it off, and you'll apologize to me in the morning for inflicting me on your social life. That's fine. It's all in the name of family."

"This is another thing I'm really good at." Hope's voice was matter-of-fact. "I know you guys think I'm tacky because I show a lot of skin, but I'm not. I just *can* show a lot of skin. There's a fine line. Most people are on the wrong side of it. I know what works and what doesn't." She stepped back and scrutinized her handiwork. She showed me her dimples. "It's not taking a risk if you know you'll look good."

"I don't know I'll look good," I pointed out patiently. "I know that *you* think it's fun to dress up your elderly sister in silly, teenage clothing."

" 'Elderly'? Jesus Christ." Hope sighed. "You're twenty-eight."

She towed me over to the full-length mirror that graced the back of the closet door. We both stared at the creature she had created.

I was no longer the well-coordinated, conservatively cute Atlanta girl. I was someone else entirely. Someone with tousled and sexy hair. Someone in skintight jeans and a flirty little halter top that made me look more like Jessica Simpson than the Meredith McKay I carried around in my head and expected to see in the mirror. My eyes were smoky and glowed like old gold coins. My lips were practically a banquet. And the wicked heels on my feet could do serious damage.

"Wow," I breathed. "Check *her* out!"

"Wow!" Jeannie echoed as I catwalked through the family room on our way out. "You look . . ." She ground to a halt, evidently at a loss.

"Like Hope," Christian said with significantly less enthusiasm. Jeannie smacked him on the leg, and I felt a sudden, small pang of guilt.

I chose to ignore it, and followed Hope out into the night. I felt the way I remembered feeling a million years ago when I was a freshman in college. When I thought anything might happen before morning, and it often did.

"I'll drive," Hope said.

I was more than happy to recline in her passenger seat and let her take control. All the thinking I couldn't seem to keep from doing wasn't getting me anywhere anyway, so why not turn it off? Why not set it all aside for the night?

I couldn't change the increasingly awkward conversations I had with Travis on the phone, the ones that were all my fault, the ones I had to pretend weren't awkward at all when he asked. I might have realized that I couldn't lay all my guilt on him, that it was my betrayal and therefore my cross to bear. But that didn't mean I was any good at it.

Hope, I imagined, would never have such problems.

My little sister was something of a celebrity, I realized, as the people in the local bars scrambled to greet her, to buy her drinks, to bask in her circle. The bars were all the same, I noticed, despite my extended absence. The same people, more or less. The sad regulars, who tended to be former high school luminaries with landscaping businesses. The usual girlfriends and buddies, and then the latest crop of young ones. Of these last, Hope was queen.

Hope had that elusive quality that some people spent their lives trying to achieve. It was innate, and I had never seen it shine so brightly before. It wasn't just that she was lovely—she exuded something else, something all her own and marvelous, that made all the men flock to her and all the women want to be her confidante. It was a certain form of power, and Hope was so comfortable with it that she didn't even bother to flex it. She just basked in it.

And I got the reflected glory, because I was with her. It didn't matter that there were years separating us, or the fact that I was a stranger to Hope's legion of friends. Everything was loud and raucous and men looked at me as if I was an extension of Hope: vibrant and sexy and halfway to celestial. It was almost as intoxicating as the margaritas I let myself have in celebration.

The place we settled in had a bustling restaurant section, which overlapped into the noisy bar area. I took myself off to the bathrooms, which were typically revolting, and was navigating my way back to the table in my killer heels when I came face-to-face with Scott.

He was exiting the restaurant portion of the place with three other men, all in business suits. He stopped dead, and we stared at each other, as if we were the only two people in the bar.

"I'll catch you all later," he told his companions, but never took his eyes off of me. I had the impression of some laughter from them, but I was too trapped in Scott's gaze to really notice, much less care.

"Hi," I said. I smirked. "Or am I supposed to say something else, being exorcised and all."

"I never said I wasn't an asshole," Scott replied in that low, husky voice of his. "I just said your family was first."

I searched his face, but it was the same one I saw in my head. The picture of little Scotty Sheridan, all elbows and geekiness, was forever burned away. What I saw now when I thought of him started and ended with sleek muscles and that look in his eyes.

"Look at you." He sounded delighted. "You look edible."

"I'm not on the menu," I retorted.

"And with a new personality to match," he said, completely unfazed. "I like it."

"That was, of course, my goal."

"Sarcastic too. Be still my heart."

"Your what? That's funny, I thought you said 'heart.'"

"That approached humor, Atlanta. The total transformation is almost too much for me to take. Was there a body-snatching?"

"You know what I can't figure out?" I glared at him. "I get the whole hate-fuck concept."

"You do." It wasn't a question.

"Sure, and congratulations by the way. You've been building up to that since the fourth grade, so it must have been a big night for you." I treated him to my best placid smile. "I just want to let you know that *I forgive you*."

He blinked. He didn't like that. "You do?"

"Of course," I said, smile widening, dripping sincerity as only southern girls could. Even transplanted ones. "I think it's *sweet* that you spent *all those years*—"

"Fuck that," Scott said, and his hand wrapped around my arm. When I didn't jerk away he towed me out the front door and started down the empty sidewalk.

"Where are we going?" I asked calmly, at odds with the riot going on inside my head. The riot I was choosing to ignore.

"Shut up," Scott said in the same tone.

He maneuvered me down the alley behind the restaurant, and then farther along, until I was confused about where exactly we were in relation to the street.

"Fantastic," I said brightly. "Are there rats out here too?"

"Probably," Scott said.

He backed me into the wall, reached down, and pulled me up so that our hips were flush against each other. The shock of it was like a punch. I shuddered. And then he stared at me, leaned his forehead against mine, his mouth just a breath away.

I forgot how to do anything but stare at him.

He was much bigger than I was, and he used that fact to his advantage. He traced the skin my halter top left bare with his hands, using the leverage of his chest to keep me pinned to the wall. Not that I was trying to get away.

And his mouth was still just a breath away.

His eyes dared me. I was breathing too hard. He was breathing too hard.

"I thought you exorcised me," I taunted him. He laughed a little bit.

"So did I."

He bent and fastened his mouth to my neck. Fire licked

through my veins. He backed away slightly. His hands were like electricity across my skin, tracing my hips, and then they came around to the fastening of my jeans. I caught his hands, and he reared back slightly to pin me with his narrow gaze.

"Say it," he told me.

"Say what?"

"Say yes or no," he said. "I'm an officer of the court. Be very clear."

It was a long, endless pause. I could feel my pulse in every part of my body—hair, elbows, heels. It was maybe a few seconds, maybe whole lifetimes.

"I don't want to say anything," I whispered.

"That's not no."

Our eyes caught and held. I couldn't look away.

"It's not no," I agreed.

I dropped my hands and saw his mouth curve slightly. Never breaking eye contact, he unbuttoned my waistband, and then slowly lowered the zipper. He hooked his fingers in the strings of the bikini underwear I was wearing.

"Ready?" He was taunting me again.

I could hardly breathe. I forgot how to speak.

In one fluid motion, Scott pulled my jeans and underwear down to my knees, sank down in front of me, and fastened his mouth between my legs.

I felt my knees buckle, and I stopped thinking altogether.


He stood across the alley and watched in brooding silence as I readjusted my clothing.

"What was that?" I asked quietly.

"I don't know." He shrugged. "I had an urge."

"I have to go."

I smoothed my hair with hands that shook, and knuckles I'd scraped across the bricks. I frowned at the scrape, and caught his brooding look.

"My sister will be missing me. So."

"Of course," Scott said with acid politeness. "I'm glad I could be of service."

Something rolled inside me and rushed straight to my head.

"I didn't ask you for anything!" I yelled at him. "I didn't ask for your 'I had a crush on you' or 'your smile almost made up for the things they did'! Your whole crappy adolescence is not my responsibility, and *exorcism*? How long did it take you to come up with that one? Entire years?"

He had the gall to smile—a real smile.

"Well," he said. "Yeah."

I didn't smile back.

"It was a shitty thing to say."

"It was." His smile faded and he held my gaze. "I'm sorry."

We looked at each other for a long moment. I could feel the insanity of his mouth on me still jangling around in my nerve endings, and the impossibility of the way he made me feel—all those dark and addictive physical things I had never believed in before.

He reached across the space between us and carefully tucked a strand of hair behind my ear. His thumb brushed against my cheek.

He didn't follow when I broke away and stumbled back toward the bar.


"Where were you?" Hope had to yell to be heard over the music.

"Bathroom!" I shouted back.

"What kind of soap do they have in there?" Hope asked archly in my ear.

I frowned at her in confusion.

"You appear to be having an allergic reaction," Hope informed me solemnly. Her eyes zeroed in on my neck, right where Scott had fastened his mouth against my skin.

"Son of a bitch!" I clapped a hand to my neck.

"Or maybe not the soap?" Hope asked with a twinkle in her eye.

# Chapter 8

Long after midnight, I was exhausted but determined to keep going as long as Hope did, no matter how much I wanted to crawl under the table for a quick nap. I was losing myself in the crowd, the music, and half-formed memories of other nights I'd spent in this same bar—possibly even on this same barstool—back when I was someone else.

Which was to say, I may have been zoning out like the old lady I was when someone materialized in front of me.

"Hi, Meredith," she said, as if it had been minutes since we last spoke. Instead of years. "I've been trying to get the nerve to come over here all night, and I think I've finally mustered up the courage, so, hi."

I stared at her, confused. And then it hit me.

"Rachel Pike," I said in wonder. "I don't believe it. Look at you!"

"I know," she said, and grinned. "Behold the wonders of Weight Watchers."

"You look amazing!"

She really did. Back in school, Rachel had fulfilled the funny fat girl stereotype so necessary to our group of girls. She had been the comedian of our little clique and like the rest of us spent most of her time alternating between vying for Jeannie's positive attention and trying to avert the inevitable, gut-wrenching putdown from Ashley. I couldn't remember ever seeing her without about fifty extra pounds, starting sometime way back in elementary school. Tonight she looked toned, tanned, and fantastic.

A far cry from the last time I'd seen her.

I cringed as the memory swept over me. I had gone out of my way to put Rachel Pike out of my mind. Rachel, who had inadvertently been *the last straw* between Jeannie and me—and *Jeannie and me* was what I had concentrated on when I thought about what had happened. Not Rachel, who had been chubby and harmless and who I'd liked, but not enough. Not when it counted.

"Oh no," I said in remembered horror. The margaritas got in the way of what I wanted to say, and I shrugged, feeling helpless. "That summer . . . I'm so sorry, Rachel."

Our eyes met, and even through the haze of alcohol, I felt small. Rachel Pike was one of the things I'd hated most about who I was around Jeannie. But I didn't have the slightest idea how to begin making up for that. Or even mentioning it directly. After all, she hardly looked like it was bothering *her*, in her toned little body.

"You don't have to apologize," she said. She smiled briefly. She glanced around. "I figured Jeannie would be around if you were, though. I imagined you guys continued to hang out?"

I groaned.

"That is such a long story and I am really so tired of thinking about high school and high school people," I confessed. "It's unavoidable when you come back to your hometown, I guess, but all I remember from high school is desperately wanting to grow up and escape." I took a deep pull of my drink. "And yet here I am again, which is my worst nightmare come to life."

"Yours and mine too, believe me," Rachel said, and laughed. She considered me for a moment, as if making her mind up, and then nodded at the barstool next to me. "Mind if I sit down? I'm on a break."

"You work here?"

"I have the great pleasure of tending bar here every weekend." Rachel grinned. She slid in next to me. "You think *you're* sick of thinking about high school. I feel compelled to mention that I'm in business school, and that bartending in this ridiculous town is not my life's ambition. For the record."

"I'm just back here taking care of my father," I told her in the same tone. "Car accident. And tonight? Out with my little sister."

"Because we're grown-ups," Rachel said at once, in solidarity. "And are in no way reliving our glory days, not that I remember any kind of glory."

"Amen."

We smiled at each other. I felt a surge of something like relief flood through me.

"So I have to know," Rachel said in a sudden rush, "because I vowed to hate her until the day I die—although, in a strange way, she inspired me to deal with myself. Do you know what Jeannie Gillespie is up to? Please tell me she's living a deeply unhappy life, and is really, really fat." She leaned forward. "She was like the evil black cloud that followed me around, always saying those things I thought I would die if someone said out loud." She grinned, clearly over those things.

I blinked. "I hardly know where to start with that, although I'm sorry to report that she's not at all fat—"

"Oh my God," Rachel interrupted me, her bright and sober eyes fastened to my neck. "Is that a *hickey*?!"


It was still there in the morning. Small but unmistakable.

*What are we, fourteen?* I stared at myself in the mirror. The glorious creature of the night before had been reduced to melted mascara bags and scary hair.

To say nothing of the hangover and the goddamned hickey.

I stood in the shower, face tilted into the hot water, when it hit me that I had forgotten to feel guilty and dirty for what Scott had done to me the night before.

What I had let Scott do. What I had wanted him to do.

The remorse was even more flattening for being delayed. I leaned against the wet tiles and squeezed my eyes shut tight. I didn't know what I was doing. There was no "stuff happens" clause for this. And now there was no "it's just one night" clause either. Scott had given me the opportunity to say no. And I hadn't. That was the entire situation in black and white. Stark and true.

I wasn't the nice girl, the good girl. I was a cheater and a liar who bore no resemblance to Saint Meredith, Miss Perfect, me.

I was turning into someone else, and I didn't have the slightest idea how to stop it.


When I hauled myself into the kitchen, Jeannie was in the midst of preparing a feast. So maybe the "turning into someone else" thing was going around. My face must have showed my confusion.

"Sunday brunch!" she said merrily when she saw me. She had a bright, broad smile across her face. "You shouldn't have to do all the cooking around here."

Okay, that was alarming. Since when was Jeannie helpful? Much less thoughtful?

"Wow," I managed. I looked at the fresh fruit and bacon, and inhaled one of the best smells in the world: French toast. "Where's Christian?" I asked, a little warily. "And what did you guys do last night?"

"We just watched some television," Jeannie said, still in Stepford mode.

I settled into a chair at the kitchen table and watched Jeannie fiddle with pans and chop up more fruit. For once, I felt no urge to leap in and help out. I was too hungover and it was nice to let someone else be responsible. Particularly when that someone was Jeannie. I hitched the collar of my sweatshirt up a little bit higher. Scott's mark was on my collarbone and, luckily, easily concealed.

And yet a small part of me wished it was the size of a plate and impossible to hide at all. Because then someone would notice, someone less forgiving than Hope and far less amused than Rachel, and I would have to face my actions and what they made me.

"Did you have fun?" Jeannie asked.

Her tone was suspiciously devoid of inflection. We might not have been close in years, but I could still recognize alarm bells when I heard them.

"It was nice to get out." I gave her an automatic smile. "Hope is actually a lot of fun."

I wanted to mention Rachel, just to see what reaction she might have, but restrained myself. Barely.

"You and Hope are bonding, huh?"

"I guess we are," I replied noncommittally. What did she want?

"That's great," Jeannie said. "She's such a force."

"She sure is."

Was Jeannie complimenting Hope? Had the world started spinning in the opposite direction?

Jeannie turned and faced me then, her face set along determined lines.

*Here we go.*

"I know this isn't any of my business," she said quickly, as if she'd been rehearsing. "But I just . . . Go easy on Christian, would you? He's all tied in knots. I don't think he's dealing with your dad's accident very well." Her big eyes were pleading. "You know how he hero-worships your dad."

I didn't know anything of the kind. I hadn't ever really considered Christian's relationship with Dad. I'd kind of assumed we all had the same distracted, puzzling relationship with the man, but, if I thought about it, it made sense that the two of them would have a different guy thing going on. It disconcerted me that Jeannie took as a given something that hadn't even crossed my mind. I coughed slightly.

"I don't know what to say," I hedged. "I didn't think anyone *wasn't* going easy on Christian."

"You made a few comments about his not being here to help out," Jeannie reminded me, in that same sweeter-than-sweet tone. She sighed. "Part of him thinks that if something really bad happened to your dad, he'd have to step in and be the man in the family. You know."

Something flickered in Jeannie's eyes as she held mine, and I knew suddenly that there was no way Christian didn't know about this conversation.

*I'll say something, honey*, I could practically hear Jeannie promising him with her usual matter-of-fact confidence. *If I get a minute with Meredith, I'll just say a few things.*

I was saved from having to answer Jeannie further by the appearance of my father and Christian. Dad was leaning heavily on him, and I was struck anew by how much he took after Dad. With their heads so close together, they looked like a before-and-after picture.

Christian looked at me for a moment, then helped Dad toward his seat at the table.

"Look at all this," Dad said. He sounded genuinely pleased, which was so unexpected that I smiled just hearing it. Christian and his issues went right out of my head. "What a spread!"

He aimed a faint smile at Jeannie. His smile was contagious for all its faintness, the way it always had been, and we all returned it. With varying degrees of relief.

"You're looking pretty good, Dad." Christian beamed at him, every inch the jolly and supportive son. I had a hard time thinking of him as a man in the first place—that sounded way too adult—much less "the man in the family."

"Did you sleep well?" I asked Dad, instead of disturbing myself further with thoughts of Christian's adulthood. If Christian really was an adult, thinking about it would only depress me as I reenacted my adolescence. Better not to engage with such unpleasantness.

"In fact, I did." Dad settled into his seat and propped his leg up on the stool next to it. "I hadn't been sleeping well at all, and then last night I think the exhaustion caught up with me." He focused on the food before him. "This looks terrific," he said. "I might beat this thing after all."

Later, we maneuvered Dad out onto the front patio as a little Sunday treat. Fresh air could only be good for him, I figured. And if I felt stir-crazy, imagine how he must feel? At least I was physically capable of leaving the house.

Christian kept up a running commentary, mostly about his job and its frustrations—things Dad could understand, after his years as a corporate executive. He had woken every morning before dawn and made his way to the train with a good percentage of the rest of the town. He had been a managing director at an investment bank before his early retirement just last year. He and Christian liked to bore everyone around them to tears with pompous commentary on the intricacies of the business world. Maybe it was a guy thing. Maybe this was a sign of the hero worship Jeannie had been talking about.

"Nice day," Dad commented into the small silence left after Christian exhausted his *Wall Street Journal* synopsis.

It really was a nice day. The humidity had dropped off the night before, and the usual breathless mugginess of the air was gone. The sky was blue and clear, and the sun was bright.

I decided to take it as a benediction.

There was no sign of Scott in his mother's house across the street, and I found I hated myself for both the anticipation I felt and the accompanying disappointment. I tried to crush them both.

Eventually, Dad grew tired, and Christian, still in jolly son mode, leapt to help him indoors. I stayed out on the front step with Jeannie, and probably should have stopped staring across the street.

Especially when Mrs. Van Eck and the loathsome Isabella appeared in my line of vision.

"Oh Christ," Jeannie swore.

As if she heard—and who knew, the woman bordered on the supernatural as it was—Mrs. Van Eck turned her sour and disapproving gaze on the two of us. She was standing on the sidewalk, some fifteen feet away, and yet both of us jumped.

"Hello, Mrs. Van Eck," we chorused.

"Aren't the two of you thick as thieves," she said with a sniff that suggested she'd thought something a whole lot worse than "thief."

"Beautiful day!" I chirped. Out of the corner of my eye, I could see Jeannie's fake smile crumpling around the edges.

Mrs. Van Eck harrumphed and tugged on Isabella's leash to move her along.

The nasty little creature gave us a malevolent look from beneath the bobbing bow, turned her back, and aimed her hairy ass at the front porch. Still holding our gaze from over her shoulder, she squatted—deliberately—and peed.

If she'd had fingers, she'd have been waving the middle one.

"I love all dogs," I said through my teeth. "Except that one."

"Surely she can't live forever, right?" Even Jeannie whispered, until the old lady disappeared around the corner.

"They've both been living on meanness for the last fifty years," I said. "Obviously, Van Ick feels it's her calling to maintain the status quo around here. God forbid the town change in any way."

"People don't like it when you change, but they don't like it when you stay the same, either," Jeannie said after a moment. "Lately I keep running into people we went to high school with. All of them make this big deal about saying hello and seeing what I'm doing and I know perfectly well they all hate my guts. I would have so much more respect for someone if they actually said so."

I looked around at her, skeptical. "Really? I think I would just burst into tears."

Although, I hadn't burst into tears when Scott had said something a lot like that. *This was an exorcism.* Asshole.

"No one would say anything like that to you, anyway," Jeannie said, and grinned. She leaned back on her hands. "You were so *nice* in high school." There was laughter in her voice.

"How come everyone says that like I should be ashamed of it?" I demanded.

"You worked so hard at it," she said. "I think you actually plotted ways to be *more* nice, didn't you?"

"Someone had to be nice." I tried not to sound grumpy, with minimal success.

Jeannie suddenly laughed out loud, and put a hand on my shoulder. She gave me a quick squeeze.

"You weren't always so nice," she reminded me. "Remember? You know what I'm talking about. Two words: Party Girl."

"Oh my God," I groaned.

"You were so determined to show the entire school that you were a badass—"

"Because Christian told everyone at that stupid party that I was the most boring girl he knew, which was horrifying!"

"So, obviously, you choose to do this by going shot for shot with those idiots." Jeannie laughed. "My God, I don't think I've ever seen you drunk before or since!"

"That was really more than enough," I said dryly. "I can't believe I did that."

"I can't believe you went nuts on Christian in the middle of the party," Jeannie agreed. "That might be the funniest thing I've ever seen."

"He really didn't know what to do." I smiled, remembering. "I don't even remember what I said."

Jeannie giggled. "I think it was all pretty much a variation of 'go to hell, big brother.' "

"I wanted to be cool and maybe a little dangerous," I said. I wrinkled up my nose. "Sadly, I was just drunk."

We both smiled, and subsided into the quiet of the moment.

"Sometimes I miss high school," Jeannie admitted after a while. She considered. "Not the school part, or the living at home part. Or even the teenager part, actually."

"What other parts were there?"

"I had fun." Jeannie shrugged. "Not everyone can say that."

"That's because most people hated high school." *Most normal people*, I thought. "There's an entire teen movie genre dedicated to how much most people hated high school."

"High school was like an extended four-year test," Jeannie said. "We just happened to test well, that's all."

"An extended four-year test that leaves permanent scars." I shook my head. "Or requires years of therapy."

"I think that's because most people didn't know who they were in high school, and had to go through some huge drama later on, figuring it out," Jeannie said. "But I'm not really like that. I knew who I was then, and I know now too. So, no scars." She smiled at me. "You and I were always the same that way."

*   *   *

Dad settled into his recliner and we all took seats around the den to continue having Family Time. Family Time without Hope, that was, who was still sleeping.

"So," Dad said, beaming at Jeannie. "How's my favorite wedding coming along?"

Jeannie launched into a description of the latest wedding nightmare, and I zoned out. There was only so much discussion of peonies versus lilies that anyone could be expected to take and remain fully conscious, especially since Jeannie refused to listen to anyone else's advice concerning floral arrangements. I'd actually had to plan floral arrangements many times for alumnae events at the Morrow School, but did Jeannie want my help? Of course not.

Christian met my eyes from across the room and rolled them ever so slightly, the way he'd done when we were younger and trapped in endless family functions. I hid my grin behind my hand.

It felt good, I thought.

It felt good to feel in harmony with everyone. It felt good to hear my father laugh again, and to share moments like that with Christian. It even felt good to reminisce with Jeannie, despite how wrong she was about me and how little she knew me.

It was so easy to slip back into place. To smile and let everything swirl around me and be okay with it.

Except it wasn't okay.

Was this how it happened? Was this how you went about deceiving and betraying the people closest to you? Atlanta felt far away—like something I'd dreamed up. An escape plan instead of my real life.

And Travis was just a voice on the phone, not my boyfriend. Not someone real I was betraying.

*This* felt real—sitting in the den with the family I'd worked so hard to distance myself from. I was different from them, I'd told myself. I was someone else, someone they couldn't understand, someone *better*.

I suddenly felt cold.

The longer I sat there, slipping back into old intimacies, the dizzier I felt. How much further from myself was I going to get?

I couldn't take another minute of it.

"I'm sorry," I said, surging to my feet and heading for the door. "I just have to go."

And even though part of me had always wanted to get up and just walk out of the house, I discovered that doing it didn't feel good at all. It felt like running away.

Again.

I walked outside and called from my cell phone. I was surprised that I had the number committed to memory, even though I hadn't dialed it in years.

"I dialed your phone number from memory," I announced. "What do you think that means?"

"That you have to do some spring cleaning in your head," Rachel replied. "What are you doing? Come over right now."

She met me on her parents' front porch and rushed me all the way upstairs to the attic, yelling something vague toward the back of the house.

"Best not to engage," she assured me, shooing me up the stairs toward the third floor.

I was embarrassingly out of breath when we made it to the

final landing, and took note of the many stacked boxes and clothes in long-term storage crates. There was an ancient sewing machine, an appliance graveyard, and beyond all that, in the smallest room, Rachel's new bedroom. The old one, I remembered, had been all pink and white and canopied, with a dollhouse to die for and a window seat stretched across the second-floor bay window.

How times changed when you returned to the nest.

"My humble abode," Rachel drawled, with a wave of her hand. "Please note the Night Ranger decals attached to the windows. That would be evidence of the eighties rock and roll lifestyle of my brother Timmy."

"This is a very serious attic," I acknowledged as I looked around. The ceilings sloped toward the roof at a dizzying angle and there was that pervasive musty smell—old paint and years of dust. Possibly centuries of dust, come to that.

"Oh yeah," Rachel agreed. "I'm almost thirty years old, I bartend in town, I live in the attic like a serial killer. What's better than this?"

"You could be in the basement," I pointed out, flopping into a beanbag. "The basement has a whole different connotation. The attic is kind of starving artist, right? The basement is where the serial killer thing comes in."

"Maybe so," Rachel mused, lounging across her bed, which appeared to be just a box spring and mattress piled on the floor. "But I think that no matter your geographic location inside the house, if you're actually *in the house* at all, you're a big fat loser."

"Boomerang," I corrected. "I believe the term is 'boomerang.'"

"Loser," Rachel repeated, drawing the word out into several syllables, and all manner of definitions.

We grinned at each other, as if there had never been space or group dynamics between us. Or anything worse.

"So . . ." She waggled her brows at me. "Want to listen to my Duran Duran records?"

I slunk back to the house when it was nearing 8 p.m. and Rachel was headed off to another night of bartending. I felt about seventeen years old—the kind of wild, reckless seventeen neither she nor I had ever been. I'd spent the entire day giggling and allowing myself to lust over inappropriately young boy musicians on MTV. Now I roared into the driveway with my music blaring out of Mom's speakers, and enjoyed the feeling entirely too much.

How sad that it took so little to make me feel so good. So very little, and yet I'd never done it before. I was twenty-eight years old and a mystery to myself. How incredibly pathetic was that?

I knew that I would have to do a lot of thinking, about the things I was doing and what that made me—but for one moment, with the radio jacked up too loud and the sound of squealing tires just fading away, I thought of none of it and just grinned.

I swung out of the car, and saw Scott's car parked in his mother's driveway. The grin, and the feelings that had occasioned it, disappeared immediately. I felt unsteady. Were my knees weak or was I just physically repulsed by myself? There was no sign of Scott himself, for which, I told myself sternly, I was grateful. I hurried toward the door.

"Dumb and Dumber left around two," Hope said, with a yoga-like stretch of her arms.

She hadn't bothered to get dressed at all, all day. It was a close call as to which one of us was scruffier, and me with half of the dinner I'd cooked across my shirt.

It was nearing nine-thirty, and we were cleaning up the kitchen together. Upstairs, Dad was still making some settling-down noises. I hoped his improved energy level meant he was on the mend, and wasn't one of those scary flukes I'd read about, where the sick person gets suddenly better and seems to be improving and then bam! Dead.

Not that I was morbid.

"Were they pissed that I had to leave?"

It was a silly question, I knew. They'd all just stared at me when I'd bolted for the door.

"How would I be able to tell?" Hope murmured dryly. "Their normal level of rudeness around me is hard to penetrate. Jeannie said to tell you she would call you, though."

"Won't that be fun."

Hope wandered off into the family room, and I joined her to watch some summer reruns. She was engrossed in the show, but I couldn't concentrate at all. It was as if there was something beneath my skin, trying to claw its way out. I couldn't sit still.

"Stop fidgeting!" Hope ordered, not looking away from the screen. "I take my television seriously."

"I'm going to bed," I informed her, and headed upstairs.

Once in my bedroom, though, I was at a loss. I thought maybe I should take a bath, except that promised far too much time for quiet contemplation. Or maybe I should go for a nice long run. Except there was absolutely nothing nice about running, and even if I could force myself to do it, it raised the same issue—time alone in my head.

I brushed my hair, trying for the hundred strokes I'd read about throughout my youth. It didn't make my hair shine and glow as promised, but it was something to do—and Lord knew my hair needed as much attention as I could give it. But too soon, even that was finished. I heard a car race by on the street outside and smirked at myself.

Of course I was going to look, although I imagined Scott had left long before, while I was carefully ensconced in the back of the house, deliberately uninterested in his comings and goings.

*Liar*, I scolded myself.

I leaned over and stared out the window.

And stopped breathing.

Scott's car was still parked in his mother's driveway.

And Scott himself was leaning against the trunk, arms folded across his chest, head tilted up, staring directly into my window.

I didn't have to be able to see his eyes to feel that stare right down to my toes.

I could pretend that there was no thought involved. That's how it was in all the books I read. The heroines would do stupid things "without thought," but in real life there was too much thought and no getting away from it.

I could pretend that I was so overwhelmed by the fact of him standing there, waiting for me, that it drove me right out of the house before I knew what I was doing. And it was almost true. I wanted it to be true.

Except I knew what I was doing.

I wasn't necessarily thinking rationally. On some level, I knew that this was different from what had gone before, things that I had hated myself for but that I could convince myself were accidental. His fault. His idea, his move, his mouth. But even I couldn't persuade myself that he was doing anything more than standing outside the house. Everything else would be entirely my responsibility.

A brief, searing image of Travis flashed across my mind, but I dismissed it. I ignored it.

There was no accident in each step I took, each stair I descended. There was no alcohol involved in the excited pounding of the blood through my body. There was no mistake. I walked down the stairs myself. Scott wasn't there to grab my arm or lean in with his clever mouth. There were no taunts, no jibes.

I just stepped out the front door, closed it quietly behind me, and walked to him.

# Chapter 9

Guilt made me stupid.

I pestered Travis at his office.

"How come you never call me?" I demanded when he picked up his phone.

"Because you call me." He sounded lazy and amused, the way he always did. *He is solid and real*, I thought: *I am the one losing my grip*. "You doing all right, hon? You sound pretty uptight."

"Everything's fine." I gripped the phone so hard it made my hand ache. "Except my boyfriend doesn't care enough to keep in touch with me. Should I be wondering what else is going on that's so much more important?"

Guilt made me project.

"Just work," Travis said, in a tone I recognized immediately. His *I-know-you're-trying-to-pick-a-fight-with-me, but-I'm-not-rising-to-the-bait* tone.

"I'm sorry." I couldn't seem to stop being snotty. "Am I bothering you?"

"I'll tell you what," Travis drawled. "I'm going to hang up now, but I'll call you later this afternoon. This is not because

I don't want to talk to you, but because I definitely don't feel like being in trouble when we're not even in the same state, okay?"

I didn't like how funny he found it. *Patronizing jackass.*

But that only made me feel worse. *Projecting.*

I hung up the phone and sighed heavily.

"And how is the boyfriend?" Hope asked from her position at the table. She was idly flipping through a magazine while she shoveled in some cereal.

"Great," I muttered.

"Is he coming up north?" Hope asked innocently. Too innocently.

"He's very busy. It's his father's consulting firm, you know. Someday Travis is going to have to take over the whole business."

I slammed the phone back into its cradle.

"Mmm-hmm." Hope sounded entirely too amused.

Making a face at the top of Hope's head, I picked up the sponge from the sink, aimed it, and winged it at her. Score.

"You," Hope said with malice, wiping the splattered soap and water from her face, "are so dead."

"Yeah?" All OK Corral.

"Oh yeah," she said, and lunged.

I squealed, and bolted.


"How are they?" Dad asked when I came into the den.

He was in his usual position: leg propped up before him, pillows at his back. The agitated tone in his voice and the undue look of concern were new.

"The fish seem fine," I said, handing him the clipboard.

I wasn't aware that fish offered a particularly broad range of

emotion to choose from. In my experience—limited, it's true—
they were either fine or they were dead.

Dad took the clipboard almost too eagerly, flipping through
the pages and frowning at the flowchart and graph. I watched
him do this, aware that I was frowning myself.

It was disconcerting, to say the least, to watch a parent be *so*
invested in something you were pretty sure you could trot out
as evidence against them at a commitment hearing.

"So," I said, perching on the edge of the couch. "You really do
have a lot of fish, Dad."

Would that ever stop—that overly formal way of talking to
him? As if I wasn't sure we could *just talk*, and so had to work
harder at the usual words?

"Some of the fellows at the conventions have a great deal
more than me," he said with a dismissive chuckle. "I'm strictly a
hobbyist."

Wow. That was a sentence with a whole lot of information
packed into it.

*Conventions?* Was he *kidding*?

"Conventions?" I echoed, in a far less accusatory tone than
the one I'd used in my head. Let's hope.

"Sure," he said, still focused on the clipboard pages. "I go a
few times a year. I like to see what's out there."

I pressed my fingers to my temples, visions of commitment
hearings flooding my brain.

"Huh," I said, trying desperately not to *sound* the way I *felt*.
This required clearing my throat. "Why do you like fish so
much?" I asked him.

He raised his head and focused on me. "What do you mean?"

"You know," I said, and smiled. "You spend so much time
with them, and you go to conventions—"

It cost me to pronounce the word with no particular inflection.

"—and I guess I didn't really know it was such a huge part of your life." There. That sounded diplomatic, right?

"So," I continued, gathering steam, "since I'm spending so much time down there while I'm home, feeding them and everything, it would be great if I knew *why* you're so excited about them."

*And why you've transformed the basement into a scene from a creature feature*, I added silently.

"I don't know that I'd say I was *excited* about them," Dad demurred.

Naturally. Excitement was an emotion, after all, and he couldn't admit to *those*.

"You have about sixty tanks down there," I retorted. "You have a seventeen-page flowchart. If it's not excitement, what is it?"

I tacked a smile onto the end of that, to cushion the tone.

Dad eyed me for a moment.

"The thing about fish is that you can control the breeding," he said after a while. "So if you're interested in fins, for example, you can breed for fins. You can see the results quickly, you know. It's about a thirty-day gestation period."

"You like fins?"

"For example," Dad said.

Fins, scales, bulging eyes, and slimy tails—who really cared? He was obviously insane! But he looked back down at the flowchart, and I noticed that his hands looked old: knobby and tired. I remembered them from when I was small and thought they could block out the sun. I had to catch a sudden breath.

"So you like the breeding part," I said, determined to make sense of it.

"I like that I can control their environments," Dad said. "They become what I want them to become. There are very few surprises when you get the science right. You get out what you put in."

*Unlike your family*, I thought, watching him.

"Well," I said when it was clear he'd not only finished speaking, but had possibly forgotten that he had *been* speaking. "I'm glad you found something that makes you happy."

I wanted to rush over and hug him, but I restrained myself. He might swoon.

As if he could read my mind, he stiffened.

"What would make me even happier," he said gruffly, "would be a fresh ginger ale, if you wouldn't mind."

He didn't look up from the chart, and still, I felt a deep ache inside my chest. I didn't move.

"I'd appreciate it, Meredith."

"Of course," I murmured, and then went to fetch it.


"I want to see you, and I want to see the movie," Scott said with a show of great patience. "It's a matter of convenience and is in no way a date. You might want to consider getting over yourself."

"It seems pretty datelike to me," I sulked at him, slumped in the front seat of his car.

The window was open and the marginally cooler night air swirled inside, scented with cut grass and flowers. Summer smells.

They didn't make me feel any better.

"And yet you haven't flung yourself from the car in disgust," Scott pointed out. "So I guess you don't really mind."

I turned my head to look at him. He glanced at me, then back at the road.

"Don't," he said, before I could speak. "I don't want to have this conversation."

"We're going to have to." I watched him narrowly. "Sooner or later."

"Later." He kept his eyes on the road. "I've been wanting to see pretty girls die gruesome deaths all week and I know you're going to ruin it."

"We can't pretend—"

"No one's pretending anything!" He flicked me a look. "Well, I guess you are. But I just want to go and see this movie, Meredith, okay? And I definitely don't want to have this discussion while operating a motor vehicle, because I think we can both be sure you're going to piss me off."

I'd been feeling sad and a little angry all day, thanks to that conversation with my father. Part of me wanted to lash out. Another huge part of me wanted to sink into Scott and forget about everything, including all the reasons that was a terrible idea. And I didn't want to *think* about any of it.

"Just for that you can buy my ticket *and* popcorn," I replied after a long moment.

"I can't do that." He sounded smug. "That would make it a date."

Later, having laughed away the urge for serious discussion in the delightfully bad movie, we sat in a shadowy bar on the outskirts of town—a bar that I had long associated with the sketchier graduates of our high school. I played with my beer bottle absently and periodically peered through the haze of cigarette smoke and classic rock to see if I recognized anyone.

I didn't. Thank God.

"So exactly what do you do with your days?" Scott asked. "You can't sit in that house all the time. Do you have friends in the city?"

I frowned. "Actually, no. Not really."

He waited. I sighed.

"You know, I don't actually have so many friends around here anymore," I admitted carefully.

There was Rachel, sure, but she was something so new and also so old—not to mention complicated—that I wasn't sure I could use her as evidence. I was fairly certain we would both have to cry and maybe hug before we could be sure of each other again.

"I've always had Christian," I reminded Scott. "And there was Jeannie. You know, that group in high school, they were mostly Jeannie's friends and I don't really keep in touch with them. She does."

I shrugged. Scott smirked.

"What a loss. And here I wanted to know all about what that evil little monster Ashley Mueller was up to these days."

He took a pull from his beer, and I decided not to mention that Ashley Mueller was, in fact, Jeannie's maid of honor.

"What about college?" Scott continued. "Don't tell me you sat in your dorm room for four years to make up for your high school sins. Though that kind of appeals to me."

"I had friends!" I made a face at him. "My freshman year I ran around with this whole group of girls from my dorm. We had fun. But then I met Billy." I felt unaccountably embarrassed, saying his name and seeing the look on Scott's face. I hurried on. "And so then I mostly just hung out with him."

"Billy?" Scott pronounced the name with far too much amusement. "Let me guess. Blond, tall, and oh so charming?"

"He was just my college boyfriend." I ignored his tone, and also his alarmingly on-the-nose description. I sat back, thinking about the Billy years. "We dated for a long time in college, and then, less successfully, out of college. It turned out I didn't think his being a complete pothead was all that attractive off campus. So I moved down to Atlanta and met Travis, literally my second day of work. We started hanging out immediately."

"Uh-huh." Scott watched me closely. "I'm going to bet you have all the same friends, and they were his friends first."

"We have mutual friends, yes," I said. Defensively.

He smiled at his drink, and then slanted a look my way.

"I can't decide if that's sad or just pathetic," he told me. "Or maybe scary. Have you ever thought about making your own friends?"

"Are you an example of what that would entail?" I asked crisply. "Because so far, it hasn't been a great success."

Scott snorted. "Nice comeback, Atlanta, but we're not friends."

"Oh, of course not," I scoffed. "Because men and women can never be friends, blah blah blah, *When Harry Met Sally*—you know, you might think about updating your—"

"We're not friends," Scott said very distinctly, "because you don't want to know anything about me. I know something about you, but you, Meredith, have never even asked a question about me."

He watched me with his eyes sharp again, and I wanted to shrink away in a sudden intense burst of shame.

"Then you should probably think about hanging out with someone else," I said finally. Weakly.

"Maybe I should," he agreed. "In the meantime, though, I'm

fine with being your sex object." He smiled, but I didn't entirely believe it.

"Ugh," I groaned, but I was thankful to change the subject, and to look away. "Do you ever think about anything else?"

"Around you?" He shook his head, and played with his beer bottle. He smiled. "No, not really."

He just watched me, in a silence that I found unnerving.

I looked away, back into the haze all around us.

"Why are you cheating on him?" he asked, very quietly. *With me*, his eyes clarified.

Of course, I thought dimly, part of me should have been expecting this question. *Because you're here*, I wanted to say, but it was mean. And untrue.

"I don't know," I said instead, which was closer to true. "I didn't know I could . . . I mean, I never have before, if that's what you wondered."

"Because you're such a nice girl," Scott supplied, his mouth curving. Although not in a smile. Not exactly.

"I think we should go," I said at length. "I'm tired."

"Yeah," Scott agreed, and laughed. "I bet you are."

"Guess where I am?" Travis asked.

"On vacation?" I asked. I was washing Dad's lunch dishes. I almost dropped the phone into the sink while transporting a plate to the dishwasher, and had to clench it harder with my shoulder. "Did you go up to the lake? That's so unfair, it's boiling hot here—"

"Nothing quite that scenic," Travis said, cutting me off. "I just landed. I'm at Newark. You gonna come pick me up or what?"

Then I really did drop the phone—happily, not into the sink. It clattered across the linoleum and lay there, staring back at me. Balefully, I thought.

This time, I actually did move without thought. It was panic mode.

I calmly informed Dad that I would be running out for a bit, and that we would be having a houseguest. I navigated the labyrinth of New Jersey highways to Newark with intense concentration, the radio up high.

I even sang along.

When I had picked the phone up from the ground and laughed uneasily to explain dropping it, Travis had said he would be waiting outside at the arrivals hall. And there he was, as promised, lounging in the sunshine, grinning when he saw me sitting high behind the wheel of Mom's huge SUV, so far off the ground I practically had to use a ladder to get in and out.

I put it into park and climbed out. *He is so blond*, I thought. *He needs a haircut*, I thought, and then I was enveloped in his arms, in the familiar heft and scent of him, which should have felt like coming home but instead felt strange and unusual. As if we had stopped fitting. Even his mouth felt odd on mine, his kiss old and forgotten.

The guilt kicked in. Hard.

"I can only stay for the weekend," he said, slinging an arm across my shoulders and heading toward the car. "I have this pain-in-the-ass presentation on Monday morning that I couldn't get out of."

"The weekend's great," I said.

I smiled up at him and willed myself to be happy. My

boyfriend was here. This was my real life. This was what mattered.

Everything else was darkness and bad dreams, and barely signified.

"Well, well, well," Hope drawled, sauntering into the kitchen. "If it isn't Travis."

"Hey there, Hope," Travis said. "How's graduation treating you?"

"Oh, just fine," Hope said, with her prettiest smile and a quick glance my way. I avoided her eyes.

"We're going out to dinner," I announced without inflection. "I made up Dad's tray. Could you take it to him when he wants it?"

Normally, this request would precipitate a snort and a quick exit, but Hope only looked at me for a moment.

"Of course," she said. "I'm going out around ten, if you guys are interested." Another glance my way. "There are a few bars in town that are fun sometimes."

"That sounds a little bit late for me," Travis replied easily, southern charm on high. He didn't notice the evil eye I turned on Hope. "I'm turning into an old man."

"Bye," was what I said, and grabbed Travis by the hand to drag him out.

We sat outside at one of the sidewalk cafés. The fact that the town boasted more than one sidewalk café still amazed me, given what the place had been like while I was growing up, and I decided to comment on this.

At length.

"What's going on with you?" Travis asked after we'd ordered and were sitting there with only air between us, my dissertation on the gentrification of my hometown having finally been exhausted. "You're taking tense to a new level."

"Family stuff," I offered immediately, with a nervous smile.

I shoved a piece of bread in my mouth. Because it's always best to sublimate emotions via carbs.

"You look good," Travis said quietly. He smiled. "Different, but real good."

"Different? What does 'different' mean?" I demanded, with, I could hear, unnecessary paranoia. Could he see my infidelity marked in ink across my face? Or did he just sense it?

Travis sat back in his chair, surprised.

"It just means different," he said, sounding slightly defensive. "Your hair or something. I don't know. You usually look more— What is going on with you?"

"I don't know," I muttered. I considered denying it, but who was I kidding? "I think I'm just a little freaked out that you're here. All summer I've felt like I'm reliving my teenage years and then suddenly here you are—it's just weird, that's all. I'm sorry."

"You've barely touched me," he continued in a low tone. "If I didn't know better, I'd think you'd forgotten all about me."

His grin told me he didn't really think anything of the kind.

I smiled apologetically and reached across the table to take his hand.

"I haven't forgotten about you for even five minutes," I said. Funny how the lies kept coming. "Things are just crazy here. I'm crazy here."

"You're the most down-to-earth, reliable person I know," Travis said with an instant loyalty that caused an answering flash of shame in my gut. "I don't know why you let your family get to you. When do you think you're coming home? The place is practically falling apart without you around."

"Let me guess—pizza boxes on every available surface, laundry in huge piles around the bedroom, and the vacuum cleaner gathering dust in the closet?"

"Worse," Travis said, laughing. "I've had to order food in every night since you left. Look at me, I'm getting fat!" He patted his stomach.

"Just solid," I assured him, the way I always did.

Conversely, when I'd put on a few pounds after a few months of nonstop weekend weddings, Travis had clucked and suggested a personal trainer. I had rolled my eyes and called him a southern chauvinist.

*Stop it!* I scolded myself. *You're just trying to make him the bad guy.*

"Charlie and Becky got engaged," Travis said.

He used that as a springboard into updates on everyone else we knew. And I couldn't help but think about the last conversation I'd had with Scott. He'd been right—everyone Travis and I knew, Travis had known first.

I had originally met him through a girl at work who had long since married and moved away to Houston. The rest of our circle was made up of Travis's college buddies and the many Atlanta-born and -bred people he'd grown up with. The girlfriends came and went and the wives were nice enough, but none of them were mine. None of them knew me outside of my role as "Travis's girlfriend."

I didn't know what that meant, but I was pretty certain it spoke to some tremendous void inside of me. The one that permitted deception and betrayal on the one hand, and on the other, the smile on my face as I sat there and held Travis's hand. As if I was still that girl he trusted.

After dinner we walked out into the warm night and stood for a minute outside the restaurant. Travis ran his hands up and down my arms and smiled down at me. I smiled back into his warm, open gaze and willed myself to be good again, to be worthy of him. He kissed me gently, and then again, with more intensity, and I told myself that it felt like coming home.

I reminded myself of the life we had together, and how hard I'd worked to make it wonderful. I thought of the way he smiled down at me so proudly when we danced, all done up in formal wear, at the succession of weddings we always seemed to be attending. I thought of how he looked when he was sleepy and silly, and how I only pretended to be exasperated. I reminded myself that when our "state of the union" discussion had taken place in the spring, he'd indicated that a marriage proposal was coming, and I'd been so ecstatic about finally winning him I'd basked in it for days.

This was love. This was real. It had to be.

We pulled away from each other, and I smiled at him.

"I missed you," Travis murmured.

"I missed you too," I replied.

It wasn't exactly a lie if I wanted it to be true, was it?

There was another kiss, a sweet kiss. I thought maybe things would be okay, or at least I would be better, and things would be all right again. We had to be. *I* had to be.

So of course Scott was standing right there when I turned around.

We stared at each other. I could feel his stare in the soles of my feet and actually swayed back, away from him, like that might help.

It was a moment, maybe two, and then he turned on his heel and walked away.

"Come on," Travis said to me, completely oblivious. "Let's get out of here."

# Chapter 10

So what's the deal?" Hope asked in an undertone.

We were sitting in the backseat of Jeannie's SUV, tearing through the suburbs at about ninety miles an hour.

Christian and Jeannie had appeared in the kitchen just after ten in the morning and announced that it was Bridesmaid Time. Jeannie's maid of honor, the odious Ashley Mueller, had shown up shortly thereafter. I'd been forced to leave Travis to Christian, which was really just as well, since I felt a little bit insane whenever I was around Travis. My attempts to overcompensate just made it worse—it made *him* think I was insane as well. He'd been giving me that *what time of the month is it?* look since dinner the night before. Which would ordinarily enrage me on principle, but I was in no position to complain.

Ashley had claimed the front passenger seat as her rightful place in Jeannie's vehicle. Hope, all bedraggled and sleepy, had merely stared at her blonde blow-out in the kitchen and muttered a fervent "Oh dear Lord, no."

She'd had other things to contend with.

"Surely you're not leaving the house like that!" Christian had barked at her when she'd appeared in the outfit she'd obviously slept in: pajama shorts and a skimpy T-shirt, with her hair haphazard atop her head. And aged flip-flops to round off the ensemble.

"It's this or I'm going back to sleep," Hope had responded in a tone that was actually mild. From exhaustion rather than any attitude readjustment, I was pretty sure. "Your choice, big brother."

Now Hope was lying down in the backseat, her head on my lap with her eyes closed. In the front, Jeannie and Ashley were shrieking about a mutual acquaintance and might as well have been waving a banner that announced that they were BEST FRIENDS FOREVER. It was so deliberate, and yes, it stung a little bit.

"What's what deal?" I asked Hope, shaking off junior high school.

"Travis," she said around a huge yawn that showed off her molars. "He's looking a little annoyed. You know, for him."

"I told him I couldn't possibly sleep with him in my parents' house and made him sleep in Christian's old room," I confessed quietly. "He's not too happy about that."

Hope opened her eyes and looked up at me. She didn't look sleepy at all.

"I don't get it." Her gaze was narrow. "Do you want to be with him or not?"

"It's not that," I said helplessly. "I just don't . . . I just think . . . We ran into Scott in town last night."

"Oops." But she sounded amused. "And here I said that would never happen. Shows you what I know."

"It was fine."

Even though I thought that look on his face might have shattered something in me. Even though I'd wanted to chase after him, and the hell with Travis.

I coughed, and continued in a low voice. "He just glared and walked away, but I can't be this kind of person. This two-timing, cheating person. I hate myself and it's getting worse and I don't know what to do."

In the front seat, Ashley was telling a very loud story involving the trials of employing Eastern European maid services, pitching her voice over the strains of a guitar anthem on K-Rock.

"And like I believe that whole 'no English' act," Ashley brayed. "Like I was born yesterday! Katya knows enough English to say 'no windows' every week, doesn't she?"

They couldn't have heard us if we'd been shouting.

"Look," Hope said, swinging herself around and sitting up. "Cheating is the symptom, not the problem. There's a reason you're stepping out on Travis. If everything was good with him you wouldn't even think about it."

"I think that's what people tell themselves."

"I think they tell themselves that because it's true," Hope argued quietly.

"Or because they want to make themselves feel better about being terrible, deceitful people," I retorted.

Hope gazed at me for a long moment.

"You're not a terrible person," she said. "You're having a rough time. We all are. I am too, I just go out more and ignore it."

"Is that my excuse?" I asked miserably. "Is that what I should tell Travis? Because I don't think he'd really buy that."

Hope looked at me closely, then shut her eyes again and tipped her head back against the seat.

"I don't think it's Travis you have to convince," she said.

\*   \*   \*

"My feet are killing me," Hope muttered. Not for the first time.

She reached over and snagged a french fry from my plate, also not for the first time. I swatted at her hand, but more out of principle than with any desire to hit her. In any case, I missed.

"I don't know why we have to participate in this group charade," she said, chewing. "We were in that place for *hours*."

"Jeannie wants it both ways," I said. I shrugged. "She wants to force us to wear something she's pretty sure we won't like, but she also wants that scene where everyone squeals and jumps up and down and someone cries. That's why Ashley's here."

"Ugh." Hope swiveled around to make sure Ashley was still involved in the fractious debate she'd kicked up with a food court employee. "That gorgon. I thought you got rid of all those evil girls when you left town."

I sighed. "You and me both."

Jeannie herself was taking a cell phone call some distance away from our table. She gestured a little bit aggressively into the air, and though her words were inaudible, her tone came across loud and clear. Pissed off and tough.

"She's *hard core*," Hope whispered. She sounded admiring. "No wonder Christian loves her—she's the only woman alive who can keep his maharajah ass in line."

"You make a good point," I agreed. "The girl teaches tenth grade. That requires a thick skin."

"Jeannie Gillespie, walking body armor," Hope mused.

"Exposure to Ashley has forced me to reassess Jeannie," I continued. "Comparatively speaking, Jeannie is fabulous."

"A *very* good point." Hope wrinkled her nose in thought. "Bridezilla she's not. Unlike Miss Ashley, who, I'm pretty sure, holds the title. One more reference to her 'special day' and the 'absolutely darling flowers' and I'm taking her down."

"I'll help!" My voice took *fervent* to a whole new level.

"Back in the day, Christian definitely would have gone for the Ashley type," Hope continued. "We should count our lucky stars."

"In fact, they went out for about three weeks in the eighth grade," I said, licking salt from my finger.

"That's a terrible thing to say about our brother!"

"It's true," I assured her. "I was there."

"The people who work here are repulsive," Ashley announced, flopping into her seat.

Hope immediately frowned and inched away from her on the plastic bench, actions speaking louder than words.

"Really?" I asked, for lack of a better response.

"*Repulsive!*" Ashley said, with unnecessary emphasis, and sniffed. That snotty little *sniff* of hers that she used as punctuation. She'd had *that* since the seventh grade. It had been equally obnoxious then.

"I'm sure they're all big fans of overly entitled fake blondes who order them around," Hope retorted. At Ashley's glare, she shrugged. "I'm just saying we all have issues."

Ashley poked at her salad with unnecessary force. She glared at the forlorn piece of tomato she speared with her fork as if she'd meant to harm it. She looked up and met my gaze, and it was exactly the same look. I was suddenly transported back in time to any number of uncomfortable cafeteria meals in high school, with Ashley the Wonder Bitch gunning for me.

For some reason, the déjà vu made me calm.

"So," I said almost merrily. "What have you been doing all these years?"

"Other than getting married," Hope interjected hurriedly. "Because I think we're all up to speed on that."

"My wedding was the most beautiful day of my life," Ashley snapped. "Doug and I are as in love today as we were then. More so, as a matter of fact!"

A lovely sentiment, but I knew enough about girls like Ashley to interpret that to mean that Doug was a jerk and probably unfaithful, and Ashley had better hurry up and get pregnant.

"That's really sweet," Hope said around her Big Mac. "And your tone there was really convincing, too."

Ashley wrinkled her pert little nose, but obviously thought better of taking Hope on directly. A wise choice.

"I don't know how you can eat junk like that," she trilled instead, looking down her nose at Hope's meal. "Aside from making you fat, it's just so unhealthy."

Hope rolled her eyes and took another messy bite.

I wished immediately that I had gone with something even more fat-laden than fries, just to annoy Ashley, who—unless her metabolism had miraculously changed for the better—had to engage in a Herculean daily battle with her body to keep herself an emaciated size four. I wouldn't have been at all surprised if that was one of her wedding vows: instant divorce should she balloon up beyond a size six for anything other than pregnancy. There was a reason girls like Ashley married young, rich, and had lots of babies. It was the only time in their lives they ate.

"I saw John Ericho the other day," Ashley continued when it was clear neither Hope nor I was going to burst into tears at her roundabout fat reference.

"My Lord, talk about ancient history." Hope groaned. "I bet *he's* fat."

"He's very good-looking, actually. He's in venture capital."

"So, fat *and* broke," Hope retorted.

"Are we really talking about John Ericho?" I asked, slightly bewildered. "I haven't thought about him since the tenth grade."

When Ashley "stole" him from me in a huge drama that rocked the entire high school and was completely forgotten within a week.

"It was just so nice to see him again, after so long," Ashley cooed.

I could only stare at her. Was she serious? Did she think I had been secretly harboring the pain of John Ericho's defection for all these years?

Hope looked from Ashley to me, and then back again.

"Am I missing something?" she asked. "Wasn't John Ericho the hairy one with the monobrow who you went to the sophomore semi-formal with?"

"Yes," I said, frowning a little bit. "He really did have a monobrow, didn't he?"

"He was one of the most popular, best-looking guys in our class!" Ashley snapped.

I leaned closer to Hope. "Ashley should know, since she fooled around with him behind my back and then got him to break up with me so she could date him."

"Scandalous!" Hope murmured in feigned shock.

I eyed Ashley. "Why would you even want to bring that up?"

"Seriously," Hope agreed. "I mean, everyone has terrifying high school stories, but most people *try* to forget them. In fact, that's pretty much the rule—the minute you graduate, you get to pretend high school never happened."

"You guys have turned into a tag team," Jeannie said.

We all turned to see her standing at the end of the table. Ashley actually jumped a little bit. I noticed that Jeannie was watching Hope and me with an odd, arrested look on her face.

"We're talking about John Ericho," I told her, grinning up at her as if sharing a delightful secret. "And *the scandal*. Ashley ran into him."

Jeannie rolled her eyes and looked from me to Ashley.

"Yeah," she drawled. "About four years ago in some Red Lobster. What a loser." She glared at Ashley. "Can you act like tenth grade is over now, do you think?"


"I feel like I barely saw you," Travis said, but with a smile. It was Sunday afternoon and we were in Newark Airport, awaiting his plane. "You're definitely deep into this family stuff."

"I guess I am," I agreed. "But no more than you are. You just happen to live in the same place as your family all the time."

"Don't remind me." Travis groaned. "Diana is driving me insane. She keeps getting in these huge fights with my parents and then expecting me to deal with them. What am I supposed to do? I can't keep her from choosing bad boyfriends."

"Your sister is something else," I agreed. What Diana was, I knew better than to say, was a spoiled brat. She'd been spoiled rotten since the day of her birth, never forced to take any kind of responsibility for herself or anything else, and it was a great big shock to her parents that at twenty-five she was the pretty and feminine version of shiftless and irresponsible. Not that anyone minded, especially; they just wanted her married and settled with an appropriate southern boy—preferably one of her mother's choosing from the family's social circle.

The fact that Travis seemed to have chosen me was a subject his parents found a bit distressing. As far as Yankees went, they liked me more than most. But I was still a Yankee.

*Stop trying to make him the bad guy*, I told myself, sounding weary even in my own head.

"Why so sad?" Travis asked, smiling down at me.

"I'll miss you," I whispered. And detested myself.

"It won't be long now till you're home where you belong," Travis assured me. "Your dad's on the mend, and you won't need to be there, right?"

"I guess," I agreed, even though I didn't exactly agree.

I didn't want to get into it, especially not with Travis. I knew that he wouldn't understand the reasons I suddenly felt so tied to my family—not least because I couldn't understand it myself.

It was what it was: obligation, frustration, and mixed in with all of that, buried in the cracks, that automatic, baffling love. I'd missed the madness of it in Atlanta, even though I'd deliberately moved that far away to escape it.

*I really do miss it*, I thought in a kind of wonder, but pushed the thought aside.

We kissed and hugged and I waved him off with the big smile he expected. I watched him as he went through the strict security check, and grinned each time he looked back. I watched until he was long gone and the white corridor was filled with strangers. I watched until I realized there was nothing at all to do with the desolate feeling in my stomach except live with it.

Dad woke up a few days later in possession of his former energy level—which was to say, he was boisterous and happy. This wasn't just pre-accident energy. It seemed a lot like pre-retirement energy.

I found it more than a little bit alarming—even if it was kind of nice to see Cheery Dad in the place of Distant and Annoyed Dad. Cheery Dad could sometimes be dorky, but was more . . . *Dadlike.*

"Dad," I ventured, over a spate of manic whistling at breakfast. "Not that I'm really complaining, but why are you so happy?"

"Why *not* be happy?" he boomed. I stared at him. He grinned. I continued to stare. "It's been six weeks," he reported, as if I'd missed that. "The goddamned cast is coming off."

He didn't actually let out a rebel yell, or pump his fist in the air, but I think we both knew it was a very close call.

"Now I know how the parents of teenagers feel," Hope said out of the side of her mouth when she observed the change. It was already afternoon—breakfast, if you were Hope—and Dad had graduated from whistling to the a cappella singing of top Billboard hits from his youth. I could hear him belting one out from his room, and I was downstairs in the kitchen.

"We should be more supportive." But as I studied the ceiling, through which I could hear the strains of "Louie Louie," I was doubtful.

"You be supportive," Hope suggested. "I'm going to stick with creeped out."

"The cast is coming off," I reminded her. "I can see why that would please him."

"He's been much nicer lately, I grant you," Hope said. "But this is bordering on the manic. You should have the doctor prescribe something for the inevitable downswing, if you know what I mean."

"It's definitely the cast," I said, frowning, and went to feed the fish.

He was actually helping me help him down the stairs, instead of the spate of complaining that usually accompanied any excursion that involved the stairs.

"You've really developed some upper body strength in the last few weeks," I told him. Because positive reinforcement is everyone's friend.

Hope wandered out from the kitchen to watch.

"In another week or two you'll be able to walk up the stairs on your hands," she said.

"I'll be a regular circus performer," Dad agreed, and let out a belly laugh.

Hope and I grinned at each other.

We all froze when the front door opened.

Mom deposited her suitcases inside the door with a modicum of fuss and struggle, and then straightened. She was wearing a linen suit that seemed impervious to the heat and humidity outside, not to mention the plane ride across the Atlantic.

But if anything described my mother, it was this: even linen didn't dare disappoint her.

"Hello," she said as if she'd just nipped out to the store. "I'm home."

She swept the three of us with a swift look, and her gaze lingered only slightly on her husband. Her husband who was, I saw with surprise, smiling at her. Tenderly.

I was sure she was about to make one of those speeches—the

sort people were always making in movies, the sort that made sense of everything and might even be a little poetic.

Mom smiled.

We all leaned forward.

"I hope," she said, "that someone can tell me why Gladys Van Eck was lying in wait for me on the sidewalk, carrying on about the state of the front lawn. Surely someone in this house knows where we keep the lawn mower?"

# Chapter 11

Christian pushed his way into Hope's room, already frowning, with Jeannie behind him. He'd been summoned to a homecoming family dinner for Mom, and looked annoyed that Hope and I had dragged him upstairs for an additional summit meeting.

"I thought we knew when Mom was coming home," he said without preamble. "I did, anyway."

"Obviously you paid more attention to that itinerary than I ever did," I said, surprising myself. I hadn't meant to say that out loud. "It's worse than Dad's fish flowchart. I could only get through the first page and then I had to throw it away."

"You were the one putting her life on hold to be here." Jeannie shook her head. "If I were you I would have been counting down the days."

"Mom's finally doing what she's supposed to," Christian said, with only a slight frown at his fiancée, who shrugged. "So why do we have to have a war council?"

"This isn't so much a war council as a meeting of the minds." That was much more the sort of soothing thing I expected me to say. I shrugged. "Just to make sure we're all on the same page."

"Yeah," Hope agreed, finally weighing in from where she lay sprawled across her bed with her head upside down toward the floor. "You can tell this isn't an actual war council because when you guys had war councils back in the day, you wouldn't let me be part of it. I had to be the so-called sentry in the hallway while the three of you giggled and told each other secrets."

She subsided, possibly just then noticing that all three of us were staring at her.

"What?" she demanded, swinging into sitting position. "I feel pain too, you know. You guys aren't the only ones with baggage from the past. Of course, *my* baggage is Vuitton."

Jeannie rolled her eyes and sat gingerly on the edge of the bed, like she feared it might be infectious. Christian didn't even bother rolling his eyes. Hope looked from one to the other and then smiled to herself.

"What page are we supposed to be on?" Christian asked me as if Hope hadn't spoken. "Mom's back, Dad's in a walking cast, we can all go on with our lives. Right?"

"I'm not so sure," I said. "Mom got a little scary about the fact that her amaryllis wasn't in appropriate condition, but other than that she was acting as if nothing was weird." Which had the immediate effect of making me think that nothing *was* weird. Maybe it hadn't been such a big deal that she hadn't come home. Maybe that had been our drama.

"Like she didn't in fact prefer to spend her husband's convalescence romping around Europe," Hope said, as if reading my mind.

"And again," Christian said, impatience laced through his voice, "who cares? This no longer has to be any of our business. For which I would like to offer a hearty hallelujah. This summer has been nuts."

"My brother," Hope said with a sigh. "The humanitarian."

"We had to send out the invitations without a final list from her," Jeannie chimed in. "You probably don't think that's a big deal, but just imagine what her reaction's going to be if it turns out she forgot to put her best friend from college on the list." She shuddered. "Carnage."

"You actually have a point there," Hope said, sounding grudgingly impressed. "It's not like Aunt Marion would be gracious about that kind of thing either."

"Maybe she just has jet lag," I said hopefully. I was still holding out for one of those Lifetime movie speeches.

"I don't care what she has," Christian said, crossing his arms over his chest. "As long as she has it here at home."

I helped Dad down the rickety stairs into the basement for the pre-dinner fish feeding. He sighed with pleasure when he saw the soft, humming light from the tanks.

"You must be excited to be back down here." I was all kinds of jovial. "All the fish missed you. They could tell I didn't quite have the touch."

"It's good to have things back to normal," he said, ignoring my attempt at fish bonding. He did produce that smile of his, the genial one he aimed around the room without hitting anything.

"Mom's back home, you're back in the basement."

I was actually agreeing, but it didn't come out that way. I wasn't sure how it had come out, as a matter of fact, and tried to smile brightly so he'd overlook it.

Dad focused on me then. "I'll call up if I need help."

"But what if you—"

"Really, Meredith," he said, with more of that unfocused geniality. Almost. "I need to get back in the swing of things."

"Okay, but—"

"You've done more than enough." He turned his back then, and limped across to one of the big tanks. Only then did he turn back and offer a smile. A small one, sure, but his eyes twinkled just a little bit to match it, and it was real.

I smiled back.

"I'll admit it, Meredith," he said then, the smile deepening. "I like being down here alone with them, where I can breed them up. Whole worlds to play with. It's good to be back."

The following day dawned hazy and overcast. The clouds were low and dark. The humidity felt like a sweaty boa constrictor, and outside, the streets smelled of slate and heat. But there was no rain in sight.

Even Hope knew enough to get her butt out of bed before ten. Mom viewed sleeping in late as a direct declaration of sloth and vice. When Christian and I had been home from college on vacations, we'd gotten it down to a science—the number of mornings per week you could sleep in until, say, eleven versus the mornings you put in an appearance earlier (with the expected naptime later on). But no one would want to draw Mom's fire so soon after her return.

Which was how the McKay women found themselves descending upon the local supermarket as a big group that morning.

"I feel like someone else," Hope complained in the produce aisle, looking ahead to where Mom was frowning over a bin of apples. "Someone who *wants* to spend her summer vacation grocery shopping with her mother. Which, let's face it, just isn't likely to lead anywhere fabulous."

"Just put the carrots in a plastic bag." When she only sighed, I did it myself. "You could have stayed at home."

"Yeah, right." Hope snorted. "And face the Wrath of Mom? Not in this lifetime."

Not that the Wrath of Mom was in evidence in the supermarket. On the contrary—the supermarket was where Mom touched base with the community. Women went out of their way to say hello to her. They called out her name and told her small anecdotes she always laughed at. More often than not, they thanked her for something or other she'd done. It was like walking around with the suburban New Jersey version of Madonna.

"I thought Deborah Singer was going to talk about her hip surgery all morning," New Jersey's Madonna said now, walking up to us. "I told her to use the surgeon Mary Catherine Reading recommended so highly, but she insisted on using a friend of her husband's down in Baltimore."

Clucking her tongue, Mom took control of the cart and set off at a fast clip toward the frozen food.

"That Mary Catherine Reading," Hope whispered in my ear. "She's just such a know-it-all."

I stared at her. "Who is Mary Catherine Reading?"

"Like I know." Hope's attention was caught by the glossy magazine racks, and she drifted away to catch up on the happenings in Hollywood.

At home, we were on bag transportation duty, and marched around to begin unloading the back without comment. Mom made as if to help us, but was pulled up short by the appearance of Mrs. Van Eck at the foot of the driveway. I was convinced that the slight prickle on the back of my neck wasn't actually sweat but an early warning Van Ick alert.

"She always knows when Mom's about to pull into the driveway," I hissed at Hope, rubbing at my neck. "I think she might have telepathy. Evil telepathy."

"Actually, I've thought a lot about this and I think that she has all the neighbors' driveways wired, with sensors or something. So she can track everyone's comings and goings." Hope squinted at her. "I bet she hides the monitor in that stupid hat."

"Gladys!" Mom called warmly. "*So* sorry about yesterday, I was absolutely drooping with jet lag." She hurried over to appease the old hag, leaving Hope and me with the shopping bags.

"Mom might be the only person in the neighborhood who's nice to that woman," I said under my breath. "Seriously—listen to how happy she sounds. She might even *like* her."

"You should know better than that," Hope said, shaking her head. "As if."

"Mom always seems to see the good in irritating people," I argued. "It's a gift—one I definitely don't have."

"Mom knows how to work a room," Hope retorted. "And she knows how to make people feel so good about themselves that they can't wait to whip out their checkbooks and give money to her organizations. She's the best actress I've ever seen."

"She's not acting." But I wasn't sure. "She just thinks it's important to be as nice as possible to everyone. She's good at it too."

"Meredith, you need to wake up and smell the politics." Hope laughed. "Someday I bet she runs for mayor."

On our second trip out, Mom was still talking to Mrs. Van Eck, although it looked more like Mrs. Van Eck was doing the talking while Mom just listened and nodded at irregular intervals when the woman paused to inhale. Isabella, her tiny head festooned with small pastel bows, growled at us and lunged against her leash.

"Ugh. That dog." I'd read once that dogs were cowed by eye contact—a whole alpha dog thing—and tried to dominate Isabella from afar with a cold stare. She just howled with rage and started dancing around in a little circle on her hind legs. I averted my eyes.

"I can't believe you're letting Van Ick talk to Mom," Hope said, pausing to stretch and simultaneously display her gorgeous and *actually concave* belly. The bitch. "What if she really *was* watching that whole Scott Sheridan night? What if she tells Mom?" She considered, and I forgot about her toned abs. "I wonder what Mom would do. I mean, as heinous as it would be to have Mom know about your sex life, imagine how much more heinous it must be to be a mother and hear that your kid—"

"Jesus Christ, Hope," I said weakly. "Are you *trying* to give me a heart attack?"

"Oh." She tried to suck in her smile. "Sorry."

But I had bigger fish to fry. I thrust the grocery bag I'd been holding at Hope and practically dove down the length of the driveway to interrupt Van Ick and hopefully head her off at the pass.

Mom smiled at me. Van Ick glared.

"It's so nice to have Meredith here," Mom told her. "I'm so lucky that she was able to help out."

"Mom," I said quickly. "Don't you want to head in?"

"I was just telling your mother," Van Ick began, alarmingly.

"I think it's about to rain," I interrupted her. I turned back to Mom. "Also, I'm not sure Hope knows where to put anything and we should probably use her before she heads back to bed."

I felt bad—briefly—for throwing my baby sister to the sharks. Then I thought about her whole "musing on Van Ick" routine and got over it.

"That child will be the death of me," Mom said, in that off-hand way she had of talking to people, so no one took such statements seriously. "You take care, Gladys, and don't worry about the Hendersons' bushes. I'm sure they'll take care of them once they're back from the Vineyard."

She let me herd her indoors. I glanced back in time to see Isabella pop a squat on the lawn again, and inferred more than saw Van Ick's scowl.

"Mrs. Van Eck can go on for hours," I said, by way of explanation. Lame, it's true.

Mom just eyed me as she put her bag down on the kitchen counter. "Gladys Van Eck is just a lonely soul," she said evenly. "You kids have always given her such a hard time."

"She's the neighborhood menace," I replied, because Hope had already vacated the kitchen and it was up to me to say such things in her absence.

"She's a sad old woman whose own children left her high and dry years ago," Mom retorted. "That weirdo son of hers is off in Alaska, last I heard, and that daughter." She sniffed, as if still too affronted to comment further. I had forgotten about the Van Ick children, but was somehow unsurprised they'd skedaddled as soon as possible for points unknown. Or maybe not entirely unknown, if Hope's sensor idea had any truth to it.

"I don't know, Mom." I started unpacking the closest bag. "What gives her the right to be such a busybody?"

"I don't think she knows how else to relate to people." There was more than a faint hint of reproof in her tone. "It's not as if she would get many visitors, now is it? What you call being a busybody is probably the only human contact that woman gets all day."

Funny how my mother was so good at making me feel tiny.

"Okay," I said. "But those dogs of hers . . ."

Mom glanced at me. "She must spend hours every day with those bows. I think it's wonderful that she has something to care so much about. You don't know what it's like to grow old, Meredith. It's good to have things to love."

I should have been more specific in my wishes for Lifetime movie moments. I could see that now. I should have indicated that I wanted to be the heroine who *listens* to the speeches that make everyone else grow and learn, not the person to whom those speeches were directed.

We unpacked in silence for a while. The brown paper bags crackled, and were damp from the humidity when I tried to fold them.

"Your father can't say enough about how helpful you've been," Mom said. "I don't know what we would have done without you."

*Come home sooner?* I thought.

"Well," I said. "I'm glad I could help."

"I don't know what your schedule is, when you can get a flight out," Mom said, "but I hope you'll stay for one last supper. I'll make your favorite."

"My favorite?" I echoed. I was just looking at her blankly. What was she talking about?

"You used to love my fried chicken," Mom continued merrily. "I'd be happy to make that, if you like. Although you might want to wait and see what the storm is like before you head off."

"Where am I going?" I asked, confused.

Mom turned from the refrigerator and looked as confused as I felt.

"Home," she said.

Which is when I realized that I hadn't even thought about going home in ages. I couldn't think of the last time I'd thought longingly of Atlanta or my life there. Even when Travis had visited, I'd given lip service to the idea of leaving New Jersey, but I hadn't *really* thought about it. I hadn't been counting the days until Mom returned and I could leave. Quite the contrary. It was like I had amnesia and had forgotten I had somewhere else to be.

"Home to Atlanta," Mom continued, possibly worried by my silence. "And that nice Travis. You must be anxious to see him."

"Oh," I said faintly. I tried to rally. "I don't know where my head is today." I mustered up a smile from somewhere. "I just need to call the airline."


"I can't believe you're really going," Hope whined later that day, lounging against the door frame. I'd spent the day packing, and was changing the sheets on my bed in my old bedroom so Mom couldn't accuse me of treating the house like a hotel. *I don't know why it's so hard for you girls to think of others*, she'd said throughout our youth whenever we'd failed her exacting laundry standards, which required a PhD and far more interest in detergent than I'd ever possessed.

"You know they're just waiting to go nuts. The minute you leave"—Hope made a big arc with her hands—"*boom*."

"They'll be fine." I smoothed out the coverlet with my palms. "They're always fine. And you do what you want anyway."

"There's doing what I want without parental interference, and then there's doing what I want *with* parental interference," Hope said dryly. "It's all about the irritation level." She straightened. "I think you should stay. What's in Atlanta anyway?"

"Travis." His name stuck in my throat. I fluffed up the pillows and swatted them into place against the headboard. "Maybe if I throw myself prostrate at his feet and am the best girlfriend who ever lived for the next, oh, two hundred years, I'll be worthy of him."

"Yeah," Hope said. "Or maybe he's not the one for you and you might as well not bother."

"I've been with him a long time." My voice was low. "That has to mean something."

"Maybe it means you were with him a long time." Hope sounded unimpressed. "Are you actually happy in Atlanta? Really happy?"

"Life isn't about being happy," I informed her. "It's about making choices and sticking with them." This happened to be what my mother had told me when I'd decided I wanted to switch majors in my senior year, which would have necessitated extra years of school, way more money, and a good deal less angst on my part.

My sister rolled her eyes, but chose not to respond. Which greatly resembled my own response to the original statement, if I thought about it. Outside, thunder grumbled in the clouds, and occasional lightning fizzled through the air. Hope groaned.

"Just *rain already*!" she told the sky. "God!"

"I have a job I'm really good at, an apartment I love in a great neighborhood, the perfect boyfriend who I don't deserve—an entire life," I continued. Fiercely. Because obviously, I needed reminding. "I don't need to be here anymore. In fact, I never wanted to come back here in the first place. I had better things to do than troll Hoboken in a tacky yellow Hummer, let me assure you. I knew I should have refused to go to that stupid party, and to hell with what Mom *and* Jeannie thought!"

"Are you going to tell him?" Hope asked, interrupting my rant.

"You told me it was better not to," I reminded her, staring. "Why share the pain, I think you said. Do you think I should tell him? What's the point of confessing *now*?"

Now that it was over, I meant. Now that the madness was about to end and be nothing but a bad memory.

"Scott," Hope clarified, with a small smile she made no attempt to hide. "Are you going to tell him you're leaving?"

I made Hope drive me around his block twice, as I gathered my nerve. I had only been to his place once before, the night I had to stop pretending I wasn't a full participant in whatever it was we were doing. The night I'd gone to him when I could have stayed inside, stayed away.

Scott lived in half of a two-family house just at the border of the next town over. I could see his lights on inside the house. It was just past five, and I was surprised he was already home. Surprised or relieved?

"Looks like he's home," Hope pointed out, as if I couldn't see the lights. "I'll just be here," she continued. "So you go ahead and take as long as you—" She caught my eye. "Okay, I'm being totally silent."

I took a deep breath, and then ran for it.

Scott yanked open the door and stood on the step. His body filled the doorway, and the light spilled out around him.

"All soaking wet and on my doorstep," he drawled. "To what do I owe the honor?"

"It's actually still raining," I pointed out. "Can I come in or do you want to mock me some more?"

"You can come in," Scott said, with a flicker of his usual mischief. "But I don't think it's an either/or situation."

He stepped back and I pushed past him into his living room, deliberately avoiding looking at the stairs that led up to his bedroom. It had been a long night, that night. It was better not to think about it, or the fact that tonight he was half naked and when he'd opened the door I'd almost swallowed my tongue.

"I was working out," Scott said. "I can put on a T-shirt if you're going to go all coy and keep staring at my feet."

"I didn't even notice," I sniffed, and looked directly at him.

"Liar."

"You're setting a new record in antagonism."

"Must be a knee-jerk reaction to seeing the person I'm sleeping with suck face with some blond guy on a public street," Scott replied in a silky sort of tone, which I didn't mistake for anything but furious. "I'll try to work on that."

"That was Travis."

"Oh, good. At least there's only the two of us."

He had the television on in the background. The rain was still pounding against the side of the house, and I could hear the traffic swishing past on the street outside. I still didn't know what to say. Scott's eyes were cool and compelling and I felt far too vulnerable.

"I'm going back to Atlanta," I announced, finally.

Scott let out a breath, and looked away for the first time. His hands rested on his hips and one of them clenched into a fist. But his voice was even.

"When?"

"Tonight. When we—when I leave here."

Scott looked at me. Expressionless. "Have a safe flight."

I rolled my eyes over the sharp sting of that.

"Fine." I headed for the door. "I don't know why I bothered."

"Neither do I," Scott snapped. "What am I supposed to say? 'Please, don't go'? Would it get you to stay?" His voice was angry.

"My life is in Atlanta!" I exclaimed. "Not in my parents' house. Not in this town. Not—" I broke off.

"I get it."

"Scott. Listen. I never—"

"Why did you come here?" he demanded. "To say good-bye? To let me down easy? I kind of got the picture when I saw you and Southern Comfort. Don't be so conceited, Meredith."

"God!" I whispered fiercely. "You make me so angry!"

He made a small sound, and then:

"I realize that I started this whole thing, so I have no one to blame but myself, but I fucking hate that you're leaving, and I hate that you're going back to your life, and I really hate that guy, and *you*, Meredith—" He stopped abruptly. "It was a lot easier," he continued quietly, "when I just hated you."

"I'm sorry," I whispered, because I didn't know what else to say, and I thought it might keep me from crying.

"So am I," he said.

I realized there were already tears wet against my cheeks. I backed away from him, and then forced myself to run.

As Hope pulled out into traffic, I couldn't help but turn back to look out the window.

Scott stood there in his doorway, watching me disappear.

# Chapter 12

Every day, I woke to the alarm at six, hit snooze once, and got up at nine minutes past the hour. I turned on the coffee maker on my way into the shower, and poured myself and Travis a cup when I got out at six-twenty. I delivered Travis his coffee in the bedroom, where he was just swinging to an upright position, and started dressing when he went to use the shower and shave.

Dressed, I ate breakfast (cold cereal with a banana, toast, or a bagel with orange juice) and then dealt with my hair and makeup once the bathroom mirror cleared. At seven-fifteen, Travis left the house. At seven-thirty, I got into my car and began my daily commute—a solid half-hour of traffic from our apartment in Virginia Highlands to the Morrow School in Decatur.

At work, I kept a tidy desk and dealt with various chores: the latest mailing, alumnae calls, development meetings. All these required a ready smile and a certain chirpy confidence I produced by rote. At exactly five o'clock, I left the office and retraced my commute to the Highlands, which often took longer. I spoke to Travis on my cell phone and discussed dinner plans.

Often, I stopped at the Kroger and bought something, or restocked Travis's beer, or ran other errands for us. By seven at the latest, I was home, and usually either had dinner ready around eight or we went out around eight, which was when Travis generally made it home.

Some nights, Travis met friends out for drinks. If the other girls were there, I would also attend; if it was just the boys, I watched television without having to fight over the remote control or suffer through *SportsCenter*. We were usually in bed by eleven-thirty, where we would negotiate having sex. When we had it, it was at Travis's initiation.

On the weekends Travis liked to go out, and so we did, with his large group of friends. There were parties, certain bars, dinners, and the same people. There were more negotiations about sex. We usually did our big shopping on Saturday, and Travis played football with the boys on Sunday while I met the girls for brunch. Sunday evening we had dinner at Travis's parents' house, and Sunday night we watched HBO together, and prepared for the week ahead.

The weather was good and the people were cheerful. It was sweet and easy.

It was the perfect life.

I was so depressed I thought I might drown in it.


"Your lip gets any lower and it might hit the floor," Travis said.

He was using his joking voice, but I could hear the exasperation behind it. I looked up at him.

"I'm not pouting, Travis." I tried to speak without snapping, but wasn't very successful. "I'm not three years old."

It was his old roommate Jason's thirty-first birthday party.

The little house in Midtown was filled to bursting, people spilling out onto the back deck and the small backyard. I had taken up residence inside, on one of the sofas in the back study. I was watching something on television, some movie I couldn't identify and hadn't even turned on myself. A woman screamed into the wind. I had no idea what was bothering her, but still, I felt I could relate.

Travis plopped down next to me, making me roll across the soft cushions into him. Annoyed, I straightened immediately.

"What's going on with you?" he asked. "I don't think I've seen you crack a smile in I don't know how long. You going to share it with me or is this something I'm supposed to figure out on my own?"

"I don't know what you're talking about," I said woodenly.

"You do. Our apartment suddenly looks like a bomb hit it, and most days I think you might take a swing at me if I look at you funny."

"I don't know when you got the idea that all the cleaning was my responsibility." I no longer bothered to keep the snap from my voice. "That's not fair, is it?"

"I got the idea over the entire course of our relationship," Travis replied at once. "You never let me so much as fold a piece of laundry, even before we started living together."

"Well, things change."

"I can see that."

Travis reached over and turned the television off with the remote control, so I could either stare sulkily at the floor or look at him. I opted for looking at him like a grown-up—but it was a close call.

"Why are we having this conversation here?" I asked.

"If things have changed between us," Travis said very seriously, "then I think I need to have some say in it. I'm still one half of us, as far as I know."

I looked at him and wanted, somewhere inside, to be able to reach out and say whatever right words I had known once. I wanted to soothe him.

But I couldn't do it.

"I'm a little depressed lately, yes," I said after a long silence. "I don't know why you think it has to be some big thing. Or why we have to talk about this now."

"Meredith, you're hiding in the back of the house. Everyone thinks you're either pregnant or drunk." He cracked a grin. "And you better be drunk, is what I keep saying."

I sighed. "I'm not *hiding*. I've been at every single birthday party Jason Westbrook has thrown since I moved to Atlanta. I don't think he's really going to care if I don't feel like the life of the party this time around."

"Come on, Meredith . . ."

"I'm perfectly happy just sitting here," I told him. "You go on and enjoy yourself. I'm driving, anyway."

He made one last attempt to draw me into the spirit of the festivities, but I didn't budge, and he headed for the door—not without a heavy sigh I pretended not to hear.

I didn't know what was wrong with me.

My plan had been to dive back into the comfort of my real life in Atlanta and never once look back. I chalked up the confusion and chaos of the previous six weeks to hometown madness. Maybe it was only to be expected when you returned to the scene of your childhood. There were hundreds of miles between me and my hometown now, which I knew because I'd stared down at every single inch of land that separated me from my past, putting it all behind me as the plane flew south. But my "real life" wasn't going according to plan.

Instead of feeling motivated by my guilt to make things better with Travis, to make it perfect again the way it used to be, I thought that the guilt was eating me alive. Or poisoning me. It wasn't making me love him more, lucky as I was to have him. It was making me hate him.

Things got worse that Sunday, when I decided I would much rather sleep in than make another command appearance at brunch with the girls.

Travis refused to understand. The situation escalated quickly.

"These are our *friends*, Meredith! You can't just back out at the last minute!"

"Because why, exactly? They might have a seating plan for brunch? I just want to sleep, Travis. I'm tired." I pulled the covers up around my neck.

"Is that a dig because I wanted to stay out last night? Because you said it was fine with you, and that's about the only thing you said all night!"

"I'm just tired!" I moaned at the ceiling. "Can't I be tired? Does it have to be about you?"

"You're not going to stay in bed all day. If you don't want to go to brunch, there's about a million things you can do around here." He finished tying up his sneakers. "Are you listening to me?"

I flipped back the covers and looked at him. "Did you just tell me to get my lazy ass out of bed and clean this apartment?"

"I didn't say that."

"But that's what you meant?"

Travis stared at me. A muscle in his jaw bulged. Then his frustration took over.

"What is *wrong* with you? Why is everything so goddamned difficult these days? This is our *life*, Meredith! You never had a problem with it before!"

"Well, I have a problem with it now!" I yelled back. "Have you noticed that *our* life is actually *your* life? Why would you *want* to be with someone who doesn't exist outside of her role as your girlfriend?"

He made an inarticulate sound of frustration. A loud one.

"I don't even know what you're talking about!" Travis shouted. "Living with you is like *Invasion of the Body Snatchers*! We barely have sex anymore, you don't care about anything, and you're mad at me because you want *friends*?"

"I'm not going to fucking brunch!" I screamed at him.

Travis made as if to storm out of the apartment, but turned back before he made it to the door.

"You better get a handle on this," he told me from across the living room, his face red and angry. "I'm not kidding around, Meredith. I'm not going to live like this."

I didn't answer, and he kicked an old newspaper across the living room floor. I watched it hit the wall and flutter, and didn't flinch when Travis slammed the door on his way out.

The apartment was dizzy with the sudden silence.

I thought, *This has to stop.*


"You're hardly the first person in the history of the world to behave hideously to cause *him* to break up with *you*," Hope said matter-of-factly.

"I don't think that's what I'm doing," I said.

I had moved to the couch, and had wrapped myself in the comforter to huddle in the air-conditioning.

"Okay," Hope said. "Then what are you doing? Because I think you said that before now, you guys never fought about anything. Ever."

"It's not that we never fought." I considered. "It's that I never really fought. I mean, there might have been a sentence or two about whatever, and then I would smooth it over. But now, suddenly, I'm screaming at him?"

"Let me tell you something, Meredith." Hope sounded grim. "Anyone who got in my face about cleaning an apartment we both lived in would find himself kicked to the curb in about thirteen seconds."

"No." I sighed. "He's right."

"I hate to break this to you, but we're in a whole new millennium and have been for a few years now. Women have the vote, the Pill, and the right to share the housework. I know you live in the South, but come on." She sounded disgusted.

"He's right," I repeated, "because that was the way our relationship was from the start. I did all that stuff. If I want things to change, I can't just decide to change them alone and then get mad at him because he isn't psychically tuned to my every decision."

"I know we're different people," Hope said. She sighed. "But I don't understand why anyone would want to be in a relationship that was trying to re-create the fifties. If they were so great, we would never have had the sixties. Or, God help us, the seventies—"

"I have to tell him." It burst out of me. "I have to tell him and I have to be prepared to deal with the consequences. He's right—we can't live this way. It's awful."

Hope was quiet for a long stretch, and I heard her turn over in her bed.

"I think you should think about breaking up with him," she said finally. "But I'm not sure why you'd want to tell him you cheated on him, after the fact. It seems like maybe you kind of want to force him to break up with you by throwing that in his face." She yawned. "Maybe you want him to know that you're the bad guy."

"I am the bad guy," I replied with way too much self-pity. "The sooner I face that, the better."

There was a pause.

"Okay, *Mom*," Hope said with disgust. "Let me FedEx you a cross to hang from in your living room. Can you *hear* yourself?"


Travis didn't come home until late that night. He crawled into the bed and we lay there in silence. Although I hadn't moved or greeted him, I knew he could tell that I was awake.

"We have to talk," he said finally.

"Fine," I agreed, without turning over to face him.

"But not now." I heard him settle into his pillows. "Not tonight."

Travis was already home when I got in the next evening, which was my first clue that things were much worse than I'd thought. He sat on the couch in the late-afternoon shadows and hardly looked at me.

"I don't know how to say this," he said in a quiet voice. "I feel like a complete shit, like I'm abandoning you in your time of need, and maybe I am. Part of me thinks I should just weather this through, see what happens." He shook his head. "I'm sorry, but I can't do it. I don't know what that makes me."

I had seated myself across from him in the armchair, which felt unnatural and awkward, and I let his words sink in. They took a long time to settle. I concentrated instead on the armchair, which I'd always hated. It had been a gift from his mother. Maybe it had been a sign.

I blinked. It hit me.

"Are you breaking up with me?" I asked in sudden, complete surprise.

"I think we need a break," Travis said. Avoiding it.

"A break."

"Nothing permanent or dramatic," he continued hurriedly. "I love you, Meredith, but what are we doing? I feel like lately we've just been bringing out the worst in each other. Don't you?"

"A *break*."

"I don't want to be this angry with you. It scares me." Travis kept his eyes trained on his hands, which were fidgeting with a magazine on the coffee table. "I don't know who you are anymore."

"So—" I cleared my throat. I felt strangely removed from the conversation. I shook my head. "Wow."

"You've been a stranger since you came back," he said, looking at me directly for the first time. "But it's not just that. Before, when I visited you, it was like you didn't even want me there. I barely recognized you. I understand you were having a family crisis, but even before that, things were just . . . stale. We've been in a rut."

"A rut which, in April, you told me you thought would lead to an engagement by October," I pointed out, not without some bite.

"Fine," Travis agreed. "The summer was bad, Meredith. I

don't think we missed each other much. Not the way we should have. Are you going to say you did?"

"Is there someone else?" I asked far too politely, and then thought: *You unbelievable hypocrite.*

"No," Travis said at once. "I would never do that to you."

I looked at him, those bright blue eyes and the blond hair, and believed him. There was probably a prospect or two in the wings, but Travis was a decent guy. He wouldn't cheat.

There was a small silence. I noticed he didn't even think to ask me the same question. It made me want to cry.

"I'm going to go and stay at my parents' house," Travis said quietly. "But I'll still pay rent, of course, until you figure out what you're going to do."

"You're moving out?" I stared at him as if I'd never seen him before. Which, I thought dimly, was sort of true. "This conversation is just . . . a courtesy call? To inform me of your decision?"

Travis sighed, and stared at his hands. "I thought . . . When you came back, I thought things might work out. I really did. I wanted it to."

"I can't believe this," I whispered. "Was I on probation?"

I felt a kind of buzzing in my ears, and could almost feel words forming on my tongue . . . *Guess what?* I could say. *I cheated on you. Repeatedly. All summer.*

I wanted to hurt him, I realized with some amazement.

"When we almost broke up that time," Travis said in a very low voice. "You remember, that first summer. You cried for days. I thought you might break in two. But look at us now, Meredith." He looked up and caught my gaze, surprising me. "You're barely reacting."

"Is this a test?" I asked, my voice a little rough. I coughed. "If I cry, you stay?"

Travis ran his hands through his hair, and then looked at me, his face twisting with emotion.

"I don't want to drag this out—I don't—" He shook his head. "I don't want to hate you."

And to my horror, his eyes welled up. The sight of his tears took the air right out of my lungs, and the poison I'd been carrying around in my gut suddenly seemed to ease away.

"Don't cry," I said. Soothing him. Finally.

"I don't know what else to do," Travis told me.

I moved across the room to him, and we held each other, even though the holding couldn't help. He nestled his head into my neck and I felt a tremendous sadness wash through me.

I knew two things then: it was over—had *been* over for longer than I wanted to admit—and I would never tell him what I'd done.


For the first few days after the breakup, people called. I hadn't told anyone in the city of Atlanta about what had happened, and could therefore track Travis's movements through the condolence calls I received from the girlfriends and wives, and the odd male friend. I let the answering machine pick up most of them, and thought I could figure out Travis's future by the innuendo I detected in some of the messages. Travis was a catch, after all. By the weekend, though, the calls began to trickle away. The fact of the matter was, these were not my friends. I was Travis's girlfriend, and as such, exchangeable. Even though I'd expected it, part of me had imagined it would be different for me.

I was surprised at how much it hurt to discover otherwise.

That weekend, I hibernated. I cried more than I imagined I should—because I didn't deserve to be so upset over something I'd valued so little, did I? But that didn't stop the tears.

"Why stay there?" Hope asked with her usual briskness. "What's in Atlanta now?"

"So what? I'm just going to relocate every time I break up with someone?" I sniffed. "That seems kind of ridiculous."

"There are a lot of places to live in the world. Why choose the one where you might trip over your ex at the local supermarket?"

"I don't have any particular urge to go anywhere," I admitted. "I mean, I would move to Paris tomorrow except I don't speak French. And I wanted to live in Seattle when I saw *Singles*."

"Didn't everyone?" Hope sounded delighted. "You should absolutely move to Seattle. I'm sure it's still as cool. When did that movie come out?"

I went to work every day and, for the first time, really thought about my job. I had succeeded at it because I alone of the women I worked with hadn't had Life Stuff intervene. Yet.

After all, the job was just a job, a convenient half-career to augment the family's finances, or to mark time and keep a girl in lipstick and rent until Prince Charming proposed. Which wasn't to say development wasn't a career-oriented field, or that someone couldn't make a terrific career in it. Just not at the Morrow School.

Real development jobs with long-term possibilities were at universities, where the development offices were huge and the capital campaigns breathtaking in scope. The Morrow School was just playing house.

And the fact was, I didn't actually think the pampered little princesses who swanned about the place needed the money I helped raise. They didn't even appreciate it; they took it for granted, and their parents insisted upon the facilities only that sort of financial support could provide. It was hardly changing anybody's life. And when I was finally honest with myself, I knew I only did it because I was good at it. Not because I liked it.

I'd known all this before, of course. But suddenly I was looking at my life as it was, instead of the way I'd wanted it to be. My entire life in Atlanta was carefully built on my own belief that I could be the shiny, happy, *nice girl* I'd decided to be. The one I'd been trying to be my whole life. Except it turned out that I didn't like where that girl ended up. I didn't want to be a happy robot anymore. I wanted to be me.

Whoever the hell that was.

My mother picked up the phone, and I launched into a defensive explanation. After all, she'd predicted this, hadn't she? All her dire warnings about Travis as she kicked up her heels canalside in Venice. Not that I was thinking about that. It would make me bitter.

"It would make so much sense for me right now," I argued. "It will only be for a while. I just don't think Atlanta is the place for me and I want to take a break and figure out where the place for me is—"

"Just come home," Mom said, surprising me into silence.

"Um," I said eloquently. "Are you sure?"

"Of course I'm sure," she said. "That's what it's for."



Travis was stunned. I told him on the same day I gave notice—not even two weeks, I was sorry, I had to go. No one argued.

That weekend Hope drove down to Atlanta, informing me from her cell phone that she was on her way. When she arrived it was late Friday night and Christian was behind the wheel.

"I'm surprised you came," I told Christian. "I mean, it was hard enough for you to make it to the house while I was there."

He blinked, possibly at all the passive-aggression in my voice, and then shook his head at me.

"You're my *sister*, Meredith!" He sounded offended.

The three of us packed as much of my stuff as we could fit into two cars, which was a lot more than you might expect.

"We don't have any more room," I said at one point, defeated by my inability to force another carton of books into the backseat.

"I refuse to accept that," Hope retorted, a wild gleam in her eye. "There is always room. Step aside."

"You definitely need to get the hell out of here," Christian informed me during one of our breaks, sitting out on the stoop in the soupy southern air. "I still don't know why you moved down here in the first place."

"I don't know." Every item I took from the apartment and packed away in the car made me doubt myself. "Maybe I need to stay here. Maybe what I really need to do is make my own life, somewhere far away from . . ." I remembered who I was talking to. "Somewhere that's mine."

Christian gave me an intent look, then returned his attention to the street in front of us.

"That sounds like a hell of a lot of unnecessary work, running all over the place and living in *Deliverance* country just because our family can be a little overwhelming." His lips curved slightly. "I'm not saying I don't understand the urge."

"I'm moving back home. With Mom and Dad. I'm twenty-eight years old." I let the words lie there for a moment. And then winced. "There's no prettying that up into a rousing chorus."

Hope staggered through the door then, knees buckling under the weight of the carton she carried. She teetered over and steadied herself against the wall. Panting, she eyed us.

"When I'm the one who's not slacking, there's a problem," she bit out.

Christian let out a long-suffering sigh, but I could see he was biting back a grin as he hauled himself to his feet.

"I got it." He wrenched the carton away from her.

Hope winked at me and then headed back inside. I made to follow her, but stopped when Christian called my name.

"I'm the first one to be hard on you," he said when I turned to look at him. "But if it helps, I think you're doing the right thing."

When everything was packed and Christian and Hope were sitting in their car, fighting over the music and ready to caravan north, Travis and I stood in silence at the curb. He'd come over to help, which had mostly meant he'd stayed out of Christian and Hope's snarling way. They'd never liked him, they claimed loudly, and were prepared to prove it.

"I didn't think you'd leave Atlanta," Travis said, with some difficulty. "I guess I didn't think about what you would do."

We stared at each other. I imagined I could see his future, spilling out in front of us, my own figure growing smaller and smaller in his consciousness until I was forgotten entirely. It was better that way. I reached up and touched his cheek with the hand that would never wear his ring.

"I'm sorry," I said. "About—" I tried to smile. "About everything. I wish . . ."

"I do too," he whispered.

Neither of us said good-bye.

# Chapter 13

I moved back into my childhood bedroom, the room I'd been more than delighted to leave just a few weeks earlier, and quickly discovered that my return to the house as *resident* was actually *more* depressing than any of my previous returns as a *guest*. Go figure.

The first few days I was home, I woke up early and made lots of noises about rediscovering myself and my purpose in life.

"I feel like this is a new direction!" I enthused over coffee. I was betting my parents would find this sort of presentation impressive.

"Please pass the jam," my mother responded, without looking up from the op-ed section of the *New York Times*.

I spent the rest of my time skulking around the house with Hope, but this was short-lived. She took off for her long-anticipated trip to Costa Rica, and I promptly discovered that I didn't feel like doing much besides sleeping. So I slept whenever I could, which meant my life back at home turned out to greatly mimic the kind of nocturnal hours I associated with being a college student. Except this time, without a dorm full of people in the same boat.

When I was awake, I bundled myself in my comforter and took over Hope's room and its entertainment center. I watched every Molly Ringwald film I could find in the video store. I watched the daily *Buffy* reruns on cable. I watched so many hours of MTV that it was possible whole days slipped by with me staring slack-jawed at Eminem, Justin Timberlake, and the many pretenders to their thrones. I flicked through the channels, one after the other, and watched whatever caught my fancy, whether it was one of those seductive Time-Life music infomercials or Spanish soap operas with all their black mascara and gesturing.

I wore a daily uniform of sweats and a raggedy T-shirt that I'd stolen from Christian sometime in the eighties. I ate Brown Sugar Cinnamon Pop-Tarts directly from the box because I didn't have the energy to toast them, and I ate fistfuls of Cheez-Its because they were alarmingly addictive and no one could eat *just one*. Sometimes, in the afternoons, when I was having my breakfast of a pot of coffee, I would watch strange reality programming with my father in the family room, where he was usually resting his leg.

"I hate these shows," Dad said one day, during a commercial.

I focused on him, bleary-eyed.

"I love them." It was possible that I hadn't spoken aloud in some time. Maybe whole days. "The best part is that real people actually act this way."

"Real people act just as foolishly every day," Dad retorted. "You don't need a camera to figure that out."

I felt my eyes narrow at him. Was he referring to my life? Did he actually know anything about my life? Not that I was feeling at all defensive, and what did he know, anyway? His real world took place in an aquarium under artificial light, hidden out of sight beneath the house.

"I'm just going to close my eyes and see if I can get a nap in," my father said, almost as if he could read my mind.

"I'll let you know what happens," I muttered, settling deeper into the couch and shoving my hand into the box of Pop-Tarts. "Reality can be tricky."

Finally, after a week in which I did not leave the house even once and showered even less, my mother appeared in my bedroom at the outrageous, dawnlike hour of ten-thirty one morning and began tossing open curtains.

"What are you doing?" I croaked from beneath a pile of bedclothes.

"It's time to get up," she announced, in a voice I remembered all too well from childhood. Two parts steel, one part ice, and a big portion of ass-about-to-be-kicked. I hadn't heard that particular voice in a long, long time.

I struggled to a sitting position in the bed and scraped at my hair, which was embarrassingly greasy and lank.

"That's a tremendous start," Mom said crisply. "You have fifteen minutes to take a shower and put on any article of clothing other than that revolting ensemble you've been shuffling around in."

"What happens in fifteen minutes?" I asked, doing a good impression of surly.

"You and I have a conversation in the kitchen." My mother could wilt surliness with a single arched brow. "I suggest you shake a leg. You won't like it if I have to come back into this cave."

I made a huge production of rolling my eyes, and huffed and puffed my way into the shower, but I pulled on a pair of shorts and a clean shirt and managed to make it downstairs with five minutes to spare.

*Take that*, I thought triumphantly. Never let it be said I couldn't follow instructions well.

My mother looked up from the *New York Times* and smiled calmly, as if she had never doubted for a moment that I would follow her instructions to the letter.

In fact, I was quite certain she'd had no doubts at all.

"It's nice to see you," she said. "You've become something of a zombie."

I was more familiar with that tone. Light, amused, and deadly.

"Yeah," I muttered.

I poured a hot cup of coffee. I hadn't fallen asleep until dawn had begun streaking the sky with blue, and my head throbbed. The first, delicious sip went right where it hurt. I sighed in pleasure.

"Do you have a particular time frame in mind for your deterioration?" my mother continued. She might have been conducting an interview. "I only ask because we're actually having a wedding here shortly."

I swiveled my eyes from my cup to my mother.

"Very funny, Mom."

"And imagine my shock when I discovered the kitchen fairies came in the night and ate a week's worth of dessert. By the pint."

"I'm a little depressed, I think," I allowed after a moment, thinking about all of that ice cream and feeling significantly more depressed.

"This is what's going to happen," Mom said, very crisply. "You will get up before ten every day and you will leave this house. Preferably to get a job. If you feel that you're too depressed to get a job, you need to find yourself a decent therapist. But there will be no more wallowing. And if I were you, I would burn those clothes."

"But . . ." I wanted to argue, but I knew she was right. "But I don't know what to do," I admitted finally. "What if I never figure out what I want to do? What happens then?"

"You keep looking," she replied, with compassion. "But you're not going to do yourself any favors if you keep on going like this."

I fiddled with my cup.

"I'm surprised at you, Meredith," Mom continued. "I never expected this sort of thing from you."

Something stilled inside me. "What do you mean?" I asked.

"I thought you were the responsible one," Mom said, laughing slightly. "But if this is how you behaved when you went back down to Atlanta . . . Well."

" 'Well'?" I echoed. I felt more alert than I had in days. Anger began to pool in my abdomen. This, finally, was it. The *I told you so* portion of the program. I'd been waiting for this since I moved home.

"No man wants to live with a zombie," Mom told me. "It doesn't surprise me at all that Travis couldn't handle it."

I blinked at my cup, because there was a sort of dim ringing in my ears and my eyes seemed blurry. The anger in my gut liquefied into fury and shot through my veins. But I couldn't seem to form a single word.

I thought about how hard I'd tried to do what she seemed to do so effortlessly—make a perfect home, have a perfect life, all the while being so nice, so approachable. When I looked back on it now, it seemed as if my whole life had been about me trying to do what she did. Hope had said it was an act, but I'd never thought so. I'd figured it was the way you were *supposed* to be. And maybe that was why my whole relationship with Travis had been doomed from the start, because the truth was, I *wasn't* all that nice. Because if I was, I wouldn't have the intense urge to fling my coffee mug at my mother's head.

"I think," Mom continued in that infuriating, calm tone, "that you should start thinking about your future, Meredith."

"I think about it all the time!" I snapped at her. The anger was simmering in my blood like some kind of drug. I felt like someone else entirely, and my throat ached from all the things I didn't know how to say. Like—*If you hadn't gone on your trip, I wouldn't have had to stay here, and if I hadn't stayed here, I wouldn't have become this stranger to myself, and I would still be able to be happy in Atlanta with Travis.*

My head swam with the effort of not saying any of that. I ignored her look of surprise, lurched to my feet, and staggered from the room before I lost control completely and started shouting.

I called Rachel that afternoon.

"I'm really embarrassed," I said when she picked up the phone. "I was so insane and I meant to keep in touch because I really liked hanging out with you and now I'm back in town—"

"I love this groveling!" Rachel laughed. "But the phone works both ways and I think you were the last one to e-mail. Come on over. I can't bring myself to study anymore anyway."

We ended up in a local hamburger joint that did double duty as a watering hole, and a hole it was.

"It looks like a dive, I know," Rachel said as we walked toward the bar's front door. "But it's crawling with cops and lawyers."

"So it's still a dive, it's just a *really safe* dive?"

"Exactly." Rachel laughed. "And I insist on coming here once a month to get myself a cheeseburger fix."

Inside, we slid into a booth along the wall. Rachel raised an eyebrow at me as I looked around, feeling furtive.

"I was just thinking that I've never actually had a single run-in with a cop in my whole life," I admitted. "This is the closest I've been."

"These are cops from affluent suburbs," Rachel said, with a negligent wave of her hand. "It's a whole different thing." She tilted her head to one side and smiled slightly. "You remember Kevin Bigelow, right?"

And there it was, on the table between us.

I had the sudden, giddy urge to lie and pretend—that I didn't know who he was, or that I only vaguely remembered him but he had no significance. After all, I was getting good at lies to save my own ass, wasn't I? I could turn over a whole new leaf and *just be* the sort of person who lied. To everyone. About everything.

But: "Of course I remember him," I said.

This time my voice didn't betray me, as it had with Travis. "I owe you an apology from about ten years back," I told her.

"You don't," she said. "Not really. Anyway, you already apologized the night I ran into you in the bar. Enough apologizing."

"I can blame Jeannie for a lot of that situation, and I do," I said, "but at the end of the day I should have told you myself."

"You should have," she agreed. "But it was just stupid girl stuff, Meredith. Didn't you see *Mean Girls*?"

Stupid was the word.

It was difficult, looking back, to explain the undercurrents and dramas that played out in our group of friends that summer. We'd all had our freshman years at different colleges, and yet had banded back together with the unspoken assumption that nothing had changed. In some ways that was true. In other ways, we were total strangers.

Jeannie still ruled, and Ashley was still her most devoted minion, even though I was nominally her best friend. Things were silly and histrionic that summer. Rachel was still the target of choice when we got bored, and the easiest thing to concentrate on was Rachel's age-old crush on Kevin Bigelow.

"Do you remember what he looked like in high school?" Rachel asked now, snickering.

I had a brief flash of memory, all swagger and a cocky grin. And something far more horrifying:

"Didn't he have a mullet?"

"He sure did," Rachel said mournfully. "And how self-destructive was my crush on him? He only dated anorexic girls with Daddy issues."

"Sandy Marconi and Tara Silverberg," I supplied automatically. "So very tiny, and so very lost."

"Exactly," Rachel agreed.

We ordered food from the waitress and then leaned back into the booth and lingered over our beers.

"At the junior prom," Rachel said, playing with her beer bottle, "Kevin Bigelow finally appeared before me and asked me to dance. Thinking I had died and gone to heaven, or woken up to find myself in a teen romance novel, I agreed."

"Why don't I know this story?" I demanded. "Where was I?"

"Jeannie knows this story," Rachel said. Meaningfully.

I winced. "This can't possibly have a happy ending, then."

"After the dance, which I remember was to 'The One I Love' by R.E.M., just to twist the knife in, he whooped it up and ran back over to his boys to claim his bet money."

We both paused to consider that.

I blew out a breath. "What a shit."

"Please." Rachel shook her head. "That was par for the course."

The worst part was, she was right.

Jeannie and Ashley spent hours setting Rachel up for humiliating interactions with Kevin. They told her he wanted to meet her places and then would drive there themselves, to laugh at her as she waited, so hopeful, for a boy who would never show. Meanwhile, I would be in the backseat, telling them they were horrible but not doing anything to stop it.

And why not? First of all, because I didn't go up against Jeannie. I never had. But that summer, that was just an excuse.

The truth was, I liked Kevin Bigelow myself. I went out with him on a few dates, in fact, all secret, because Rachel's crush was well-known. Obviously, I couldn't tell her. I didn't value Rachel enough to be honest with her about my feelings back then, but I didn't want her to hate me.

It only made sense if you were a teenage girl.

"It's actually worse than you know," Rachel told me now. "I lost all that weight in college, I spent some quality time in therapy, and *then*, when I found myself living at home, what do you suppose I did when I discovered that Kevin Bigelow is one of our town's finest?"

"Justifiable homicide?"

My memories of Kevin, happily, involved only very minor fooling around. But he was inextricably linked with all the fall-out that came after that summer.

"Much worse," Rachel said, almost gloomily. "I dated him." She waited for me to absorb that, and nodded. "I *slept* with a guy who once *won a bet* by dancing with me." She frowned at her beer. "How did I get on this subject?"

"I think that's another girl thing," I ventured. "You have to do really horrible things sexually just to, I don't know, hate yourself enough to force yourself to change."

A chill snaked through me then, and I thought about Scott suddenly. Wasn't that what I had done? Used him to feel just badly enough about myself that I couldn't possibly work things out with Travis? Because just feeling vaguely dissatisfied wasn't reason to end things with someone, but cheating on them was. Cheating, in fact, was pretty much the breakup trump card. I shook my head to clear it of that unpleasant realization. Had I really done that?

"It was a really rough time," Rachel was saying. "I had just completely failed my first-year law school exams because I didn't really want to be a lawyer but I had somehow ended up in law school and I didn't know how to get out of it. Except fail. Spectacularly."

"Ouch," I murmured. I would save the speculation about Scott for another time. Maybe when I was feeling less fragile.

"Seriously," she said. "Kevin Bigelow seemed like a girl power move in the middle of all that."

"I can't even remember why it was so important I keep it a secret," I told her. "Jeannie and I had a huge fight, and we were never really close after that night she told you about Kevin and me. I guess that summer was just the last straw."

"Everyone did crazy shit in high school just to survive." Her voice was quiet. "I don't blame you for that. You were always nice to me."

"I wanted everyone to think I was the nice one," I agreed.

The word "nice" stuck in my throat a little bit. "It turns out I wasn't nice at all. I'm not very nice now, either."

"Bad news, Meredith," Rachel said with a grin. "You might have to be human and flawed like the rest of us."

We sat there for a moment, with Joe Cocker on the jukebox, rasping and wailing like some kind of classic rock absolution, and then we toasted each other and moved on.

# Chapter 14

Temp jobs came in two distinct types: boring or humiliating.

Applying to temporary agencies was just the latter.

I learned that I had wasted my time and my parents' money on a college education, when a secretarial degree would have garnered me an immediate position with a starting salary larger than any I'd seen in my employment history. I learned that no one was interested in my academic record anyway, because I had attended a liberal arts college, and as such, my studies were *too vague*. At the same time, no one would be likely to care about my *actual* work experience, because it was *too specific*.

The only thing I was good for—and there was unanimous agreement on this point between Pat, Debbie, and Sheila at the Temp-o-Rama—was scrub work. Filing. Answering phones, in the sense of literally picking up a phone and taking a message, because real "switchboarding" required years of training. And, last but never least, the ever popular data entry.

And yet temping was the least of my humiliations.

It wasn't that my parents went out of their way to make life difficult, it was more that *difficult* was the way they liked things.

Talk about being set in their ways—they could set records. I was reprimanded for using the laundry room when my mother wanted to and not cleaning up after myself in the kitchen fast enough. Every morning there was a silent pitched battle over the first section of the *New York Times*. My father demanded absolute silence over breakfast and my mother preferred nonstop chatter about the day ahead. If I avoided controversy and hid in my childhood bedroom with my boxes, I was chastised for treating the place "like a hotel." If I joined in family dinners, I felt like I was a particularly unhappy seventeen all over again.

This is why, I reminded myself daily, adult children were not meant to live at home.

It was a Thursday night, and Rachel and I were considering another round of drinks. We had fallen into a pattern, which was: we went out as much as possible to pretend that we weren't actually living in our parents' houses. It was only moderately successful.

I was just about to launch into another tale of parental oppression and humiliation—a daily occurrence, not unlike high school—when Rachel's attention was caught by a group just coming in from outdoors. She waved.

"My friend Jessica and some of her coworkers," she told me, her eyes sparkling. "Jessica was my roommate in law school. They're all really cool, actually, for a bunch of lawyers."

Since my back was to the door, I decided not to expend the energy it would require to turn around and watch the approaching group.

"This is the most relaxed I've been in days," I confessed. "For some reason, being forced to explain why I can't type ninety words per minute is starting to get on my nerves a little bit. Especially when the person asking is an evil temp manager who really just wants me to—"

"Meredith," Scott said.

My head snapped up.

His eyes locked with mine and it was exactly the same as it had always been. That catch in my breath, that clutch in my gut.

His hair was slightly longer, and he still looked edible in a suit. His eyes were still that gray and bright with his private amusement.

"You guys remember each other, right?" Rachel asked in a tone I recognized as intrigued.

"We grew up together," I mumbled, and could feel myself flushing. "Of course we remember each other."

I couldn't seem to drag my gaze away from Scott's.

He had no such difficulty. He smiled at Rachel.

"We grew up on the same street," he corrected, with that lazy undercurrent of laughter. "Not exactly the same thing."

Rachel looked at me. I just rolled my eyes.

Scott swung into the booth next to me, and proceeded to ignore me as introductions were made around the table. The names went in one ear and out the other, and I wondered if everyone could see the turmoil going on beneath my skin. I felt as if it must be tattooed across my forehead, for all I was trying to be casual.

I had convinced myself that when I saw him again, all of that heat and yearning would be gone. Scott was just a symptom of the breakdown with Travis, I'd decided. I'd *needed* Scott so that Travis was no longer an option for me. Scott *himself* had nothing to do with anything. It had all become perfectly clear to me after the Kevin Bigelow conversation with Rachel.

I'd imagined that when I saw him again, I would feel embarrassed and then move on with my life. Isn't that what people did? Granted, Scott represented one-third of the people I had slept with in my twenty-eight years, but that was neither here nor there. Until Scott, I hadn't even known that sex could be a compulsion.

One that was still with me. What the hell was wrong with me? It didn't help that Scott was so close beside me, completely focused on the group, completely unaware that I could feel the warmth of his body and smell the soap he used. Irish Spring, I happened to know. Only the fact that I had to drive home kept me from diving headfirst into a pitcher of martinis.

"Stop fidgeting," Scott said, turning to look at me.

"I can fidget if I feel like it." Because I was so very mature.

"You can," Scott agreed. His eyes laughed at me. "What are you doing here?"

"Here in New Jersey or here with Rachel or here in this bar?" I asked.

"Pick one."

"I live here."

"In what sense?" Scott asked, with an exaggerated sigh.

"In the sense that this is where I live." I sniffed. "This may come as a big shock to you, but sometimes people change their geographic location without your express permission."

"I never thought you were incapable of change, Meredith. Just flailing around in an identity crisis."

I opened my mouth to fire something back at him but then considered. I grinned a little ruefully.

"That's not a bad way to put it." I grabbed my beer bottle. "I think I've evolved to treading water now. No more flailing."

"Is the object to swim or to get out of the water?"

"To decide what I want to do," I said quietly. "And then do it." Like most things in life (i.e., "grow up"), this sounded very simple but was, in practice, enormously complicated. But I wasn't prepared to get into that with him.

"Not a bad plan," Scott said. He sat back, and then angled his body slightly, adroitly cutting me off from the rest of the table and Rachel's obvious eavesdropping.

"That was a nice move."

"You like that? I'm actually pretty slick."

"If you really believe that, you need to get out of New Jersey."

"Why are you back in New Jersey?" he asked. "Your dad? Is he okay?"

I looked at my hands rather than at him.

"Things fell apart in Atlanta. I didn't see any reason to stay there."

"Are you really going to make me ask?"

"Yes, we broke up." I searched his face for some reaction. "Satisfied?"

"Interested," Scott amended. A beat. "Why did you break up with him?"

"I didn't."

He watched me as the color rose in my cheeks.

"What?" I could hear the belligerence in my voice. "Do you want a play-by-play?"

"I really don't."

We sat in silence. The music and the conversation swelled around us. Our last interaction hung there, rainy and awful, between us. But there was that damned attraction as well, which just seemed to grow the longer we sat there. Whatever he might have been while Travis was in the picture, he felt like something else entirely now. I felt a lot of things, but *embarrassed* wasn't one of them.

"*So*," Rachel broke in pointedly. "What are you two whispering about in the corner?"


"I can't believe you're not going to tell me the whole story!" Rachel cried much later. She was outraged. "You two were sporting underlying sexual tension! You were *whispering*!"

"It is almost three in the morning," I pointed out. "Can we get some coffee if I'm going to be attacked?"

"Do you know how much of a legend Scott Sheridan is?" Rachel continued as if I hadn't spoken. I gave up and concentrated on the road. "He is by far the hottest attorney in the prosecutor's office. I know certain people who have claimed to risk arrest just to have a whole trial to gaze at him. My friend Jessica has had a crush on him for the past three years!"

"She should date him," I said through gritted teeth.

"She's married," Rachel said dismissively. "It's a nonproductive work crush. The point is, you're holding out on me! After our post–Kevin Bigelow bonding! I'm wounded to the core!"

"No, you are not." I looked at her as we came to a stoplight. "You just want the gossip."

"Well." Rachel grinned. "True."

I returned my attention to the road as the light turned green. "The hottest attorney in the prosecutor's office, huh?"

"Yup." Rachel yawned, then made a face. "I mean, okay, that's actually not a hard category to win, but even so. Talk about overcoming a rough beginning—do you remember how nasty everyone was to the poor guy?"

"He cried in the third grade."

"Clearly you do. Except you and he definitely seem to have a history beyond any third-grade weeping—"

"He's really considered that eligible?" I was desperate to interrupt. "I think you're making that up."

Rachel laughed. "You must be kidding," she said. "Spill the dirt, sweetheart."

We had a stare-off, which I lost, but only because I was operating a motor vehicle.

I made a sigh into a minor opera. Then:

"Yes," I said. "We were . . . seeing each other. This summer."

"This summer? But you—oh."

"Yes," I said. "Exactly."

"I can see how Scott could be pretty high on the irresistible scale," Rachel said with a loyalty that fired up the shame in my gut. I wondered if it would always be there. "I'm just . . . You just seem so . . ." She shrugged and smiled. "Miss Prim and Proper. I'm surprised that you're not."

"I used to be," I said, with some regret. "Although now I think maybe that was just wishful thinking."

"I always suspected that those prim and proper girls were repressing actual personalities," Rachel assured me. "You're just confirming that."

"By being a terrible person? A liar and a cheater?" I shrugged. "But of course you already knew that."

"I don't see any point in beating yourself up over things you can't change," Rachel said matter-of-factly. I pulled up in front of her house. "Actions might speak louder than words, but only what you learn matters." She crooked a brow at me. "So sayeth the rum and Coke."


Hope returned from Costa Rica deeply tanned and unprepared to discuss the trip with our parents.

"I promise," she told Mom over dinner, "I'll show you the pictures."

"You said that about your trip to Canada and have I seen a single photograph?"

Mom's tone was a classic: the *oh, how you wound me* tone.

"That was like five years ago, and I told you, the film was ruined," Hope gritted out.

She caught my eye across the table and shrugged, then mimicked smoking. Presumably not tobacco.

"I'd love to go to Costa Rica," Dad chimed in. As ever, deaf to tones and mimed communication. "Not to collect any fish, per se, but some of the saltwater varieties are supposed to be quite amazing. I'd love to see some of those babies up close!"

"It's great to be home," Hope murmured and closed her eyes briefly, as if to summon her strength.

Later, we sat in the cheesiest of the town bars. It was filled with piano music and desperate-looking blind date types, and we thereby avoided Hope's minions, who would never allow themselves to be seen in the place.

"What happened to you down there?" I asked, when I'd depressed us both with my tales of temping and other humiliations. "You seem different. Is it Costa Rican fever?"

"I feel different." Hope frowned into her drink. "You know, I've had a great summer, more or less. We hung out, which was cool, and even hanging around here was fun. It was all good."

"I'm glad someone had fun."

Hope eyed me. "I bet you that one day you're going to reflect on this summer and think that it was actually the best thing that ever happened to you," she said. "You already know it. If you didn't, you would have stayed down south and worked things out with your frat boy."

"We were talking about you."

"Right." She shrugged, and cupped her hands loosely around her beer. "So we decided to hike up this mountain, which looked like no big deal, even though it was near an active volcano."

"How was that no big deal? How could that *possibly* be no big deal?"

"Because an active volcano down there is like a pine tree here, I don't know," Hope said, waving a dismissive hand. "There was this whole monkey incident when we were starting out which I can't talk about because I'm still freaked out, but then everything was great. Nice hike, pretty on top, except it was about to rain. And we figured, no big deal, it would obviously take a long time for the water to penetrate through the leaves and get to us, and we probably had plenty of time to hike back down before it mattered that it was raining." She smiled. "Sounds reasonable, right?"

"I don't know anything about Costa Rican rain forests." I was apologetic. Hope let out a bark of laughter.

"Yeah, well, neither do I. And neither does Katie, I assure you. It took all of fifty seconds for us to be involved in some kind of flash flood roaring down the side of the mountain, which looked like it was only going to get worse, and possibly carry us away with it, which would mean broken bones and a slow, painful death from exposure. If we were lucky. If we weren't lucky—wild animals."

"What did you do?" I asked, fascinated. I would probably sit down and cry, all things considered. Hope was far more intrepid.

"We ran," Hope said, with a certain grimness. "Down the side of a mountain. For about two hours. I was pretty sure we were going to die up there."

"Thank God you didn't," I said, unable to even think of it.

"And that's the point," Hope said firmly. "I thought I was going to die on this mountain in the middle of nowhere, and nobody had any idea I was even there. No one would even think to miss me for a week or so, since no one knew anything about our itinerary. Some guy in the office at the foot of it had our passport numbers, but how long before they would even think to look?"

"This is what you thought about?" I asked. "You couldn't concentrate on anything more positive at such a time?"

"That's when it clicked," Hope said, ignoring me. "If I die in some foreign jungle, I want it to make the nightly news—that night—in several countries. I don't want to just vanish. This was all very, very clear in the jungle, and it forced me to come to a decision." She smiled grandly. "I'm going to Hollywood."

I stared at her for a minute and let that statement hang between us.

"But not now," she amended, in slightly less ringing tones. "After New Year's, when pilot season starts."

"Wow," I said. "But, Hope. I mean, you're gorgeous, you know it, and you have this *thing* about you which is probably that X factor thing they're always talking about, but can you actually . . ." I paused, delicately. "Act?"

Hope smiled. "As a matter of fact," she said. "I can. I did a lot of theater at school." She laughed at my expression. "I don't just mean in a social sense. I was pretty good. I just didn't tell you guys about it, because I didn't want Mom giving me that speech about dreams versus reality again."

I shuddered. "I got that speech when I announced that I wanted to wander around Europe looking at art and maybe someday become an art historian. Brutal."

"I'll tell them after Christmas," Hope said, leaning back in her seat. "That will give them exactly no time to react, and then they can just harass me by telephone." She crooked a brow. "Which is always better, because I won't have to be involved. The beauty of voice mail."

# Chapter 15

That Saturday, I decided to take myself shopping.

I managed to slip out of the house without having to explain to my mother how my underemployed self could afford to shop, or having to discuss with my father the exciting reproductive developments of live-bearing guppies.

I snuck down the stairs and took off in my car like I was escaping from Attica.

I was only about fifty feet down the street, however, when I recognized the figure running in the street, and, after a moment's hesitation, pulled up next to him.

"Morning," I said out the window.

Scott rocked to a stop and looked at me, wiping at his face with one arm. I didn't think it was at all fair that, sweaty and exerting himself, Scott just looked even sexier than usual. I had once viewed my own appearance after running, had found the red face only slightly more upsetting than the frizzy hair, and knew there was absolutely nothing sexy about it.

"How can you already be scowling at me?" Scott demanded. "I haven't even said anything!"

"Why are you running in this neighborhood? Why don't you go running near where you actually live?"

"I like the route I have over here better, and why do you care?" A beat and then, more calmly: "Where are you going?"

"Christmas shopping." I arched my eyebrows at him.

Scott's hands came to rest on his hips and he squinted down at me.

"You know it's months away, right? Or has this been a really long run?"

"It's only going to get more crowded and horrible as time passes," I warned him.

"Why do women shop all year round for one day in December? It's impossible to catch up. My mother has extra gifts going back fifteen years. How can I compete with that?"

He hadn't shaved, and the stubble along his lean jaw was a revelation. I jerked my eyes slightly more north. Scott's smile was knowing.

"Want to come?" I asked, without meaning to or even knowing I was going to say anything.

I must have looked as surprised as I felt.

"Where did that come from?" he mocked me. "You want to reconsider?"

"A simple yes or no is all you need to say," I said primly.

"I'll come," Scott said, after a long, assessing look I could feel in my toes.

But first he demanded that I take him back to his house to change, which meant I got to spend an uncomfortable twenty minutes staring around his living room and remembering the last time I'd been there.

He jogged down the stairs, in old jeans and a T-shirt, and we stared at each other for a moment. I wondered what he could see in my eyes, because his own narrowed slightly. He said nothing, and angled his head toward the door.


Scott lounged in the passenger seat and propped his arm across the headrest behind my head. He looked particularly at ease, and I was aware of every single breath he took.

"So how's the big wedding coming along?" he asked. "Are Jeannie and Christian getting ready to pledge their love?" His voice was just shy of full-on mockery, so I ignored it.

"It's all fine," I said. "I mean, given what you think 'fine' means when you're talking about the most anal person alive— that would be my mother—and the scariest woman alive—that would be Jeannie's mom."

"You're not kidding. I remember that woman. I think she ate kids for fun."

"She still does," I said. "And then there's the bride, who pretends to be laid-back but is secretly high-maintenance."

"Jeannie Gillespie in a nutshell," Scott said, and laughed. "My mother predicted she would marry your brother, you know. Years ago, when we were still kids."

"Really?" How had I been so oblivious to that eventuality?

"Sometimes she can just read people," Scott said with evident pride.

"It's good that you and your mother are so close," I said. Meanwhile, mine seemed to be from a different planet. But maybe all daughters felt that way. "She must really depend on you."

"You know my dad died when I was ten," Scott said.

I nodded, not sure what else to do. Were you supposed to

offer your condolences some eighteen years after the fact? The moment to do so passed, and he continued.

"So five or six years later, I was this angry teenage boy with no life and my mother started seeing other men. And I seriously flipped out. There was this one guy in particular . . ." He shook his head. "She ended up getting rid of him to keep me happy. Meanwhile, I grew up and realized that she was just as entitled to a chance at happiness as anyone else, and who was I to ruin that for her?" He shifted in his seat and his smirk was directed at himself for once. "So, yeah. She depends on me. It's the least I can do."

"You can't blame yourself for her not finding someone else," I said before I thought better of it.

I could feel his eyes on the side of my face, and concentrated on the road in front of me with more ferocity than was strictly necessary.

"I can't?" he asked, surprised. And maybe something else.

"Your mother's happiness is her own responsibility," I told him, a little fiercely. "If she wanted to date that guy, she would have dated that guy. Maybe she's happier on her own." I remembered suddenly that I was talking about his mother and coughed slightly. "I mean, what do I know, I'm just—"

"It's okay," he said. I snuck a look and saw a smile playing around his mouth. "I'm not that fragile."

But I wondered.


"So explain to me why Southern Comfort let you go," Scott said, out of nowhere. We were strolling along one of the corridors in the mall, listening to the Muzak. "That seems like a boneheaded move."

I was so startled by the question that I was nearly mowed down by a pack of teenagers. Scott pulled me out of their path and smiled down at me.

"This was such a strange summer," I said after a long moment. "I'm almost convinced that my personal life is your business."

"I could pretend that I don't want to know," Scott said agreeably. "But I thought I'd just go for it and see what happened. It's a lawyer thing."

I smiled despite myself, and looked up at him. "It's not what you think," I warned him. "It has nothing to do with you."

"That's good, right?" He shrugged. "For you, anyway."

"The thing is," I said, looking at the ground and not answering him, "I think I just got caught up in being the kind of person who would be in that particular relationship. I think—" I broke off. "It's really hard to talk to you about this," I told him, looking him straight in the eye. "I don't know what you want from me."

"Maybe I don't want anything from you," he replied in an even tone. "Do we have to go there?"

"Look!" I said too brightly as we approached a store with both men's and women's clothes. "Let's go in."

"Nice dodge," he said, but he was smiling.

Scott tried on a ridiculous oversized shirt in an obnoxious shade of orange that he claimed to love, and I experimented with straw hats.

"You can't buy that shirt," I told him.

I flung the hat back in the bin.

"I have to have this shirt. It wants me to have it."

"It wants to hurt you."

"You're crazy!" He held it up against his chest and waved it at me. "See? How can you resist?"

"It's evil. Scott, it's *orange*."

"You have no soul," he told me with a sigh, but he didn't buy the shirt.

We had lunch in one of the restaurants attached to the mall.

"So what's it like spending so much time with your family?" He smiled at me. "Do you feel like you're reliving your youth?"

"Just paying for it," I assured him.

"Your little sister seems pretty cool," Scott said.

"She is," I agreed. "It's been great to get to know her. It's my parents who've become total strangers. Maybe they always were, I don't know."

"Parents are tough," Scott said, watching me.

I told him about my father and his fish, and about my mother's curious decision not to cut short her European vacation. Of course, the moment I'd finished speaking, I was filled with a searing sense of shame for exposing her like that.

"Your mom's always been pretty intense," Scott said. "I think the hardest part about watching parents get older is that they become more and more like caricatures of themselves. All the dramatic parts, and none of the stuff that made the drama okay."

"She's actually an amazing woman," I hastened to tell him. "She raised three kids and took over all these volunteer organizations when what she really wanted to do was go to graduate school. She's the most well-informed person I know. She reads the paper cover to cover every single day, and reads about five books a week. She could have been just as powerful and successful as my father if she'd wanted to, maybe even more so. She's amazing," I said again, my defense winding down.

Scott was looking at me in a way that made me want to curl into a ball, preferably where he could hold me.

"I don't think I understand her or her life," I confessed. "And the longer I live at home, the surlier I get. I keep expecting to mutate into a troll, so everyone can see what kind of person I am. Any day now."

There was a beat. I wondered where *that* had come from.

Scott studied me for a moment. "You're not going to mutate into a troll," he assured me. "Anyway, there would be warning signs, probably. Like falling into a vat of radioactive sludge. Let me know if that happens."

"You should be more concerned than anyone," I said. "You had a front-row seat to my bad behavior. And when the troll takes me over? You're going down."

His eyes warmed. "You're not turning into a troll."

"I appreciate that, but you know, you're the person I *cheated with*, so you're hardly in a position to judge." Because there was no need to pretend we had any kind of pretty history here.

"Meredith." He shook his head at me. "You want to feel bad, and maybe you should. I've been cheated on and it sucks."

"Thank you." For some reason, when he joined in and beat up on me too, it hurt more.

"But you weren't happy," he continued. "And now you're out of the relationship. It's not like you're off living a lie somewhere, pretending everything's okay while you're beating yourself up inside. *That's* insane, and you know what happens?"

"More cheating and lying?"

"Sometimes," he said. "Or you take it out on the person you're with. None of these are good scenarios. It maybe took you a while, but you ended up doing the right thing."

I stared at his hands. They were almost elegant, and he

drummed his fingers against the tabletop to a rhythm only he could hear. I liked that.

"I don't know why you like me," I said. "I'm not particularly nice to you either. I'm beginning to think the only person who *really* thought I was nice was me."

"I liked you because you always seemed so happy." He smiled at me. "There I was having this shitty adolescence, my family was in pieces, and there you were, always so happy. I figured if I could get close to that, to you, it would rub off on me."

I put my glass back down carefully. I said his name, softly, and then I didn't know what else to say.

"I figured out later that probably you were no happier than anyone else," he said. His eyes were warm on mine. I felt caught there. "I wanted to find that comforting but really I just resented it. How come you could fake it so well? Why couldn't I?"

"The real me must be such a crushing disappointment," I said, only half kidding. "All messy and just as unhappy as everyone else."

He smiled again, a real smile that I could feel myself answering even before he spoke.

"Not at all. Now when you smile, I know you mean it."

We looked at each other for a long moment then, and something glad and quiet swelled in me. I wanted to reach out and touch him more than I could remember wanting anything else. But then the waiter arrived with our food, and in all the chaos of plates hitting Formica, the moment disappeared.

The fact was, I admitted when I got home, I wanted to minimize time spent in the house. Not just because I was compelled by forces beyond my control to act like I was seventeen again.

Of course, that was part of it. But mostly, I wanted to avoid the wedding.

It had been my mother's idea to have the reception in our house and backyard. I distinctly recalled rolling my eyes at this news, and thinking I was lucky to live in Atlanta, where the trauma of the preparation would affect me not at all.

Karma was a bitch.

There were a scant two weeks before the Big Day, and the house was in a state of chaos. Melissa the wedding planner, who bore no resemblance whatsoever to Jennifer Lopez and wasn't at all amusing or helpful, seemed to specialize in dropping in on the house and winding everyone up. I thought that given the opportunity, I could do a far better job. Every time she whipped out her little book and started talking about schedules, I could think of at least ten different and more efficient ways to do the same things.

I even suggested a few of them.

"Who knew you were so interested?" Jeannie sounded more amused than anything else.

"Seriously, all you have to do is move that aisle, and you don't have to worry about the table," I said. I noticed the way she was looking at me, and sat back. "I just like things to be planned well."

Jeannie laughed. "And if it benefits me, who am I to complain?"

My father had disappeared almost entirely into his basement, emerging only to eat meals and make complicated statements concerning his fish tanks.

"Dad," Hope said, cutting off a particularly involved and incomprehensible rant. "Unless you've created the Swamp Thing, can we not talk about this while people are eating?"

"Oh," Dad said, seeming befuddled. Possibly he didn't even realize he'd been speaking aloud.

My mother, meanwhile, was engaged in the kind of grim housecleaning usually reserved for people moving out of rentals who are determined to get back every penny of their security deposits. Corners of the house that had never seen daylight were exposed and scoured. Mom directed Hope and me in many an unpleasant task, seeming to take a certain amount of pleasure in the sight of the two of us in bright yellow rubber gloves.

"I think she wants us to suffer," I told Rachel on the phone. "I think it makes her happy. On a cellular level."

"Weddings are a day of joy and sharing for everyone," she replied. Piously. "Maybe this is how your mother expresses her joy."

She was probably right, I thought later, having spent some more quality time cleaning out the kitchen cabinets. Which, obviously, required the removal of every item and individual dusting and wiping, as well as full-fledged scrubbing of the shelves themselves, as we could expect all the guests to pry around in the pasta section.

The wedding couldn't come fast enough.

# Chapter 16

$T$he happy couple and my mother had been colluding over the final seating chart for days, and called a new summit meeting disguised as a family dinner. Meatloaf and motivational speeches from the bride. What could be better?

"She's really marrying him," Hope said with a sigh from behind her hand. The two of us were off down the table, since it was predetermined where we'd be sitting at the reception. The perks of being family *and* bridesmaids. "She used to threaten to do it when we were kids, but I never thought she was serious. I thought she was just blustering about the pink dresses too."

"Can't you guys even *pretend* to be interested in where Aunt Lolly is going to sit?" Christian asked, with a smirk that announced his own lack of interest.

"Honey?" Jeannie bared her teeth at him. "She's your aunt."

"Great-aunt," Christian retorted, and returned his attention to the seating chart.

"Your father adores her," Mom intoned. Obviously, Mom was somewhat less enamored of Aunt Lolly. "I think we can give her a little bit of the respect she deserves."

Dad, meanwhile, only smiled and (wisely) remained silent.

Aunt Lolly would have to twist in the wind—she was getting no help from him.

Christian stared at our mother. "We're giving her a catered steak entrée with béarnaise sauce. If Dad wants to give her anything else, he can pony up the cash to pay for it."

Hope grinned her approval.

"I love it when he gets all butch," she whispered to me.

The backyard was soon to be turned into a tented wonderland of tables and flower arrangements. Meanwhile, gifts arrived daily and it had somehow become my job to jot them all down in the book Jeannie had provided for exactly that purpose. Relatives I knew existed only because they shared our name called night and day to make last-minute travel arrangements and dietary requests. My mother was in her *Eyes on the Prize* mode—I wasn't certain she'd even thought beyond the wedding since her return from Europe.

"Your great-uncle Irwin refuses to eat anything that was ever mobile," my mother informed my father wearily now, ignoring the many rolled eyeballs around the kitchen.

"The man is eighty-nine years old!" My father actually frowned. "He can only eat food if it's pureed."

"He's your relative."

"They'll all eat what they're served," my father grumbled.

"That always worked so well with us," Hope murmured in an undertone. "Do you remember when my scrambled eggs came back at every meal because I refused to eat them?"

"Ew. Yes."

"If I actually *had* eaten them," Hope whispered, "I would obviously have dropped dead, don't you think? Do you think there's a statute of limitations on bad parenting?"

"Could you stop whispering over there?" Jeannie snapped at

us, clearly losing whatever tenuous hold she'd been exerting on her temper.

"Brunch!" I smiled brightly. "We were wondering about the Sunday brunch. Just family and travelers, right?"

Christian slid a look my way at that one, and flashed me that wry little grin of his that told me he wasn't at all fooled. It reminded me of back in high school, when the two of us would end up in the same classes despite the efforts of the faculty to prevent that from happening. We had an entire language of looks and signs, smiles and lifted eyebrows. A secret form of communication that led most of our peers to think we were twins and had that twin telepathy thing going on. Sometimes it had felt as if we really were twins.

But then college had separated us, and after that, Jeannie was his girlfriend and we just drifted apart. Maybe that was the way things happened. Maybe that was just growing up. I shook it off, and concentrated on the wedding details.

Two hours later, after we'd all discussed and debated the Wedding Day Schedule to death, Hope and I were allowed to leave. We were upstairs debating a night out when Jeannie appeared in Hope's bedroom door.

"I want to talk to you guys," she said. Her eyes were on me.

I sat up from my lounging position across Hope's bed. Hope paused in the act of arranging her hair, peering at Jeannie instead.

"We have to pick up our dresses and shoes, and be at your house at eleven-thirty for pictures." She didn't make much of an effort to sound interested. "We get it, really."

"What's going on with you two?" Jeannie demanded, but she was still looking at me. "How do you think it makes Christian feel to know his sisters don't care enough about him to even *fake* being happy for him?"

"Who said we're not happy for him?" Hope asked, genuinely taken aback. "I don't do *enthusiasm*, if that's what you mean, but that doesn't mean I'm not happy for him."

I met Jeannie's gaze. "We're happy for Christian. What are you talking about?"

"Please!" She scoffed. "I had to drag you to get your dresses fitted. You never helped with a thing—"

"I offered to help you about a million times, Jeannie," I reminded her, with a little leftover bitterness. "You told me you had all the help you needed. Remember? At the engagement party at Christmas?"

Jeannie pinched the bridge of her nose with her fingers. "You offered," she agreed, "but don't think I didn't get the subtext. I know you didn't even want to come up for the bachelorette party. You've made your feelings perfectly clear from the start."

"You know what?" Hope broke in, her eyes moving from Jeannie to me and back again. "Whatever is between you two really isn't any of my business."

Jeannie just glared at her. "And you were *busy*? Nice, Hope."

Hope made a face at me and strode from the room.

"Thanks, Hope," I said sarcastically. To her back.

"Guess you can't hide behind her anymore," Jeannie said. It was a taunt. "Like you've been doing all summer."

I didn't want to deal with *that* comment. I decided it was better to soothe than to respond. She was the bride, after all. They were notorious for going loony right before their Big Days.

"I understand that you're incredibly stressed out right now," I said, trying to sound completely sympathetic. "And who can blame you?"

"Just stop it!" She shook her head. "You know, when you decided to stay and take care of your dad, I was actually excited. How pathetic is that?" She laughed a little bit. "I actually thought we just needed to spend some time together, and things would be the way they used to be. I thought *distance* was the problem."

"I don't know what you're talking about."

"So I've been racking my brain trying to remember what actually happened, and I still have no clue," she continued, ignoring me. "You would think that I might remember why I lost my best friend in the whole world, right? You'd think something might stick out."

"You have Ashley." I couldn't help myself.

Jeannie rolled her eyes. "Ashley is a stuck-up, evil little bitch." She shrugged. "She makes me laugh, but let's not kid ourselves. If she *could* make new friends, she would."

"I don't know what you want me to say," I said, holding myself very still.

"It was that summer, wasn't it?" Jeannie asked. "What was so terrible about that summer? Could you *finally* tell me, please?"

"You must be kidding!" I folded my arms across my chest. "We had a big fight, Jeannie."

She threw up her hands. "We fought all the time!"

I sucked in a breath, and then blew it out in a sigh.

"Fine," I said. "You told Rachel that I was dating Kevin Bigelow. And you took *pleasure* in it, because you wanted to hurt her and because you wanted me to look bad. It was the last straw."

Jeannie blinked. "You were dating the love of her life behind her back," she said. "I don't think even you can come out of that looking *good*, Meredith."

"It's pointless to even talk about this." I tilted my chin up, as if that could make me rise above it. "It was a long time ago, you don't remember, and Rachel doesn't care."

"Rachel doesn't care?" Jeannie repeated. She gave me a hard look. "Oh. I get it. You're hanging out with her now?"

"She's back in town."

"And let me guess, you both like to bond over what a super bitch I am, right?" She didn't take her eyes off me. "Swap stories about high school and how evil I was?"

I couldn't resist. "If the shoe fits, Jeannie."

"You're lucky I don't kick that shoe right at your head." She looked like she might do it, too. "You are unbelievable."

I didn't like the way she said that.

"That summer was just the last straw," I told her. "The truth is, I was tired of being 'the nice one.' You were just . . ."

"Just what?"

"Mean." I looked at her. "You can be so *mean*, Jeannie."

She looked as if I'd hit her. "I'm not mean!"

"Being mean was your favorite high school pastime and you know it."

She blinked in confusion. "It was just stupid teenage girl stuff. We all did it."

"Maybe you did. I didn't."

"Of course you didn't! I forgot that Saint Meredith the Pure and Righteous never had a bad word to say about anyone." She rolled her eyes. "I forgot how good and sweet you pretended to be."

"I wasn't like *you*," I threw at her. "I didn't play people off of each other just because I was bored."

"No," Jeannie said in a hard voice, "you just pretended. You never had the guts to actually admit how you really felt about anything. I bet every single person we went to high school with thinks you liked them."

I blinked at her. "And what's wrong with that?"

"You're full of shit!" she exclaimed. "Take Rachel Pike. I bet you've conveniently forgotten how many times you were involved in the things we did to her. Poor, innocent Meredith," she mocked me. "Swept along by evil Jeannie and forced to do horrible things."

"They were *your* horrible things," I retorted. "Not mine. I never wanted to do any of that stuff."

"And what?" she demanded. "You were born without a spine? If you didn't want to do something, no one was going to force you, Meredith."

"No, I'd just have to be Ashley's target for a week!"

Jeannie dismissed that with an impatient toss of her head. "Ashley was wildly jealous of you and always will be. You didn't have any reason to care what she thought."

I clenched my arms tighter around my chest. "This conversation is getting us nowhere—"

"You really do blame me for everything, don't you?" Jeannie interrupted. "You have such a convenient memory. It lets you make believe that you were Miss Mary Sunshine, doesn't it?"

"My memory is pretty specific." I had to talk from between my teeth.

"You're a liar," Jeannie told me, her voice quiet and sure. "You have this fantasy in your head that you're the good girl, the nice girl."

"That's because I am!" I retorted.

"Whatever. You wish." She leaned close. "The difference between you and me is that I don't pretend to be anything I'm not. Sometimes I'm nice and sometimes I'm good. Other times I'm a raging bitch. That's the way it goes." She studied me for a moment. "It's called a *personality*."

"You'll have to help me out here," I said in a snotty tone that managed to do the snotty thing while also throwing in some dripping condescension for good measure. "I'm drawing a blank on your *nice* and *good* versions."

That hung there for a moment, alive in the air between us.

"You're making my point for me," Jeannie said. Quietly. "The reality is, you couldn't handle the fact that you did something fucked up to Rachel Pike. Because in your head, that made you as bad as me, and God knows you love feeling better than me, don't you? So instead of dealing with it, and possibly hearing some stuff you didn't want to hear about yourself, you decided I was out of your life and you ran away to Atlanta."

"You don't know what you're talking about—"

"Where, from all I hear, you paid penance by becoming a boring plastic girlfriend to some guy who was lucky you even looked at him and probably has no idea what you're *actually* like," she continued.

"You're crazy." But I was shaking.

"That version of me you have in your head? The one you're so righteously indignant about?" She almost smiled. "That's actually *you*, Meredith. It's always been you."


Naturally, I blew that off, and put it with all the rest of the crazy things Jeannie had said to me across the years. It was her way of ending that pointless conversation—and it had worked. I'd walked out of the room and left her to stand there with her revisionist history and her insults.

But the things she said echoed around and around in my head. It actually kept me up that night, staring at the ceiling, practically itching with rage.

Obviously, she was insane. Truly mean, and vicious, and after all, she'd always had an amazing talent for striking right at someone's weak spot, like she was some kind of psychic or something. I hadn't listened to a word she'd said in years, why start now? What did she know, anyway? She was just mad because I had dared to move outside her control. That was all she cared about: her power over other people and the shitty things she could do if anyone let her down—

She'd called me *mean*. She'd all but called me a bad person, delusional, hiding from myself and blaming it on her. What kind of person would I be if that were true?

I turned over and glared at the window, hoping it might shatter from the force of my anger. It remained whole. Taunting me.

I was nothing like Jeannie. I was the good one, the sweet one, the nice one. My smile made up for the things she'd done—wasn't that what Scott had said?

I was *nothing* like Jeannie.

*Except*—a tiny voice whispered. *What makes you so different?*

I'd cheated on my long-term boyfriend, never told him about it, and had made him feel like the bad guy for breaking up with me.

And much as I wanted to deny it, Jeannie had made some points about how I'd ended up with Travis in the first place. Playing perfect. Paying penance. Those words hit chords in me I wanted to deny.

I'd moved back into my parents' home to take care of my father, of my own free will, and had used my *great sacrifice* as a weapon with which to bludgeon my siblings.

I had spent years ordering the world around one central concept: how much better my life was far away from everything and everyone in this house. And in case someone missed the memo, I'd beat everyone over the head with my own *perfection* for years. I'd gone to great lengths just to make sure that *everyone knew* how *incredibly perfect* my life was.

I sat up in bed, stunned.

I wasn't sure I could breathe.

Jeannie was right: I'd been on the fast track to Bitchville for years.

The only person who thought of me as *good* and *nice* was me.


"It's the single scariest thing about being a woman," Rachel was ranting. "You know that one morning you're going to wake up and realize: *I am her.*" She shrugged. "It's unavoidable. It's why men insist on meeting your mother before they get serious—it's a sneak preview."

It was a few days later and we had just finished lunch in town. I had concluded a temp job at a scary manufacturing plant in Secaucus the day before, and Rachel had no classes on Thursdays.

I had thought a lot about Jeannie's take on my relationship with Rachel too. Maybe she had a point that I'd liked allying myself *with* Rachel and *against* Jeannie. I could admit it. But the fact was, I liked Rachel just because I liked her. That was all that mattered, wasn't it?

In any case, there was no one else I liked enough to do the lunch and coffee thing. I figured that counted for something, and the rest would come.

But anyway, we were talking about becoming our mothers, one of Rachel's favorite topics.

"Surely it should be like a buffet," I argued, using my latte for emphasis. "You pick and choose the traits you like, and skip over the ones that drive you insane with rage and which you vowed you would never, ever have yourself. You'd die first."

Rachel eyed me over her own cup. "Genetics isn't a buffet," she pointed out. "Try a time bomb. I've seen the future, and it involves breasts to my knees and a map of the greater New York metropolitan area across my face."

"At least you're spared the personality defects," I countered. "No one's exactly lining up to date the Early Christian Martyr over here, you know."

"What part of 'breasts to the knees' do you think is okay?" Rachel demanded. "I'd much rather have the personality of a bull terrier and *perky* breasts, thank you very much."

We moved on to less emotional topics—namely, my continuing attempts to find nonhumiliating employment opportunities.

"Hope is working at a bookstore now. I could work at a bookstore."

"Hope is what? Twenty-two?" Rachel shook her head. "What do you *like* to do?"

"I like not having this conversation," I said after a moment's pause to think about it. "I think it's only a very select few who have all that *drive* and *ambition*. I'm mostly looking for something to pay the bills. If it's kind of fun also, well, that's just icing."

Rachel considered. "Why not go to graduate school? You don't have to have this conversation again for two to seven years."

"Why would I go to graduate school? I don't have any idea

what I want to do." I frowned at her. "And it's not as if I thought college was so much fun. I couldn't wait to get out."

"I'm not unsympathetic to this, really," Rachel said. "After the whole law school debacle, I flailed around a lot and did my share of hideous temp jobs." She swept her latte through the air in an arc. "You don't know pain until you are crawling around in a freezing cold warehouse, affixing stickers to things and pretending that you actually counted all the eight million and seven hundred thousand buttons in the carton."

"That sounds like big fun." I shuddered.

"So I figured that since the fact that it all sucked was a given, the idea was to get the most out of a bad deal. Since you can make more money with an MBA, I thought: Why not? So here I am. If you have to have a corporate job, might as well be the best corporate job, right?"

"That's not a bad theory," I mused. "But I don't think I could make it through an MBA course. Isn't there a whole thing about statistics?"

"Hold that thought," Rachel commanded, squinting up at the building we were passing. "I have to pick up a prescription."

I opted to stay outside and enjoy the Indian summer. Most of the actual summer had been a haze of high humidity and higher temperatures, but today was gorgeous. Blue skies and a warm sun.

It was still hard to believe that I was back in New Jersey. If I could only find an appropriate career and stop having fights with various members of my family, maybe everything would be okay after all.

"Well, well, well," said a smug voice. "If it isn't Miss Meredith McKay."

Kevin Bigelow, of all people, stood before me.

It hadn't occurred to me that I might actually run into him. He was just part of a story. He wasn't *real*.

But here he was, standing with his legs planted wide apart and his meaty hands on his hips. The remnants of his high school hotness were evident in the way he held himself, even if his waistline was starting to rebel against his belt. Happily, he'd rethought the mullet.

"Hello, Kevin," I said politely. "It's great to see you. Gosh, it's been a long time."

"You're looking good," Kevin told me. "Look—Ing—Good!" His voice was overly familiar and his smile could really only be described as shit-eating.

*This*, I told myself, *is the reason Jeannie and I stopped being friends, why I betrayed Rachel's trust, and the proof to every single thing Jeannie said to me the other night.*

He didn't really seem worth all the trouble.

He remembered that summer, I could see, thanks to that smirk of his. Moreover, he seemed to think we were having a moment.

"I haven't seen you in years," he told me, as if I needed him to point that out for me. "But I remember that summer, believe me."

As if we'd torn up the sheets across Bergen County. Ew.

"I remember it too," I said, and regretted it. Because Kevin gave me a wise nod of his head and a smug little twist of his mouth. The pig.

"I'm a taken man, I'm afraid," he confided, as if he could see the yearning written across my face after so many years. He actually winked at me. "You're still pretty cute, though."

"I don't know what to say," I gritted out through the horror. Which wasn't a lie.

"I have a call," he informed me. "Good to see you, though,

Meredith. Maybe we'll catch up one of these days." He smirked.
"If you know what I mean."

He strode away, his radio squawking at his hip.

I stared after him with rage in my heart and murder in
my eye.

The worst part, of course, was that I deserved it. I'd brought
it upon myself almost ten years ago.

"I'm sorry," Rachel said from behind me. "I just couldn't
bring myself to come out here and talk to him. I threw you to
the wolves and I hate myself for it." She sounded remarkably
chipper for all that self-hate.

"You enjoyed that." It wasn't a question.

"I sure did. I'm a bad, bad person."

I eyed her. "He's 'taken,' apparently. Be still your broken
heart."

"Taken by what?" Rachel was deeply unimpressed. "Aliens?"

# Chapter 17

The Sunday before the wedding, the McKay family succumbed almost entirely to wedding fever.

By the time Christian arrived that evening to spend his last week as a bachelor under his childhood roof, the rest of us had hit a particularly stellar level of family interaction: feigned deafness (I'm sorry, what did you say? I was in the other room *actually doing something*, and couldn't hear you yelling from across the house—), slammed inanimate objects (Oh no, everything's fine—SLAM—why do you ask?), and overly hostile responses to even the most innocuous questions (Do you know—Do I *look* like an *information booth*—).

"You people need to relax," Christian said, staring around at each of us in turn, after Hope had predictably stormed out. My mother actually averted her gaze, and my father blinked. I just grinned. "I'm the one getting married here."

Much later, I had lost a battle with insomnia and was dealing with my defeat by rereading my collection of Sweet Valley High novels, thoughtfully preserved for all time in a box at the back of my closet. There had been a time when Jeannie and I had pretended to be the Wakefield twins, and had enacted their glamorous California lives around the neighborhood. Jeannie, naturally, was the reckless and exciting Jessica, while I was always the bookish and sweeter Elizabeth. I was reliving some of those memories when the door was pushed open.

"I thought you were escaping." I laughed, expecting to see Hope, but it was Christian. "Is something wrong?" I frowned at him. "It's almost 3 a.m."

"I couldn't sleep," he muttered, and raked his hands through his hair. He was wearing a T-shirt and those Adidas sweatpants that all men our age seemed to own. He let out something like a sigh. "Partly it's being back in this house. Jeannie and I agreed that it was good to spend this week apart, but I really hate being back here."

"Are you okay?" I watched him, feeling cautious.

I didn't think this was a social call. He was probably here as Jeannie's emissary after our fight, and I definitely didn't want to talk to him about it.

*That's actually you, Meredith*, I heard her say, pitch-perfect in my head, and steeled myself.

"The thing is, I need to talk to you," Christian said at last.

"You're kind of scaring me." I waved a hand at the foot of my bed. "Of course we can talk."

He came over and sat there, and sighed again, and then he looked at me with the crooked smile that had once inspired so many teenage girls to carve his initials across their notebook binders. But his eyes, unlike then, were troubled. He looked away, down at his hands.

We sat there so long like that I thought he might not speak

again at all. Or that he'd forgotten and maybe slipped into some kind of zombie state.

"Am I doing the right thing?" he asked finally. He couldn't look at me.

The question hung there between us.

Of all the things in the world I thought he might say, I didn't expect this. It threw me. I blinked at him.

"I walked in the house tonight and it was like walking into the Ice Age." Bitterness laced his voice. "And I started thinking about all the ridiculousness this summer, you know? Like how Mom and Dad only get along when he's either away on business for years at a time or hiding out in the basement to get away from her."

"The fish are more interesting than you might think," I ventured.

"If you say 'flowchart,' I'll smother you with that pillow."

"I'm just saying, he's maybe running *to* the fish as much as he's running *away* from Mom."

"Anyway." Christian frowned at me. "That's not the only thing. We've been paying a lot of attention to how Mom didn't want to come home, but did you think about the fact that Dad didn't *want* her to come home? The more you think about it, the more you realize how incredibly fucked up that is."

"Christian . . ." But I didn't know what I wanted to say, and he carried on.

"Jeannie's so incredibly *sure* about things," he said. "She always knows what she wants, and she always gets what she wants. You know this better than anyone."

"You're allowed to not be as sure as Jeannie." I tilted my head so I could catch his eye. "No one is as sure as Jeannie."

He shrugged. "That's what I usually think but lately, I don't know . . ." He shook his head. "There's only one other woman I know who always gets what she wants. And I don't want to end up in a basement trying to convince my kids that fish are more fun than the life I've completely given up on."

I let that sit there for a moment.

"First of all," I said, "you're not ending up in the basement."

"You already think the fish are cool," he pointed out. "It's a slippery slope."

"And second of all, Jeannie is not Mom."

Although there could be worse things, I thought then, than being a supermarket Madonna.

"I don't know," Christian said. "I mean, I don't *really* think she is, obviously, but sometimes they get along a little *too* well and this whole wedding thing has brought out the obsessive psycho side . . . I just don't know."

I laced my fingers together and frowned at them.

"I think you have wedding jitters, Christian," I announced. "It doesn't make you a terrible person. Marriage is a big deal. Maybe you *should* be jittery."

"I think 'jitters' is what happens when someone thinks he's about to make a huge mistake," Christian replied, sounding sad. "And then he sucks it up and gets married anyway, and thirty years later realizes he's miserable."

"You are not going to be miserable!"

"How do you know that? No one's miserable when they start out. Maybe miserable is how you end up, without even meaning to."

I stared at him until he looked at me.

"When we were in the fifth grade, you gave Jeannie six red carnations for Valentine's Day when she liked Eric Katz because you heard he wasn't going to give her any."

"Yeah, and she beat me up at recess," Christian reminded me. "Is that supposed to be a tender story of young love?"

"When we were in eighth grade and that idiot Dave Revello dumped Jeannie the day of the dance, what did you do?"

"Smacked him down," Christian grunted.

"Yes, *and* danced with Jeannie during 'Crazy for You' even though you were going out with Hannah Green at the time and she was not at all amused."

"Jeannie was *crying* over that loser," Christian said, as if he still couldn't believe it.

"And then, come on, you remember when she had mono? You practically nursed her, and you were a freshman at NYU. You certainly didn't have to take the train out every day to wait on her hand and foot."

"I remember all these things too," Christian said, but I thought he was faking his impatience. "I'm not sure why you're reminding me. I would have done the same for you or Hope." He paused. "Well. For you. Hope would beat me up for subjugating her or some shit."

I let that pass. "I heard Jeannie tell Ashley that when you guys kissed for the first time, it was as if everything just fell into place." I smiled. "You always fit. Nothing in the world makes more sense than the two of you together."

"I want to believe that's true," Christian all but whispered. He shook his head.

"The thing about Jeannie is that you always know where you stand," I told him, and even though I would have said it anyway, I realized it was true. "She doesn't play games."

"This means a lot, you know," he said after a moment. He crooked his smile at me again. "You're the one who knows us both the best."

"Listen," I said, very carefully. "Jeannie and I haven't exactly been close in a while—"

"Yeah," Christian interrupted. "She told me about that." He frowned at me. "When did you turn into such a drama queen? I knew the South would ruin you."

"What?" Because what else was there to say?

"You and Jeannie were practically joined at the hip your whole lives." He looked exasperated. "Of course you'd want a little distance. I still don't think you had to go all Georgia Peach to get it, but it doesn't *surprise* me."

I just stared at him.

He looked at my expression and laughed. "I kept telling Jeannie that you just needed time, and it wasn't personal."

"It *was* personal!" I was surprised to see my hands trembling. I shoved them under the comforter. "And it wasn't just her, Christian, it was you too."

"That's why I said it wasn't personal," he said. As if we were agreeing.

"We used to be so close, and then we weren't anymore," I said. Very. Slowly. "How could that not be personal?"

He gave me the exact same look he'd leveled at me on the porch of my old apartment house in Atlanta.

"You're my *sister*," he said. "That's a lifetime thing. You don't get to get out of it." He scowled at me. "What the hell goes on in your head?"

"People change," I began. His eyes flashed impatience.

"Whatever," he said. "You're the same person you've always been; you're just more wound up about it suddenly."

"Maybe I'm not who you think I am," I countered.

"Was there a body snatching? Because seriously, I think I'd notice."

"I'm not particularly nice, and I'm not particularly good." I was throwing it down like a challenge.

"I never thought you *were* a saint," Christian pointed out. "You just *wanted* to be a saint. Everyone has dirty laundry, you know. It's how you know you're alive."

He wanted dirty laundry? I could do that.

"Oh, I'm alive." I eyed him. "In fact, I cheated on Travis."

Christian shut his eyes briefly, and shook his head. "Why are you telling me this?"

"Because I'm not—"

"I know that you *have* dirty laundry," he interrupted me. "That doesn't mean I want the details, okay?" He shook his head again. "Jesus Christ."

He sounded disgruntled, I thought, but no different than usual.

A sudden, unwelcome thought began to bloom in my gut. What if the distance between me and Christian had been of my own design?

That was entirely too huge and frightening. I shoved it aside and concentrated on Christian instead.

We sat in silence for a while, until something seemed to settle in him. He nodded just a bit, to himself. Then he looked at me and smiled.

"Thanks," he said.

Just the one small word, but it was the look in his eye that made tears clog in my throat. Something sweet. Something ours I'd thought we'd lost forever.

It made my heart hurt to think that it had only been lost because I'd been too blind to see it. Was that possible?

He reached over and ruffled my hair with his hand, and then let himself out.

Leaving me with chaos on the brain. Again.

Christian had seemed so irritated at the very *idea* that we'd grown apart. As if he hadn't ever even *considered* such a thing.

It made me rerun through the past ten years, seeing things from his perspective and not really liking the picture. I'd been the one who'd pulled away. So I'd also been the one who'd been pretending through all those holidays. Christian hadn't been doing anything more than what he usually did.

Could I really have convinced myself that he'd been responsible for something I'd done? Had Jeannie pegged me so well?

That one hit me like the shoe Jeannie had threatened to kick upside my head.

That was exactly what I'd done, and more to the point, that was what I'd always done.

It was Jeannie's fault Rachel Pike found out I wasn't as nice as I pretended to be. It was Scott's fault I'd cheated on Travis. It was Travis's fault I'd cheated in the first place. It was Jeannie's fault we weren't friends anymore. It was Christian's fault we weren't close anymore. It was never *my* fault. As if I didn't exist. As if all those relationships carried on by themselves. As if I was only involved in them in theory.

As if it was anyone's fault but mine that I wasn't that imaginary Meredith, all sweetness and light and a glimmering halo.

As if she was such a prize in the first place.


The following night, Hope and I were watching one of the many incarnations of *Law and Order* when Christian and Jeannie appeared at the back door, shaking off the sudden rain, arms filled with something Christian referred to in an aggrieved tone as "usher gifts, not that they deserve anything, the idiots."

I studiously avoided looking at Jeannie while Christian dumped his armload behind one of the couches.

He straightened and frowned. "Where are Mom and Dad?"

"You don't want to know," I assured him. "Think tent in backyard and freak rain shower." Christian winced, and went to peer out the window.

"How come you were like the incredible disappearing couple this whole summer?" Hope whined. "And now you only appear during my favorite TV shows?"

"Oh, did you want to watch this?" Christian asked sweetly, and proceeded to collapse on top of her. They had a brief, violent scuffle. When Christian finally stood, Hope was rubbing her arm and he was rubbing his thigh, but they were both smirking.

Rolling my eyes at them, I got up and headed into the kitchen to get myself another drink.

I wasn't entirely surprised when Jeannie followed me, but I braced myself.

"I wanted to apologize," she said without preamble when I turned around and faced her. "I think I got a little bit carried away."

"I think I'm the one who should apologize," I replied before she could say anything further. "And anyway, I think you were right."

"I never should have attacked you," Jeannie said, still in that oddly stiff voice. "I was really just having a wedding fit, and anyway, I've been informed it's none of my business."

The stiffness was because she was apologizing. I realized I'd heard her do that only a scant handful of times before, scattered across the years.

Which is when the rest of it hit me—that Christian had

heard the whole story and hadn't agreed entirely with Jeannie, just because. *I've been informed*, she'd said.

I felt that dizzy sensation again, the one that I was beginning to figure out signaled that I was the one who'd been lost for years. Not everyone else.

"I shouldn't have called you mean." I could apologize too. "Especially while being mean myself."

Jeannie smiled, and hunched her shoulders up beneath her ears.

"See, here's why I don't understand why we . . ." She cast around for the word, and then shrugged it away.

"Christian said he figured we were going through something," I offered, feeling hesitant. "That maybe we needed some time apart, anyway."

"He told me he freaked out all over you," she said, and grinned at me. "Men are so fragile."

"He wasn't really freaking out." I went for the diplomatic spin. "You know, he just wanted to talk about the general state of marriage in the world, not really about *you guys*."

"He spazzed!" Jeannie laughed that wonderful laugh of hers. "But thank you for talking him down."

"Anytime," I said, and smiled.

"I miss you," she said simply. She raised her hands up from her sides and then dropped them down again. "I never wanted Ashley to be my maid of honor. It doesn't even make sense. I only ever wanted you."

"I know," I said. "It's okay, though." I felt our history shift again inside of me, turning until I saw only the years together, not the pitfalls along the way. "Ashley can have the wedding. We have the rest of our lives."

We both looked away—at the floor, the cabinets. We were

both in that pre-weepy but no-tears stage when we dared look at each other again. We both laughed a little bit.

"Come on, honey," Christian called to Jeannie from the other room. "We still have to deal with your mother tonight, and if I get caught up in the tent thing my head will explode."

Jeannie made a face, but we both walked back into the den, just in time to watch Hope wing a throw pillow at Christian's head. He caught it easily and flipped it around between his fingers. He headed toward the door, tossing it over to me.

"While we're young," he said.

Hope muttered a good-bye and slumped back against the couch.

Jeannie followed him, already back in wedding mode. "Don't mention anything about the tent to my mom—you know what she's going to say."

"Your mother has a swimming pool. There's no room. Why is this even an issue?"

Both Christian and Jeannie turned to look at me, each wearing an identical expression. The *she/he must be kidding* expression.

I looked from one to the other, and grinned.

Because finally, after so long, I felt like I'd come home.

# Chapter 18

The morning of the wedding was a blur. Hope and I managed to get ourselves showered, coiffed, gowned, and into the car within minutes of our eleven-thirty deadline. Hope was still working on her panty hose, and wriggled around in the front seat like an eel.

"You better not ruin that dress," I warned her. "Jeannie will kill you."

"You just keep driving," Hope told me, her hips in the air.

At the bride's house, the commotion was at near fever pitch. I didn't know what was worse: Jeannie's mother, who seemed to be unclear about who was traditionally the center of attention on a wedding day, or Jeannie's trio of other bridesmaids, who, with Ashley as the ringleader, were involved in a catty battle for supremacy. All of them in shiny, shiny pink.

"I'm the maid of honor," Ashley was snarling at the other two girls, both from Jeannie's college days. They had been indistinguishable at the bachelorette party and now, in matching gowns, were even more so.

"I think it's *matron* of honor, actually," I said. But only to Hope.

"You mean matron of horror," Hope sniffed. "I did not put on control-top panty hose for *this*. I'm going to find some more coffee."


The reception was already swinging by the time we reached it, after an endless round of the inevitably cheesy photographs. The pouring rain, rather than ruining the celebration, seemed to make everyone a little more giddy instead.

Everyone, that was, except Mrs. Van Eck, who sat in her seat at the neighborhood table with a face like a sour lemon.

"I suppose no one could have predicted the rain," she said when I ventured too close. Clearly, she'd predicted it. And assigned blame where she felt it was due, no doubt.

"Aren't they a cute couple?" I gushed.

She actually *harrumphed,* which I took as my cue to leave. Van Ick the Horrible looked human and a little bit naked without Isabella the yip dog at her feet, bows trembling. I had a delightful fantasy involving little Isabella shut up in the house next door, able to see the party but not participate. It warmed my heart.

When the first dance segued into dancing-with-parents, I wandered toward the house in search of some food.

The wedding planner, I thought as I looked in on the carnage in my mother's usually pristine kitchen, had completely misjudged the capabilities of the caterer. I felt myself snap into my own obsessive mode, the one I'd more or less turned off since I'd left my job in Atlanta. The situation looked ugly.

Melissa, the wedding planner, was becoming increasingly loud, while Tina, the caterer, was becoming increasingly belligerent.

"One more word!" Tina snarled about an inch from Melissa's chin. "One more word and you can feed the entire reception yourself!"

"But the entire catering concept springs from the fusion of mini quiches and egg rolls!" Melissa shrieked. "There is no place for those—those—"

"They look like pigs in blankets," I observed sweetly, and helped myself to one. "Who doesn't like pigs in blankets?"

I smiled my brightest, most encouraging smile, the one that had bilked old ladies of their money. I was pleased to see that lack of use had not dimmed it any.

Both women blinked at me—a vast improvement over glaring as if they were about to start throttling each other.

"The catering concept . . ." Melissa began weakly.

"I'll let you in on a little secret," I confided.

I grabbed the contested tray of pigs in blankets, and handed it off to one of the servers. With my other hand, I indicated my dress.

"As you can see, I'm a bridesmaid. I've known the bride and groom my entire life, and let me tell you, they love nothing more than pigs in blankets. Which are delicious, by the way," I told Tina.

I snuck an arm around Melissa and eased her around and away from the caterer.

"You are doing such a lovely job," I whispered. "Who could have known the weather would be so terrible and look at how well you've kept things running. I don't know how you do it."

I talked her out of the kitchen and down the hall to the bathroom, where she caught a glimpse of her reflection and started.

"I'll just be a moment," she murmured.

"Of course," I replied sunnily.

The door closed and I heaved a drawn-out, and silent, sigh, and turned around to rejoin the party.

"That was very well done," said the sleek-looking woman at the end of the hall. I smiled automatically.

"I'm Meredith McKay," I announced, extending my hand as I approached.

"Gloria Delgado," she replied, with a matching smile. "Don't worry, I'm not your long-lost cousin, I'm the wedding coordinator."

I glanced back toward the bathroom. "But I thought—"

"Melissa is one of my associates," Gloria told me. "She's a genius with anything floral. This was her first big gig, and it appears that grace under pressure isn't one of her strengths."

"I think you're being too hard on her," I said, rushing to the other woman's defense at once. "You may not know the bride, but I do, and she takes her catering concept very seriously."

"Melissa's not going to lose her job," Gloria guffawed. "She's my niece." She eyed me. "What do you do?"

"I—" I just couldn't bring myself to announce that I was a temp, living at home in my parents' house. I just couldn't do it. "Until recently I was the assistant director of the Annual Fund at a small girls' school in Atlanta," I told her. It sounded almost impressive when I put it that way.

Gloria smiled. "That sounds like a very worthwhile profession."

And that was when something alien overtook me.

"I've always been interested in wedding planning," I lied. Her eyebrows arched. "It was my idea to reorganize the space in the tent."

"Really?" she asked, looking intrigued. "Or are you interested in becoming Jennifer Lopez's character? You'd be surprised how many applications came in when that movie hit the theaters."

All I could remember about the movie in question was that I'd lusted after Jennifer Lopez's hair and wardrobe. Nor would I be likely to turn down Matthew McConaughey anytime soon.

"My Annual Fund experience means I can soothe even the most demanding donors, and it requires a serious eye for detail," I told her.

Gloria considered me for a moment.

"I could use someone like you," she said with a grin and another assessing look. "Calm enough to keep the most obnoxious caterer in the world from having a hissy fit and even looks pulled-together in a froufy pink bridesmaid's dress." She laughed at her own joke and presented me with a card. "Give me a call on Monday."

"I will," I said, as if I received job offers every five minutes and the whole thing left me blasé.

She brushed past me and went to pound on the bathroom door.

I stared down at the card in my hand. Had I really just done that?

I tucked the card away in the bodice of my dress. Damn right, I'd done it. It was long past time I took charge of my life.

I looked around at the familiar wallpaper and the pictures so old I'd stopped seeing them years ago. Moving home had seemed like the thing to do in the wake of my breakup with Travis, and I hadn't thought much beyond that. How long was I going to keep living in this house, playing the same teenage games around the dinner table? Summer was over. It was time to get on with my life.

I snuck into the den, called Information, and left a message on a local Realtor's machine. No more waiting for life to happen to me, I promised myself fiercely. I had a new career to kick ass at, a new place to find and move into, and a brand-new attitude. No more pretending. No more trying to be someone I wasn't because it was so much easier than figuring out who I was.

I'd spent my entire life defining myself by the people around me and what I thought they thought of me. My mother, Christian, Jeannie, Hope, Travis. I'd wanted so much to be "the nice girl" that I'd forgotten to figure myself out along the way. All I'd cared about was how others perceived me and I'd tried so hard to be someone, anyone else depending on that perception.

It was about time I was just me.

I was coming out of the bathroom when I saw Scott's mother in the front hall.

"Are you going?" I asked. She smiled at me.

"Such a nice party," she said. "But it's getting late."

"It's dark," I pointed out. "Let me walk you home."

"Don't be silly, dear." She dismissed me with a wave. "It's just across the street and I wouldn't dream of stealing you away."

"I insist."

She took my arm as we made our way down the steps, and I was glad the rain had finally stopped as we headed across the street.

"A lovely evening," she told me with a smile when we reached her door. "Thank you so much, Meredith. You go back and dance now."

I smiled, and was about to go do just that when the door opened and Scott stood in the wedge of light from inside. He smiled down at his mother.

"I was just about to go looking for you," he told her tenderly.

"You are a sweet boy," Mrs. Sheridan said, and patted his cheek. "But I'm old, dear, not addled."

She went inside and disappeared from view, and I felt a smile start up from deep in my stomach and take over my whole face.

Scott stepped out onto the porch and shut the door behind him.

"How's it going over there?" He grinned at the loud music. "I heard something earlier that sounded suspiciously like the Chicken Dance. Please tell me that even Christian McKay would not allow the Chicken Dance at his wedding."

I rolled my eyes. "My younger cousins have strange customs. I can tell you that Ashley Mueller's husband is, as expected, a drunken idiot even now leering and pinching the server's ass. Just like high school all over again."

"Didn't I tell you?" Scott sounded smug.

He stood next to me and rocked on his heels. For some reason the light brush of his shoulder against mine made me feel as close to him as if we were embracing. I wanted to tilt into him and stay there for a while.

"My mom insisted I sit in the house to scare off any burglars," Scott said, in a long-suffering tone. "Because, you know, with all the neighbors invited to the wedding reception, it was pretty much open season."

"You should have come," I said. He smiled, and leaned in slightly, so we touched just that slightest bit more.

We stood there, as the band played something funky. From a distance, the reception sounded sparkling and a little bit wild. I couldn't identify individual voices, just the general din of my family making merry.

"I want us to be together," I blurted out, much more loudly

than I'd intended. I heard the rebound of my voice and felt my face catch fire. Thank God there wasn't very much light.

"What?" He sort of laughed, but he angled his head down toward me.

"I should go," I mumbled. He really did laugh then.

"Are you kidding?" He crossed his arms across his chest and regarded me with an inscrutable expression. "You can't throw something like that out there and then just run away. It's the emotional equivalent of yelling, 'Tag—you're it.'"

"That was pretty much all I had to say." I was suddenly aware of all the ways I was uncomfortable, from the shoes pinching at my toes to the yards of satin that constricted my breathing.

And everything else.

"That's not good enough, Meredith," he said in his lawyer voice. "You want us to be together? Define 'together.'"

"Is this a deposition?" I snapped at him. "Because I don't actually feel like playing lawyer games with you, Scott."

If he'd snapped back, I would have known what to do with it, how to keep that antagonistic flare going. But he shook his head instead, and reached over to hold my face between his hands for a moment.

"I don't feel like playing at all," he said quietly. "I keep trying to tell you."

I sucked in a breath as his hands fell away, and felt a shiver down my back.

"I think about you all the time," I confessed. I looked at him, and felt that emotion in me, rising up through my chest as if it might choke me. I didn't know whether I wanted to cry or laugh. "I want to see what happens when I'm not so guilty. When you're not performing exorcisms. When it's just us."

"Are you asking me out?" Scott asked, laughing. I laughed too then, but had to wipe moisture from my eyes.

"See, but I don't understand why you would want to be with me." I couldn't tell if I was crying or not, but the words kept coming. "You know firsthand that I'm a cheater, and a liar, and I'm mean when you don't deserve it." I waved him off when he made as if to move closer. "Why would you want to be with someone who is only just this minute figuring out who she might be? What's wrong with you?"

He closed the distance between us and tucked a stray tendril back behind my ear, and then smiled a little bit as he wiped away the tears beneath my eyes.

"I've had this thing about you, Meredith, in one way or another, since I was five years old. And you have some stuff to work on, but so do I." He stared down at me, his eyes almost silver in the light. "Trust me."

I let out a laugh, which sounded more like a sob.

"We're just about to start," he said, and suddenly he was even closer, and I had to tilt my head back to look at him. "All you have to do is believe in the possibilities."

He cradled my face between his hands but it was me who stood up on my tiptoes and kissed him. All that heat and magic, and a sweetness to it as well.

It was about as close to perfect as I was likely to come.


"I have too many people to talk to tonight," Christian said, "so I have to dance with both of you at the same time."

"That's genius in terms of the photo op," Hope replied brightly. "But you might have presented the whole thing in a more attractive package."

"Leave the man alone!" I chided her. "It's his wedding day!"

"My wedding night, actually," Christian said. "I'm an old married man."

"Is that excitement or terror?" I teased him.

"Definitely excitement." He laughed.

All three of us went out onto the floor and commenced dancing together, the way, legend and photographs had it, Christian and I had done with little toddler Hope at Uncle Martin's wedding some twenty years ago. I could hear the combined "aw" from the relatives.

"You really can't dance," Hope observed, looking down at Christian's feet.

"Shut up, brat," he replied easily. "Did you guys see Jeannie's uncle rocking out to Elton John? How scary was that?"

"Please," I scoffed. "Aunt Marion has been downing rum since noon and ran barefoot and half-dressed down the street. Uncle Jules had to force her to lie down in the guest room."

"I love family events," Hope said with a smile. "It's always such an excellent way to remember that I'm really not the black sheep Mom would like to believe." She glanced over to where most of our cousins sat gathered around a single table. "I mean, I have no visible tattoos, I didn't try to sell the younger cousins marijuana at the church, and I'm not pregnant. That's pretty much a home run in this family."

All three of us laughed, and then the song came to an end. Jeannie wandered over from her own dance, and the way she and Christian smiled at each other made even Hope grin.

"Two girls at once?" she asked archly. "Good thing they're your sisters. This is the wedding, not the bachelor party."

"Very funny," Christian said.

"And now"—Jeannie tipped her head back and smiled up at Christian—"I want to dance with my husband."

"You know what," Hope said as they danced away from us, "I actually really do think they'll be happy. Not that they're not boneheads with untold issues."

"Of course."

"But I think it'll be good."

"I agree," I said. I slid a sideways look her way. "Is that a tear I see in your eye?"

"Don't be ridiculous," Hope said. "I don't do emotion."

But she smiled at me as she wiped at her eyes.

Much later that night, the guests were dancing up a storm and I was taking a breather at one of the tables. I had lost track of my shoes hours ago, and my sides ached from laughing at Hope's antics with some of our cousins. Jeannie and Christian were still out on the dance floor, both of them possessed of enough energy to light up the tent on their own, which was a good thing, as everyone expected the power to go out next.

"Well," my mother said, settling into the chair beside me. "Isn't this a lovely night after all?"

"You did a great job," I told her, and watched her smile.

"I remember when your father and I got married," she said now, her eyes far away. "My mother insisted I wear the most uncomfortable pair of shoes, and she wouldn't let me take them off all day." She laughed. "That should tell you how happy I was to be marrying your father—I danced all night long and when we finally took the shoes off that night, my feet were bleeding. I hadn't even noticed."

Which is when I thought I finally understood my mother. She'd given up a lot to be the Madonna of our town. It wasn't a small thing at all. There were costs I would never know about. And love, of course, in forms I'd overlooked my whole life. All those smiles—they weren't my mother pretending, or acting. They were her way of loving.

"I don't know what made me think of that," she said, and shook her head.

I looked around at my family, scattered across the reception. Jeannie and Christian couldn't bear to let go of each other's hands, and had yet to stop beaming. Hope was holding court in the corner, no doubt wowing our cousins the way she wowed everyone else with what could only be called her star power. My father looked dapper and charming, taking care of Aunt Beth so she wouldn't feel lonely at her first big event following the divorce.

My father had his little worlds to rule, all in separate tanks in the basement. My mother ran their life together. Everyone found the things they were good at, and those things didn't necessarily make sense to anyone else. It was pointless to look, or judge. It was possible my mother would confound me until her dying day, but then again, that was her job. She was good at that too. As Rachel said, we all ended up as our mothers in one way or another. It was all a question of degrees.

And, possibly, a good plastic surgeon.

In the meantime, I could be exactly as free as I wanted to be. I'd gone out of my way to wreck my so-called perfect life, after all. If I'd really wanted it, I might have fought for it, but doing so had never crossed my mind. It was time to stop licking my wounds and start living the life I had. It was time to stop worrying about being nice, being good. Saint Meredith was well and truly dead.

*Love*, I thought, *is dancing for joy when your feet are bleeding*. Because the joy was what mattered. Feet would heal. Everything healed, given enough time. All you had to do was want it.

"Come on, Mom."

I surged to my feet when the band swung into a new song.

"Let's dance," I said, and held out my hand.

# Author Note

      I wrote the bulk of *Everyone Else's Girl* while in-
volved in what I like to call an "extended move" from York, En-
gland, to Los Angeles, which really means I spent six months
hidden away in my parents' attic finishing up my dissertation,
something I felt I was unlikely to do once I escaped west.

What, I thought at the time, was more likely to make a
grown woman revert to her absolute worst than an extended
stay right smack in the middle of her adolescence? I knew what
that was like, after all. I spent most of my twenties living in
short-term housing in random cities (four months in Hoboken,
NJ, I'm looking at you), student housing (as detailed in my first
novel, *English as a Second Language*—that communal kitchen
cured me of being a slob where years of my mother's tutelage
never could), or crammed into my childhood bedroom on the
second floor of my parents' house. Complete with twin beds,

rules concerning the use and placement of towels, and all those surround-sound memories of my hideous teen years. And that was just in the bedroom.

I hope you enjoy Meredith's journey back to the family home!

Come visit me at www.megancrane.com.

**5 reasons you should *never* move back home with your parents (No matter how many times you tell yourself *"It's different now because I'm an adult!"*)**

**1. No more privacy.** Close your eyes for a moment and consider what it was actually like to be sixteen. Sure, no responsibility, no bills, yada yada yada—but now *really* think about it. Intrusive personal questions. No independence. Shared mealtimes. No such thing as escape, or *alone* time! Kind of makes that pesky utility bill look good in comparison, doesn't it?

**2. Not that story again!** You know when you visit home for the holidays and find yourself stranded with your parents' friends and neighbors for sixty hours as they tell that story about the time you [*insert humiliating teenage adventure—which you only recovered from after years of therapy—here*]? Okay, now imagine having that conversation *every single day*.

**3. High school reunion.** You keep running into all those people from high school who you can't even identify when you look through the yearbook. You know the ones—they all run together in a strange mush of bad hair, weird extracurricular activities, and terrifying fashion decisions. There's a reason you "grew apart" before the end of the graduation ceremony.

**4.** **Forget about dating.** Oddly, being in your mid-twenties and living with your parents is not considered a big pull for attractive members of the opposite sex. For some reason, the idea of having to greet Mom and Dad when entering the house puts a bit of a damper on social engagements.

**5.** **Watch out, you'll become your mother!** First you hear yourself using some of her catchphrases, which doesn't even bother you *too* much, because it's along the same lines as arranging the kitchen in your own home to resemble hers. But then you start joining her for the semiannual sale at Talbots, because good quality is good quality. After that it's a downhill race to a house in the suburbs and a constantly revolving selection of festive sweater vests to celebrate the seasons. *Mark my words, young lady.*

# Acknowledgments

To Julie Barer, who continues to be the greatest agent in the world, and Karen Kosztolnyik, who makes editing seem easy and even fun. Thank you both from the bottom of my heart. And thanks to Michele Bidelspach, Keri Friedman, Brigid Pearson, and everyone else at Warner for all their support and hard work.

Thanks to my writing/therapy/you-are-not-a-hack group: Josie Torielli, Kim McCreight, and Louise Austin. Special thanks to Dan Panosian for last-minute artistic suggestions. Thanks also to Lani Diane Rich, Charmaine DeGrate, Amanda Lower, anyone else who read this book in one of its various drafts, and all my wonderful friends and relatives. Extra thanks to my parents for their support while I was writing this novel—and for not being the parents described here, despite the fish!

And a million more thanks to Jeff Johnson, my clown in reverse, for everything else.